MW01147901

Figure EIGHT

CALIA READ

Figure Eight

Interior design by Angela McLaurin, Fictional Formats
Cover Design by Cover Couture
Editing by Marie Piquette Editing

ISBN-13: 978-1544632001
ISBN-10: 1544632002

To the real Sam and Noah.

I am poured out like water, and all my bones are out of joint.
My heart has turned to wax; it has melted within me.
—Psalm 22:14

Figure EIGHT

PART I

1

"BE HONEST WITH me. How's my hair?"

Those are the first words that Claribelle Sandoval asks me.

I shouldn't be surprised. When she was contacted about the one-year anniversary taping of the small city tragedy, the first two things she asked were: would she get paid and would she get a wardrobe?

The answers were no and no.

That didn't stop her from agreeing to have us to interview her. Who could possibly pass that up? The tragedy surrounding Selah Kerrington was severe enough to catch nation-wide attention. Front pages for weeks. Journalists from local newspapers all the way to *The Wall Street Journal* were running stories about this elusive woman from central Illinois.

And now it was almost the one-year anniversary. We knew that if we wanted an authentic take on the story we were going to have to go to the very place it happened. The crew and I arrived two days ago.

"Now, I've always been told that my left side is my best angle.

Feel free to tell me differently."

I nod, barely listening to her rambling. This woman was going to make me take up smoking, and I quit five years ago. Right about now she was starting to turn into one giant cigarette. Besides, the truth of the matter is the camera will love this lady. She's a beautiful person. Even if she wore no makeup and a trash bag for a shirt she'd be beautiful.

Her dark brown hair has caramel highlights—which I'm willing to bet a pack of cigarettes were done yesterday; her eyes are amber; and she has the kind of pale skin that make her red lips look bold and daring.

Her interview isn't for another ten minutes but she sits primly in her seat, sipping on a Diet Coke. Every time she takes a sip the makeup artist had to redo her lipstick.

The only tell of her nerves is her right leg slightly bouncing up and down. Whether she wants to admit it or not, she's nervous, which can mean one of two things: she's camera shy or she has secrets that she doesn't want getting out.

There are a few orange ladders around the room with people standing on top of them as they fix the portable light stands. Multiple cameras are being angled her way. Cables are running to and fro yet no one trips. Claribelle is sitting on a single stool watching everything. The longer she stares the paler she becomes.

"Do you prefer Claire or Claribelle?" I ask.

I already know the answer from executive producers and past interviews.

"Claribelle," she replies.

"Pretty name. Anyone ever tell you that?"

She perks up at the prospect of conversation being focused in her direction. "Oh, yes. All the time."

I smile and she smiles back.

"Okay, here's what's going to happen. I'm going to ask you a series of questions. You have to pretend that the cameras aren't here. Don't look at them. We're just having a normal, easy conversation. Alright?"

She swallows before she nods.

In a perfect world we'd get this shot in one or two takes, but the film crew and I both know that's not going to happen. Claribelle may look good for the camera but she's not used to the camera.

We do a sound check in which everyone on set eleven, including Claribelle, stays silent. Her hands are laced together so tightly it looks like she's cutting off her circulation. Audio and video switchers are studiously working in the makeshift control room.

I glance down at the questions on the page in my lap. I give her one last smile. "Remember. Don't look at the screen. We're just talking one on one, right?"

She nods just as a crewman walks into the shot with a clapperboard. Written in the title line, in white messy handwriting is, 'The Selah Kerrington Story: Victim or Villain?'

"You ready, Claribelle?"

She lifts her chin up a notch and gives me a brief nod.

"Take one!" I shout.

The clapperboard snaps together.

There is a brief moment of silence, and then I dive into the questions. "Claribelle, how well did you know Selah Kerrington?"

Her lips purse into a thin line. "I hardly knew Selah. I'd met her only twice." I watch as she looks away momentarily and tucks a piece of hair behind her ear. Right then, I knew she wasn't telling the complete truth. I could push, but it's too soon for that.

"And what are your thoughts about her?" I ask.

Claribelle surprises me by completely ignoring the camera and looking me dead in the eye. "She's an evil, manipulative bitch who can't be trusted."

2

DO YOU REMEMBER me?

Of course you don't. So I'm going to give you a refresher course.

I've known you for years and years. We used to have beautiful conversations. There was no one that knew you better than me. Right now, if I told you that we used to be close, chances are you wouldn't believe me.

But it's true. You have to believe me on that.

Selah, not so long ago you needed me. You relied on me. I was your comfort. Your escape. But you left me. Patiently, I've been waiting for you to come back.

You haven't.

If you don't remember me, then you certainly can't miss me, but sometimes I feel a certain tug in your direction. And I know you feel it too. It's like extending your arm for something out of your reach. The muscles in your arms burn but you keep going and going until at the last minute your arm gives out and drops heavily to the ground. Instead of giving up, you keep reaching. And reaching. And reaching.

This shows me that you have hope. And that you're also a fighter. I like that about you. But it's achingly obvious that you're miserable.

It covers your shoulders and drapes itself across your figure. A few times, you've tried to fight it off. But it's hanging on for dear life and now you've realized that it's no use to try and put up a fight. So it starts to pull your body down with every breath you take. Pretty soon your shoulders will hit the ground, but by then it will be too late.

You deserve light. The brightest colors out there. Your mouth needs to smile and laughter needs to spill out. Your hollow brown eyes need to be filled with hope and the promise of tomorrow. No matter how many times I try to tell you that, you're slowly breaking apart. Everyone around you sees your suffering, but they're not willing to help you.

But isn't that how it always goes? There for the happiness, but never the hurt.

Cowards.

They're too afraid that what you're feeling is contagious and they'll catch the darkness that whirls around you. But I'm not afraid, and I know I'm stronger than your agony.

I like you; there's something special about you.

I might love you; your heart is just like mine.

So I'm going to make you something special. It's something that I've been working on for months. And it's something that will obliterate your pain.

If you want, I'll wrap it in a pretty package and hold it out to you.

Please, go ahead. Take it.

But if you take my gift, you're accepting me, too. Don't worry, we'll become fast friends. We'll pick up right where we left off.

You seem to forget that I'm your figure eight. Your infinity. You try to run but I will always find you.

3

I BLAME FEBRUARY.

It's such a pathetically small month, wrapped up in the comfort of hot chocolate, snow angels and candy and flowers from your very own Valentine. But that's all smoke and mirrors so you don't notice the Antarctic winds and frosty pavements. Then you blink and you find yourself wondering, *How is it already March?*

February… it takes away your opportunities and chances. It leaves you with nothing.

Yes, that's it. That's why I haven't got a job. It's all February's fault.

I pull back from the screen and rub my eyes. Picking up my pen, I cross out office manager. Another job down the drain. The sad part about all of this is not my pathetic attempt to blame my calendar, but the fact that this office manager position was the most promising one I've seen in days.

I'm trying to keep an optimistic attitude. Tomorrow, a new job might pop up. And who knows, it might be the right fit for me. But I thought that yesterday morning and the day before that. The selection is getting smaller and smaller, each job sketchier than the last one.

My pen taps against the notepad as I pick up the newspaper on my lap and re-scan the job ads, as if I'd missed a good one the first few read throughs. I tilt my head back and stare at the ceiling, reminding myself to take a deep breath in. Deep breath out. Everything's okay. There's no reason to panic.

Another deep breath in. My left hand forms into a fist. I drop my chin onto my knuckles and glance out the window and stare at the backyard. From this angle I have a view of both neighbors flanking our house. The one on the left have two kids, but you'd never know it judging by how spotless their backyard is. The other has one but it looks like a Toys R Us warehouse blew up in their backyard.

Snow is steadily falling, like sprinkles of sugar. A little girl dressed in a leopard pink snowsuit builds a snowman with her daddy. She laughs at something he says. It's so picturesque. So charming, I'm almost tempted to open up the window and shout out to them that moments like this won't last forever. Sooner than later life bites you in the ass and when it does it bites hard.

A new e-mail pops into my inbox. I sit upright and turn my attention back to my laptop. I squint at the screen, staring at the e-mail address: Jackvan_dosis@gmail.com.

Curiosity gets the best of me and I click on the e-mail even though there's no subject line and I have no idea who it's from.

The e-mail only says on word: ***Hello***.

Instinctively, I click delete and continue on with the job search, which, if I'm being completely honest, is just a futile attempt. In the four weeks I've been home I've had a total of two interviews. Both of them were teaching jobs. I came out of the interviews telling myself that I did well. I've had a steady career as a second grade teacher for years now and good references. Well, I used to have good references. But that's a whole other story.

Yet the call backs never arrived.

My next interview is tomorrow. And even though it's only my third, I still feel the beginning of panic creeping in. It's the fear of the unknown, treading on uneven ground, that scares me, because all I can see is the money that *isn't* coming into my checking account and the money coming out of my savings. Things may be okay for now, but my savings is quickly turning into a well that's about to run dry.

There was a small stack of bills next to the front door when I moved back in with Mom that crisp January morning. I remember stomping the snow off my shoes and staring at it as though it were a foreign object. Mom always kept the home in perfect order. Everything always had a place. She was the mom who, when you were finished with your food, would grab the plate from your hand and put it in the dishwasher.

Yet that stack is turning into a small mound. This morning I attempted to open a few. I was determined to put a dent in the pile. But I became overwhelmed and put it aside to come upstairs. I've been upstairs ever since.

Another ping. New message from the exact same person.

Where have you been? is all it says.

"Buddy, I think you've got the wrong person," I mutter to the screen before I once again click delete and go to a different web page.

"Selah? Honey? I need you."

I squeeze my eyes shut and push away from the desk. I miss the days when I could be relaxed and complacent at the sound of Mom's voice. Now it just makes me bolt upright in alarm. My first thought is, *What's happened now?*

"I'm coming," I holler.

Before I walk out of the room I glance at the computer. The

blinker taunts me, saying, *Don't leave! You need to keep searching!* For a millisecond I'm tempted to stay. Then I think of Mom downstairs, by herself.

She needs me.

I suppose this moment was bound to happen. That period in time when the parent stops being the parent and the child does the taking care of. It's part of life. I just always pictured this moment fifteen to twenty years down the road. Not now.

At fifty-three my mom's perfectly healthy. Happy. Hardworking. There's no disease ravaging her body. That is, if you don't count depression.

No one saw her downward spiral. Especially me. Maybe if I did I would've been more prepared. But I'm not and now I'm back in my hometown, living in my childhood home and taking care of my mom.

Quickly I bound down the stairs, my hand lightly grazing the bannister. When I reach the last step I stop and look to the right, into the living room. The green and white checkered chair that she always sits in is vacant. The TV is on. The couch is covered with wadded-up blankets, the coffee table littered with piles of *Good Housekeeping* magazines, newspapers, and old food wrappers.

There's been an aberrant odor wafting throughout the house recently, so even though it's the dead of winter I've cracked a few windows open in the hopes it would find its way out. A few times, in a desperate attempt, I've sprayed some Febreze but it did nothing.

The bay window behind the couch is cracked, causing the curtains to lift up lightly, as if ghosts are toying with the gauzy material of the curtain.

"Mom?" I call out.

She doesn't reply.

I step out into the hall. "Mom?"

Panic, large and powerful, threatens to seize me. It doesn't matter that I locked the front doors and repeatedly told her I'd be upstairs, she could've up and left the house and wandered down the street. She could be anywhere.

I walk through the dining room, but I know there's no possible way she's in here. There are boxes, opened and unopened, everywhere. About two weeks after I came back to my childhood home, I realized it was just too big for both Mom and me. I talked it over with her and she agreed that it might be time to downsize. Yet downsizing required getting rid of clutter and Mom had a lot of it. I wouldn't call her a hoarder but she's damn near it.

There are light square marks on the wall from pictures that have been taken down and are now leaning against the wall. I'd packed up some photo albums and some fine china, but I still had a ways to go. Quickly, I weave my way through the maze of boxes toward the kitchen.

Oh, God, I think, *someone might find her and call the cops. And then they'll take her away and I don't know if—*

All my terrible thoughts come to a halt when I enter the kitchen and see her sitting at the table. A coffee cup is placed in front of her. Slowly she pours a Sweet'N Low packet into the cup. When it's empty she gently places it to her left, where a neat stack is starting to form. She grabs another pink packet to her right and repeats the process.

Loudly, I sigh in relief, not even caring that she's making a mess. "Why didn't you answer me?"

Slowly, she lifts her head. She shrugs and stirs her drink slowly. Mom has her good days and then some bad days. Today is a bad one. She may physically be here, but her mind is clearly elsewhere.

Two months ago she was placed involuntarily in the psychiatric unit at St. Mary's hospital for seventy-two hours. A stranger found her walking down the street in her robe and slippers. Later on, I learned that she was laughing manically and crying out in pain.

Signing her out wasn't hard. The doctors monitored her and saw no reason to keep her. They said she was in a depressive state, encouraged that she look for a therapist and we were on our way.

Repeatedly Mom reassured me that she'd had a bad day when she was a found on the streets. That's all. Doesn't everyone have bad days?

I agreed with her but told myself to check in on her more often. Call her to see how she was doing. But days later the very same thing happened and this time it was harder to sign her out. Doctors wanted her to stay for two weeks for further treatment. They thought it was more than depression. A 'psychotic breakdown' they'd said. They continued speaking, but I blocked them out because I knew my mom wasn't psychotic. Depressed, maybe. But not psychotic.

Leaving her there was out of the question. It was a struggle, a back and forth between the doctor and me. The only way I could sign her out was if I agreed to take Mom back for a follow-up. When we left, dread took root in my body. There couldn't be a third-time visit. If there was, I knew I wouldn't be able to sign her out. I had to be with her. She needed me.

So I moved back home. I did all of this knowing that Mom needed me more than anything. Until she was better, my life was on hold. To me, it seemed fundamentally wrong to leave the woman that raised me all alone during a rough time. She was, no, *is*, a good mom. No, better than that. She's poured all her energy into giving me a good life. Now it's my turn to return the favor.

But that doesn't mean that every day has been easy. At first I couldn't sleep for more than three or fours hours. My racing mind would rip me out of my slumber and I would have to go check on my mom. I was so afraid that she was going to leave that I refused to let her out of my sight.

Sometimes she was fine. Other days she stared blankly at the television or sat at the kitchen table with a cup of coffee in front of her. She never drank it, just stared into its muddy depths as if the secret to her insanity lay there. Maybe insanity is a harsh word, but there's no other explanation for what made her snap.

There is no income coming in. My savings is dwindling. But it's next to impossible to find a job that would give me a schedule to fit my mom's and my unusual circumstance.

"What are you doing?"

"Putting sugar in my coffee."

"That's fine, but first you need to make some coffee," I say gently.

She stares into the coffee cup. At this point, it's halfway filled with sugar.

"You want me to make you some?"

She shakes her head no.

"Are you hungry?"

Another head shake.

"Are you sure?" I persist. "I can make something simple like a ham sandwich."

Minutes roll by and I'm close to giving up and going back to my job search. Then she looks me in the eye. "I guess a sandwich sounds good."

Instinctively, I smile. Because this is good. Really good. "Excellent!" I say, wincing at my own voice. I sound like an eager beaver.

There are days where it's an all-out war to get Mom to function like a human. If I didn't remind her she'd go days without bathing and eating. If it were up to her she'd live off Sweet'N Lows and home makeover shows.

I go to the fridge and pull out food to make a sandwich.

My mom has always been an introvert, the kind of person that doesn't vocalize her thoughts. She'd rather sit in silence and endure the pain. She'd rather go slowly insane than reach out to someone.

I look at her out of the corner of my eyes. She stares straight ahead.

What brought her to this point? What made her turn in on herself and become a shell of her former self? Out of this entire situation, that was the scariest part.

"Tomorrow I'm going job hunting," I say conversationally.

She says nothing.

"I found a few jobs that look pretty promising," I lie. I don't know why. Maybe I'm hoping it will snag her attention.

Silence.

"There's one job opening at a credit union in Decatur. It's not my dream job but it's only ten minutes away from here. So if you needed me I could be home in a heartbeat."

This one-sided conversation is par for the course.

"Of course I'm still holding out hope that I can find a good teaching job." I place the sandwich in front of her and start to put away the food. Out of the corner of my eye, I look at Mom. She continues to sit there; she doesn't touch her sandwich. What was the point of even making the damn thing?

I wipe down one of the counters before I turn around and face her. "Good talk," I say sarcastically. "We should do this again."

I start to walk out of the room when she finally speaks. "I'm so sorry, Selah," she says very softly.

I stop in my tracks and walk back to her. "Mom, it's fine."

"No, it's not. It's not fine. You shouldn't be here."

"Of course I'm going to be here. You're my mom."

"I can be alone," she replies earnestly, like a child trying to prove her parents wrong.

"No, you can't," I say slowly but gently.

4

TWO WEEKS AGO a man moved into the house across the street.

For the twentieth time this morning, I peek through the blinds and peer at him. As usual, he's sitting on the porch. It doesn't matter that it's freezing out. He seems impervious to it. A newspaper rests on his lap and a coffee sits on the end table. He has a golden retriever that normally follows him around but is now loyally resting at his feet. His tail lazily shuffles back and forth as he looks at the world around him.

Nothing about this picture should be even remotely interesting. But there's something… strange about this man. I can't put my finger on it. For that reason alone, I can't stop watching him. I need to figure him out or it'll drive me crazy.

I'm not obsessive or compulsive or anything but I'm damn near close. When I don't know the answer to something or can't find an item I'll keep looking and thinking until it's found. Safe to say that for the past fourteen days I've been doing a lot of staring at this man.

I suppose he could be considered attractive. He has a

weathered look about him. His dark hair on the sides is threaded with gray hairs. He has stubble that's also peppered with gray, which makes me wonder if he's one of those silver foxes or is just prematurely graying.

The one thing that I despise is his eyes. For me, that's uncommon. I truly believe that instead of people wearing their pain, they store it in their eyes. With this man, I can't get a good read on his eyes. That unnerves me. They're shrewd and closed off and say, *I'm watching you.*

Even so, I still watch him. And this is what I've gathered from my stalking sessions: he has no family. No kids. No friends. If he does, they certainly haven't by stopped by for a visit. He has a golden retriever that he frequently walks.

I'm not one hundred percent sure but I'm fairly certain that he has a nine-to-five job that he goes to everyday. It's no suit and tie job. More like jeans and a nice dress shirt that stays in the gray color wheel. He drinks so much coffee I'm convinced it's his blood type.

He never smiles. Whenever I'm outside with Mom he never says hi. Although to be fair, neither do I. When he moved in the first thing he did was rip the FOR SALE sign out of the front yard and toss it into the garage like it was a piece of garbage. There was no U-HAUL parked in his driveway, filled to the brim with his belongings. He carried in a few boxes and a duffel bag and that was it.

In a way it's thrilling—dissecting this man in plain sight. It's like playing with a Rubik's cube: just when you think you have it figured out, you see another side that doesn't have the same colors and you have to start all over again. So far I'm still trying to solve this cube.

There are times where I open the door to my imagination and let it run wild with all kinds of crazy scenarios. Maybe he was a criminal on the run, trying to lay low. Was it murder or bank fraud? Perhaps he lost a job or a loved one and had to start over somewhere different.

I know those theories are far-fetched at best, but I didn't want to latch onto the idea that he was some boring man that simply moved into a quiet suburb. It just can't be as simple at that. This man is hiding something.

As though he can sense my stare he whips his body around and stares right at me, as if he's trying to get a better look at me.

"What are you doing, Selah?"

I jump back from the window and turn around, holding my hands behind my back, like a child caught stealing from the cookie jar.

I hiked a thumb toward the window. "I was just watching the new neighbor."

Mom narrows her eyes at me and for the smallest second she's the mom I grew up with. With crystal clarity I can see her dressed in her customary long, flowing skirts. She hated shorts and very rarely wore jeans. She grew up in Tucson, Arizona so warm weather ran through her veins. During the summer she wore tank tops in a full range of colors. Her dark blonde, pin-straight hair would be pushed back with a headband. Gray was starting to creep in now, but she didn't bother to cover it up. There isn't a pair of Birkenstocks that Mom doesn't like. There were a few times that I saw her wear them in the wintertime. With socks, of course.

I just painted you a very quirky version of Susie Kerrington. But it's the best, most honest version I can give you. If she were her regular old self right now, watching me watch the neighbor, she'd say, "Your imagination is going to get you in trouble some day."

And I would've replied, "Impossible. There's no better friend than the imagination."

And she'd sigh as if being an adult, being stern, was exhausting. Finally she would give up the fight and smile broadly. "Such a dreamer. Never stop living inside that beautiful head of yours."

Any chance I could I tried to work her wise words into my life. Growing up, if I read a book that didn't end how I'd want it to, I'd close my eyes and let my imagination take control. When I got my license, I'd drive around town with my best friend, Sam. If we were at a stoplight and a car was in front of us, I'd create a story for the person driving or the rest of the people inside. Sam thought it was insanity at first, but she quickly caught on to the game.

It'd been years since I'd done that; life had dulled out that quirky habit of mine. But right now, with everything so up in the air, it felt nice to do.

"He seems nice," Mom says as she walks toward her chair. Her hands hold a fresh cup of coffee, which I don't see the point of. She'll take a few sips before she forgets about it altogether.

Mom's words do nothing to reassure me. She got along with everyone and saw the best in them. It was a trait that always seemed to hurt her in the end. She used to always tell me how nice this person was and to give them a chance. She once made friends with a lady at Curves. They started having coffee dates. Those little dates extended to shopping trips. It took three months before Mom finally realized that her little Curves friend was stealing from her.

There were rare moments when she was right, though.

Take the couple that lived in the house before our strange neighbor moved in. Mom said they were quiet, but nice. The same age as her. They'd moved in a year after I graduated high school. The husband was retired from the military. The wife had been a stay-at-home mom. The few times I'd come home to visit, I'd seen them in passing. The lady was constantly outside. Many times Mom mentioned that the flowers she'd planted in their front yard were so beautiful.

Those flowers are now dead.

Crossing my arms, I move closer. "And how do you know he's nice?"

Mom crosses her robe tighter around her waist. "I talked to him."

I move away from the window. "When?"

She won't meet my gaze. "A few days after he moved in."

How is that possible? I'm constantly keeping watch over Mom. Sure, there's been the small number of times she's walked out the front door, but I always catch her before she leaves the porch and escort her back into the house.

"I just want to take a walk, Selah," she'd protest weakly. "There's nothing wrong about that."

"I know," I'd say gently. "But not today." Or tomorrow. Or the day after that.

"I was on the porch swing and he had just finished walking his dog." She takes a sip of her coffee. "Nice dog. His name is Duke."

"Who? The dog or the owner?" I ask dryly.

"The dog."

"Mom," I say slowly as I push away from the wall. I sit down on the edge of the couch and angle my body toward her. "You have to be careful. I can't have you wandering around by yourself."

She scoffs. "I'm perfectly fine."

I bite down on my lower lip until I draw blood. Best not to reply. I stand up and let Mom go back to watching HSN and walk over to the window. When I glance through the blinds I see he's still on the porch.

"So during your impromptu visit with the neighbor did you happen to catch his name?" I ask with my eyes still glued to the window.

"Noah."

"Noah," I repeat.

Didn't expect that. I pegged him as a Steve or a Nick. Yeah, definitely a Nick. But not a Noah. Noah seems like a gentle name. A name for a little boy with a mop of curly brown hair and a toothless grin. Or a loving husband who's overworked and tired but keeps trudging on because he loves his family. Loves life. Noah doesn't fit my sullen neighbor.

"So what does Noah do for a living?" I ask, making sure to put his name into air quotes.

Mom's eyes start to glaze over. It's like a curtain goes down behind her eyes, closing her off from the outside world and effectively making her a prisoner of her mind. I wonder what goes on during those moments. What does she feel? What is she thinking?

Before that curtain completely closes, I make one last-ditch attempt to keep Mom in the present. "Mom? *Mom*, did you hear me?"

She turns toward me and gives me a carefree smile that sends chills down my spine. It's like I get to see Mom when she was teenager. Flighty and untroubled, without a care in the world.

She reaches out and grabs my hand. "Selah," she coos. "Your imagination is going to get you into trouble."

She gives my hand a final pat before she drops it and directs her attention back to the TV. I flop back onto the couch and sigh heavily as I stare up at the ceiling. This can't happen. Not today. Why today?

I've already mentioned that Mom has good and bad days. On those bad days Mom is completely vacant. She's living and breathing like everyone else but wires become tangled in her head and short circuit. She starts to speak in circles.

"If it's any consolation, I've seen the others neighbors stare at him," I point out.

It's the truth. We live in Wildwood, a subdivision straddling the edge of Decatur. It's a quaint place, with bi-level and ranch style homes. In the summertime the yards are neatly mowed. Kids walk down the sidewalk without risk of being kidnapped. Parents do carpool. In short, this is the ideal place to raise a family.

A single man who keeps to himself and has no kids of his own sticks out like sore thumb. He might as well hang a marquee above his front door that says, *Hello! Look at me! I don't belong here!*

"Your imagination is going to get you into trouble," Mom says once again, pulling me out of my thoughts.

Closing my eyes, I take a few deep breaths.

I glance down at my watch. In fifteen minutes I have to be out the door. I have a job interview that actually seems promising, something that I could be hired for and then I would have an income. And then I could pay all the bills and not just the most important ones. And then I could find a way to get Mom better.

Although all my hopes are starting to look like castles in the air. I glance at Mom. She's smiling widely at the TV screen while a blonde lady with a sleek bob prattles on about this amazing eye cream that the viewers just have to try. *You'll see results in under two weeks!*

I glance down at my watch and sigh. "We can talk about the creepy neighbor some other time. Right now we have to go. I have a job interview in fifteen minutes. I can't be late."

Mom perks up, looking more like the mom I grew up with. "A job interview? For what?"

I grab my purse from the coffee table and dig for my keys. "It's nothing special. Just a job at the Credit Union."

"That's wonderful!"

With my keys in hand, I lift my head and see Mom's smiling face. I can't help but smile back. "It is," I agree softly. For a small second I feel hopeful that everything will work out for us and we'll make it through this difficult time.

"Do you want to get dressed real quick?"

Mom's smile fades as she stares at me with confusion. "I'm not coming."

"Yes, you are."

"Selah," she sighs, "I'm a big girl. I can stay at home by myself."

Allowing her to stay at home isn't an option. I learned that the hard way and now I'm once bitten, twice shy.

"Mom," I start out slowly. "Do I need to remind you of what happened the last time I left you alone?"

"No."

"I think I do. Last Thursday I went to that interview for the teaching job at the private school. Remember?"

Hesitantly, she nods.

"You vowed that you were okay alone. I was only gone for thirty minutes at the most, yet you were gone when I got back."

Her face turns beet red. She tucks her hands beneath her thighs and stares down at the ground. "I was not!"

"You were too. I was looking for you for hours and couldn't find you. I was so… scared."

At the very last second, I switch up my words. What I really wanted to say was that I was so terrified that I almost called the cops. Over and over I kept picturing her dead on the street. Or cold and alone. The fear I felt can still make my skin clammy.

In the end, the cops never needed to be called. A nice woman who lived three streets away had been walking her dog when she found Mom wandering aimlessly. She'd been dressed in a ratty gray robe that she'd had for as long as I could remember. Her hair was wet, like she'd just got out of the shower.

Before the lady left my doorstep she leaned in, worry coating her features. "It looked like she'd been crying." She hesitated. "Is everything all right?" Translation: Is she nuts and need to be on medication?

I shook my head at the kind lady and quickly made up a lie. "She's going through a rough time. Loss in the family," I lie and nod with a look that says, 'You understand how that goes.'

The lady nodded with understanding. She patted my shoulder. "I'm sorry to hear that." And then she walked away.

My relief was palpable. Yet all I could think about was what if I wasn't as lucky next time? What if the thoughtful, kind woman didn't find her and bring her back? What if it was someone not as understanding? Mom would be taken away from me forever.

"Selah, I was here the whole time, you just didn't look hard enough!" Mom says sharply.

This is an argument that has no end in sight. Mom has her version of the truth and I have mine. The truth is somewhere in the middle but neither one of us has the desire to search for it.

"Look I don't want to argue with you right now." My hand curls around the doorknob. I twist around to look in Mom's direction. "This interview is important and I'm not leaving unless you go with me."

Mom sighs heavily and slowly stands up. "Fine. I'll go. But I'm not changing."

Impatiently, I look down at my watch. I'm down to ten minutes. "Fine," I rush out. "Let's just go."

"Oh, this is a bad idea," she mutters as I usher her out the door.

"No it's not."

"What kind of person is going to hire a thirty-year-old woman that has her elderly mother tagging along?"

I'm thinking the same thing myself, but what other choice do I have?

"One: You're not elderly."

"I'm fifty-three."

"So you're a young elderly," I say without missing a beat. "Two: They won't even notice you," I lie. "They'll probably think you're a client."

Another lie but if it makes Mom feel better then I'll lie until I'm blue in the face. Judging from her single arched brow I know she's not buying it.

As we pull out of the driveway Mom mutters beneath her breath. "I have a bad feeling about this."

"YOU CAN DO this, you can do this," I chant as I sit in my car directly outside the credit union. My stomach has been in knots all morning. I ate a bit of toast and coffee and almost threw it up. Anxiety makes my heart race.

"Of course you can, honey," Mom says.

I look out at her from the corner of my eye. I didn't realize I said my words out loud. My lips kick up into a small smile. "Thank you."

"Now remember—when you're nervous you tend to fidget with your hands. Lace them together and place them on your lap."

My confidence grows with Mom's words, which is ridiculous; I'm not a child. But for a millisecond I saw a small part of Mom, the one I'd known for so long, shining through.

"Alright," I breathe. "Lets go in."

Mom shoots the brick building in front of us a worried look. "Selah… it's bad enough that you dragged me here. But go inside?

Don't you think they'll find that strange?"

Of course they'll find it strange. What sane person wouldn't? I turn in my seat, my seatbelt strap digging into the side of my neck. "It's not a big deal, alright? Just act like you're in there to cash a check or something." I finish my words with a bright smile.

"And when I don't have a check to cash?" she challenges.

"I don't know," I reply impatiently. "Just say you're waiting for a family member!" I glance at the half-filled parking lot. "It looks relatively busy. They probably won't even notice you're there."

With a heavy sigh Mom nods before she unbuckles her seat and gets out. The sky is a slate gray as snow continues to fall all around us. A snowplow drives by on the main road, pushing the snow towards the side of the road.

It's a lazy day, the kind that makes you want to cuddle up on the couch, burrowed deep in a blanket with a cup of coffee between your hands. Hell, even the sun is too lazy to peek out from behind the clouds.

Shoulder to shoulder we walk toward the credit union. It's directly off Dividend, a fairly busy road. I take in the tan building, with its meticulous landscaping now hidden under a cloak of snow. It wouldn't be so bad to work here. The only downside is that it takes about fifteen minutes, give or take, to get here from my house. I want to be close to Mom, just in case. But if I try to stay close to Wildwood, my options will consist of gas stations, fast food, a tanning salon, a Farm and Fleet and a Kroger's.

My confidence continues to cling to me as I hurry ahead of Mom and open one of the front doors. A gust of warm air brushes against my skin. With the frigid temps we've had the past few days the heat should feel amazing. But I'm so nervous my skin feels clammy.

Confident. You are confident, I tell myself.

The pressure I feel to get this job is unbearable. Every day that

I buy groceries, fuel up my car, or take a shower I hear the sound effect of a cash register. I picture my savings slowly dwindling away until it ends up with a negative balance. There's nothing I can think of to ease my fears. No 'it's going to be okay' pep talks, because there are no guarantees that everything will be all right.

"This shouldn't take long," I murmur into Mom's ear. I gesture to the open seats to our left. "Just sit and read a magazine. If you get thirsty you can ask the—"

"I'm not a child," Mom interjects sharply.

"I know," I say slowly. "I'm just trying to give you options of things to do."

"Hello." The lady behind the front desk greets me.

All of a sudden my confidence takes off. I jerk my head to the right. Behind a large curved desk is a lady with a bright smile. Another woman sits to her left with a phone cradled to her ear and eyes glued to the computer screen in front of her.

Quickly, I glance at my Mom. "Stay here," I whisper before I walk toward the front desk. I see the lady quickly glance at Mom.

"Hi, I have an 11:30 interview with Dan McEntire," I say in a bright voice, the one I use to convince strangers that my life isn't as fucked-up as it appears.

The lady blinks rapidly. Her brilliant smile never fades. "Of course. You can have a seat and I'll let him know you're here."

"Thank you." I turn around feeling the secretary's eyes on me. On Mom. Mom pats the seat next to her. I sit down and place my purse in my lap like it's a protective barrier.

"Don't worry," Mom murmurs.

I grab one of the many magazine placed on the coffee table and blindly flip through it. "I'm not worried."

"Of course you are."

"I'm not." I pause. "There's just a lot riding on this."

"No, there isn't," Mom insists. "There are plenty of jobs."

I drop the magazine onto my lap. "Have you seen the job selection out there? It's slim pickings!" I hiss.

"Everything will be fine."

Will it though? No one can predict the future. We want to. We all want to prepare ourselves for the pain or happiness that could be coming our way. If that were possible I would've put more money into my savings. I would've kept a closer eye on Mom. I would've never left Kansas City.

"Ms. Kerrington? He's ready for you." She glances at Mom and back at me. First instinct is to defend my decision in bringing her, but I know that explaining things would honestly just make things worse.

I stand and adjust my black blazer. I paired my black blazer (and only blazer) with black slacks and a white dress shirt. To me, it screamed, *I'm responsible! Hire me!*

It was probably a good thing I didn't have a checking account with them. If I did, they'd take one look at the balance and throw my resume away.

I walk toward the hall with my head held high as though the lady behind me with limp, stringy hair, pale skin and sad eyes isn't related to me.

I KNOW THE second I leave the building that I didn't get the job.

When I step into the front lobby Mom is still in the same spot where I left her. She's in good spirits and greets me with a bright smile. The receptionist, though? Well I can't say the same about her. She stares at Mom like she's lost her damn mind.

"Have a nice day," she says as we walk out the door.

My left hand gently curls around Mom's elbow. It's so fragile. One big squeeze and I think I could snap it in half. The thought serves as a reminder that Mom needs me more than ever. She needs me to be the shield between the world and the depression taking over her life.

I look over my shoulder at the receptionist and shoot her a dirty look. There's no reason for her to judge Mom or me. I know my actions are one more check mark against me landing this job.

When I get inside the car I rest my forehead against the steering wheel and groan. "Shoot me. Just shoot me now."

"That bad?"

I lift my head and sigh. "I wouldn't even say it went bad. It's just that I could tell he didn't think I was qualified for the job and it's clerical work," I explain.

"Don't worry, honey." She pats my hand. "There's a bigger and better job on the horizon."

Mom sounds so happy and optimistic and if I were just starting out on this job search I might've believed her. I think my lack of enthusiasm shows on my face because Mom says, "How about we go get something to eat?"

I don't have dumbass written across my forward. Her suggestion is a ploy to take my mind off yet another bad interview. But Mom's starting to look like she licks granola bars for meals, so I nod.

"Where do you want to go?" I ask, as I put the car in reverse.

"Krekel's?"

My stomach grumbles at the suggestion. "Krekel's it is."

The drive there is filled with silence. We drive across the Staley Bridge, notorious for the stench that finds its way into your car and makes you want to gag. When Sam and I were younger we'd go over the bridge holding our breath and whoever made it without gasping for air won.

But I'm too distracted by my interview to be bothered by the smell. Plus, Mom is humming a song that I've never heard before.

"What are you humming?"

"A song," she replies, as she stares out the window.

"I get that but what song?"

"Just an old hymn that your grandmother loved."

"Why are you humming it?"

"Why are you in such a bad mood?" Mom counters.

"I'm not," I say, even though my hands are gripping the steering wheel so tight my knuckles are white.

Silently, we get out of the car. There's only the sound of traffic zooming by. This isn't the best area of Decatur but it certainly isn't the worst. There's a used car dealership next door and we're surrounded by ranch style homes. Cars with oversized rims and bass systems to match are parked in the driveway.

At this time of day the restaurant is almost empty so we quickly get a booth and grab the menus placed behind the ketchup and mustard. A haggard blonde with coal-black roots and makeup slowly melting off her face approaches. Before she can say anything Mom cuts in.

"We already know what we want. A Diet Coke, and a number two for me." She gives me a sparring glance before she points a finger in my direction. "And a Dr. Pepper and a number five for her. Can you put cheese on the fries, please?"

The waitress looks both dumbfounded and pleased that for once she doesn't have to rattle off the specials for the umpteenth time. "All right," she says as she takes our menus. "I'll have your orders out as soon as possible."

"Thank you," I say.

The waitress gives Mom another quizzical glance before she walks away. Not that I blame her. What she's just experienced is the self- sufficient, know-what-I-want Susie Kerrington and it's impossible to know when and where she'll decide to make a grand appearance. You just have to go with the flow. Although today I'm not in the mood for it.

"So," Mom sighs and smiles happily at me. "Any more interviews?"

I roll my neck and take a deep breath. "No. Not yet."

My fingers tap against the sticky table as my right leg bounces up and down. I feel time slipping from my fingers and what am I doing about it? Sitting here, having lunch.

"What's the rush anyway? Let the right job come to you!"

I bite down on my lip. I've always loved my mom's eccentric, hippie way of thinking. But in times of stress she tended to fold in on herself and throw her problems out to the world, hoping that someone would catch them, fix them, and toss them right back to her.

Typically that person is me. But very swiftly I'm starting to see that this isn't a problem that I can fix. I can't click my heels together and have a job and all the bills paid. Mom looks at me, her green eyes blinking with a bewildered expression as she waits for me to answer.

"There's no rush," I lie. I'm starting to get really good at that. Too bad there's no job for that. "I'm just being dramatic."

"You were always like that. Worry, worry, worry!" she says with a soft chuckle, as if we're taking a walk down memory lane.

I wonder if she'd be laughing if she knew how little I had in my bank account. The mere thought of it makes me nauseous. Something hard settles in my stomach and I push away my food.

"Mom, I may be a dreamer but this time there's no exaggeration on my part."

She takes a bite out of her hamburger and frowns at me.

"If I don't find a job soon then we are royally fucked," I say bluntly.

"Language, Selah!" Mom admonishes.

"Well, it's the truth!"

Another bite of her sandwich.

You know how people say they're emotional eaters when they're upset or sometimes even happy? My Mom is one of them and right now she is trying to push aside her fear by attacking her food with gusto.

I try to soften my approach. "We have bills to be paid, and if weren't for my savings we wouldn't be coasting along like we are right now."

She's quiet for a few second. Creases appear between her brows as she frowns down at her almost empty plate. "You may think I don't notice what's going on, but I do. I just believe panicking isn't going to fix anything. What have I always told you? The right job will find its way to you."

"Your words haven't fallen on deaf ears. I believe you. The only problem is that I don't have the time to wait for that perfect job. At this point I'll take anything I can get."

"And just waste your degree? You're an amazing teacher!" Mom says heatedly. "Any school would be lucky to have you."

"You're my mother. If you said anything different about me, something's up."

"Selah, I mean it."

"What do you want me to do? I've put out resumes all over."

Mom starts to list all the school districts around us. I've gone to about ninety-five percent of them looking for a job. She becomes quiet. Her shoulders slump. Then she says, "Move back to Kansas City."

"Sure," I say, playing along. "As long as you come with me."

Mom lifts her eyes and says stoically, "I'm not going anywhere."

"Neither am I, then," I shoot back.

She sighs and rubs her temples as if I'm giving her a headache. "Selah, how many times are we going to have this conversation?"

"Until you understand that you can't be by yourself."

"But I *can*," she repeats slowly, like she's talking to five-year old. I'm a grown woman. I can take care of myself."

I start to reply but I see the waitress plodding our way and shut my mouth.

"Are you ready for some dessert?" the waitress asks listlessly, almost as though she's forced by her manager to ask each and every customer this question.

This conversation isn't over but I can tell Mom is ready for it to be. I'm about to tell the waitress yes, but before I even open my mouth Mom smiles brightly at her and says, "We'll take the check, please."

WHEN I PULL into the driveway, I stifle a groan. After lunch I got it in my head that it'd be a good idea to stay out of the house. Maybe part of Mom's problem is that she holes herself away from the world. Maybe that's what's making her so sad. So we braved the bitterly cold weather and slowly walked the bike trail. A few ladies dressed in puffy jackets, black yoga pants and mittens walked past us, furiously speed walking.

After that we went to Kroger's. We were out of the house almost the whole day and I felt damn proud of myself. Yet there's one thing I didn't take into account: at end of the workday, there's a sudden influx of vehicles driving down our street. People filter in and out of their houses, leaving the front door open so you can hear the TV's blaring, neighbors speaking to one another, kids giggling loudly, car doors slamming. This goes on for an hour or so before everyone finally meanders into their homes for the night. And right now I'm stuck in the middle of it.

"Let's get this over with," I mutter beneath my breath as I open the car door.

Mom gleefully opens her door and it seems like the day out of the house did her good. Almost too good, because she practically skips to the back of the car. She slaps the trunk. "Open up!" she shouts. "I'll help with groceries."

I can feel people's eyes on us. My blood boils; Mom is established on this street. Like the tall oaks lining the road, she's been here forever. And that's what has made her downfall all the more depressing.

"Mom." I rush to her side. "Let me do that." I try to grab the bags dangling from her hands but she won't have it.

"There's Trina with her girls!" Mom says as we cut through the front lawn, fresh snow coating her shoes.

"Yes, I see them."

I hook my arm through hers and gently guide her toward the porch. I have to get her inside before she says or does something that draws even more attention to herself.

"Hi Trina!" Mom calls out enthusiastically. She lifts her free hand and waves.

I stifle a groan and stop walking long enough to look over Mom's head. Even without Mom's greeting it'd be impossible to go incognito. In Wildwood everyone knows everyone. There are the hermits that keep to themselves barely offering their neighbors a passing glance. Then you have the outgoing ones who greet everyone on the block like they're family. Mom is the latter.

Trina stares at Mom as though she has three heads. There's an uncomfortable moment where I think she's going to completely snub Mom and walk inside her house, but finally she waves back. Seconds later, her girls follow suit. Somehow their stiff waves become synchronized, as if they've practiced it before. It's awkward and formal and says, *Let's acknowledge the crazy person so she'll leave us alone.*

They all look at us like we are the Big Edie and Little Edie of Wildwood—two crazy ladies that taint their wholesome and safe subdivision. But they're wrong. This isn't *Grey Gardens.* I remember watching the documentary a few years back. I was fascinated by the two charming—albeit eccentric—women holed up in their once grand estate in the Hamptons, blissfully unaware of what was going on around them.

Now that I feel myself being compared to them I no longer find Big Edie and Little Edie charming.

How dare any of our neighbors look down on Mom?

Especially Trina.

I call her a one-upper. Whenever someone has good news, she has an even better revelation. You have a bad day? Forget about it because it doesn't come close to the kind of day Trina's had! People barely tolerate her, but Mom does. She would stand there on her porch, nodding along while Trina rambled on about her day.

Mom once tutored one of her daughters. I think it was the middle daughter, Jenny. Who the hell knows; they all look the same. Anyway, the girl would come over almost everyday. She would sit with Mom at the kitchen table where they would painstakingly sound out words and slowly read each sentence aloud. Mom had an infinite amount of patience. She never lost her cool, no matter how many times Jenny got a certain word wrong.

Trina, of all people, deserved to return some of that patience. It was the least she could do.

I can just picture her gossiping with one of her friends about how she had to interact with the nutso Susie Kerrington. And I can vividly imagine one of her vapid friends tilting her head to the side and patting Trina on the shoulder, saying, "God, Trina. Your neighbor sounds crazy."

"I wonder what's wrong with her," Mom says in her wistful voice.

"She's probably just distracted. With three kids who knows what she has on her plate," I reply lamely and try to steer Mom toward the front door. She slowly shuffles forward and keeps looking back at Trina and her girls.

"I bet you're right." She gives me a weak smile as I reach around her and slide my key into the lock. "Her youngest, Jenny, is in seventh grade, isn't she?" She doesn't give me time to reply. "Remember when I tutored her? Lovely girl."

"Yep." I drop my keys in the key bowl right next to the front door. "I remember you telling me that."

"I recommended that Trina get the sweet girl a tutor. But she didn't listen to me. Got all huffy on me. You know how parents can be. Oh, my kid is brilliant! My kid doesn't need help." She puts air quotes around the last word and rolls her eyes as she walks into the living room. The remote control and coffee are right where she left them.

Dammit, I should've removed the batteries from the remote before we left. I'm beyond sick of watching the Home Shopping Network and *The 700 Club*. But if the television's shut off that means silence and that might be worse than any of the mind-numbing shows Mom watches.

"Do you want to take a shower?" I ask nonchalantly.

She looks over at me with bright eyes, like I told her I'd found the cure for cancer. "That sounds wonderful. It'll warm me up." She places the remote on the end table and stands up.

I watch as she walks toward the stairs. She grabs the bannister, her pale skin almost translucent against the mahogany wood. Suddenly, she stops in the middle of the stairs and twists around to look at me. She wears a peculiar expression on her face: part suspicious, part insightful.

"What is it?" I ask.

She motions for me to come closer, so I do. When I'm right next to the stairs she bends over and whispers to me, like we're surrounded by people, "I know how they look at me."

"How do they look at you?" I ask. I don't know why. Perhaps I want her to say the words. Crazy. Insane.

"They all think I'm psycho. But I'm not." She pulls back an inch. "You don't feel the same way, do you?"

"Of course not," I say adamantly.

Mom smiles at me. "I knew you'd feel the same way."

She pushes away and goes up the stairs. I watch her, goose bumps trailing beneath my skin; I lied to her.

Sometimes I *do* think she's insane.

6

I HAVE DISCOVERED that from a distance it is incredibly easy to read people.

In the shadows, people don't notice you. They let their guard down. Let you into their life without even knowing it. After a while their movements become predictable and you start to feel more intimate with them. You know when they're irritable or sad. Happy or anxious. And while they keep desperately seeking a cure-all for their afflictions, you stand there in shadows, knowing what they need.

My last gift was what you needed. But you barely noticed. You were too busy with your despair.

Ah, despair, despair, despair. Too many people get caught in that bitch's web. And the sad truth is that they never find their way out. They never find their figure eight.

They never find me.

The truth of the matter is you didn't find me. You got lucky and had the tables turned. You may not see me yet. But you will.

Something as big as me takes time to acclimate to. Until then

I'm going to give you another present. This one you're going to take notice of. It is truly something.

I'm actually quite proud of myself with this one. It's so good that I'm going to let you think that fate, kismet or whatever bullshit you call it was responsible for it. Besides, I have a million more gifts just waiting for you, that I can take credit for.

Each one is bigger and better than the last.

You'll see.

7

"YOU'VE GOT MAIL."

My head jerks up so fast it slams into the lamp to my left. Instinctively I rub the side of my head and slowly take in my surroundings. I'm so out of it that it takes me a minute to realize that I'm up in the computer room.

In a daze, I try to remember what I was doing before I fell asleep. Looking for jobs is a given. But I remember that after awhile I gave up and then binge watched a sitcom on Netflix and that's why the volume was cranked up so freaking high.

I rub my eyes and ignore how raw my throat feels. It's two a.m.

With my palms flat on the desk I sit up straight, ignoring the crick in my neck. I click on the new e-mail, ignoring the fuzziness in my brain and the serious cottonmouth I have going on. I should technically drag my tired ass to bed but my mind is slowly starting to wake up and it's telling me two things: find a damn job and take care of your mom.

I'm doing neither of those things well lately. But I've never been good at handling stress. Typically, if I don't have the answer that I'm looking for, I move on.

I hate remaining idle and everything lately has been about keeping still and being patient. Already I'm on the cusp of a small panic attack. There's a misconception about panic attacks. They can sneak up on you no matter what you're doing. At least, that's always been the case for me. I start to think of all the things that are stacked up against me. All the things that I'm failing at and can't get to and it feels like thousands of bugs are crawling beneath my skin. My legs get itchy. Sometimes I even break out in hives. I can't focus on a single thing and it feels like I'm going to pass out.

Before I check my e-mails, I hurry to the bathroom. With my hands curled around the lip of the counter I stare at myself. Now that I'm up, there's no getting back to sleep. Tomorrow I'll be a zombie and cranky.

With a sigh I open up the medicine cabinet and look at the array of medications neatly lined up. There are so many that Mom could open her own little pharmacy. I grab the one that says Melatonin and read the dosage: 3mg. Nope, that's not enough. I place it on the counter and grab the Remeron. 30mg. That's more like it.

I grab one Remeron and two Melatonin. Once they're swallowed I neatly place them back in their correct positions and hope that the medicine does its job. More than half of those medications are Mom's but the rest are mine. With the exception of the sleep aids, I don't take the rest.

Why? Because I'm perfectly fine. I may have stressful moments here and there but who doesn't? It doesn't mean I need medication to make myself feel better.

I turn off the bathroom light and go back to the computer room. I pass Mom's room and peek inside. It's so dark it takes a while for my eyes to adjust. Finally, I see the small outline of her body. Slowly, I close the door and walk into the computer room.

When I sit down, I click on the new e-mail. It's from the same person that e-mailed me a few days ago.

Again, there's no subject. Nonetheless, I click on the e-mail but am disappointed when I see all the person wrote is: ***Where have you been?***

My hands fly across the keyboard as I write back: ***Sorry. Think you have the wrong person.*** I press send. Seconds later I get a reply. ***I don't think I do. This is Selah... right?***

The sight of my name makes me jolt slightly. Who is this person? Maybe it's a friend from high school that I haven't spoken to in years? Or a friend of a friend that I randomly gave my e-mail to? Who knows? Either way, I don't reply.

Then I receive another e-mail.

Selah from JustWrite?

It takes me a few seconds to realize what this person is talking about. Then I groan.

Over six months ago, I joined JustWrite. It's a website that is strictly for writers and aspiring writers, a place where they can go to vent and ask questions. It was an impulsive move on my part, sponsored by too much merlot and self-confidence. I had spent the entire night thinking about the coulda, woulda, shoulda's of my life. Not pursuing writing easily fit into all three categories. Writing always seemed like a shooting star: always out of reach but so beautiful to look at. At the time, joining JustWrite sounded like a great idea because it brought me just a bit closer to my dream.

I really, really, really need to deactivate my account. I haven't logged on in months. Things have been too hectic.

In total, I have about twelve manuscripts on my laptop. Only two are complete. I've only allowed Mom to read one of the books. She was biased though. I could've written a book tentatively titled *Ten Easy Steps to Grow a Chia Pet* and she would've thought it was the most moving story she's ever read. On par with *War and Peace.*

This hidden passion for writing has remained my best-kept secret for years. I like it that way but sometimes, just sometimes, I long for someone to read my stories and connect with my words. One of those sometimes drove me to create an account on JustWrite.

I ended up addicted and for a while I was constantly active. I couldn't help myself; there was this tantalizing sense of anonymity that was impossible to resist. I could tell a virtual stranger all my goals and thoughts when it came to writing and not have them rejected. In return they could do the same with me. We became a support system for each other.

My hope at the beginning was to find people like me. Yet ever so slowly, more and more of my Internet writing buddies were taking leaps of faith. Whether it was self-publishing or submitting their manuscript to agents, they were attempting to reach their goals. I never had the courage to publish. And trying to send my book out into the world right now is out of the question.

Don't reply, I think to myself. *You know nothing about this person.*

Yet my hands continue to hover above the keys. My heart starts to pound, the sound grows louder and louder until it's all I can hear.

My fingers fly across the keyboard. ***What's your name?***

Quickly, I log onto my account. I tap my fingernails on the desk as I wait for the home page to load. When it does I see I have six new friend requests, two hundred and fifty alerts and three new messages.

"Shit," I mutter to myself.

It shows my last login was a month ago. Right around the time I moved back home. Makes sense.

I reload my e-mail and see a new message.

Jackson Cooper.

I quickly type his name in the JustWrite search bar and press send. Within seconds his name pops up. Turns out, we are friends and we have been friends for approximately five months. There's hardly been any interaction between the two of us other than comments on chapters that we have posted on one another's manuscripts. People are typically very interactive so it's impossible to keep up with comments, but…

"How did I miss you?" I mumble aloud.

No, really. How did I accept his friend request and not give him a second look? Most people have pictures of typewriters, books or some aspiring quote as their profile picture. This guy has an actual photo of himself. He's leaning against a brick building. Judging from the winter coat, it has to be during the wintertime. His hands are tucked into his pockets. His eyes are dark brown and his hair is the same color. Resting my chin on my hand I lean in closer to the screen for a better look. He's smirking in the photo, as if he and the person taking the photo know something that no one else does.

It's completely cocky, but undeniably intriguing.

A new e-mail pops up and I hurriedly switch tabs.

Let's switch over to messenger.

I should really go to bed, but instead I type, ***Sure.***

It only takes a minute before a small box on the left hand corner of the browser pops up. I smile.

Are you looking me up?

No. I type back

Yes you are... I'm not a crazy stalker just so you know.

That's exactly what a stalker would say.

I assure you I'm not.

I pause for a second before I type out my reply. I can feel the smile spreading across my lips.

Don't believe me? I read the first twelve chapters of "Thread". I was the one in the comments section who

suggested that Caroline travel back and save Daniel.

"I remember you now!" I say aloud like he's in front of me.

He's talking about one of the many unfinished manuscripts just saved away on my laptop. It centers around a girl named Caroline who time travels to 1820 and meets Daniel. She's convinced that Daniel needs her help but in order to help him, she has to risk that she'll forever alter the future—including her own existence.

The fact that he remembers my story, let alone that tiny tidbit of information makes me grin. I'm a quiet person by nature but when it comes to writing and books? Well, I turn into a different person. I can't shut up even if you paid me to.

Did you ever take my advice?

Truthfully? I did and it completely altered the chapter for the better. Suddenly, it became cohesive and flowed just like I wanted. I've always wanted to say thanks to the person who made that comment, but never got around to it. Now that the chance is presented to me, I play it cool and elusive.

I did. It worked out great.

You've been pretty MIA lately. Are you still writing?

Not as much as usual. And you?

Did I really care if he was writing? Not really. But it seemed like the right thing to ask. And if I'm being perfectly honest with myself, I wanted to keep this conversation going.

There's never enough time in the day to write.

"Amen to that," I mutter aloud.

There's a beat of silence. Adrenaline courses through me and I realize that I haven't felt this way since… well, since I moved back home. There's a greedy side to all of this—the part that recognizes something good and will do anything and everything in its power to keep that feeling.

Even if it means taking a risk.

I exhale a shaky breath and quickly type out, ***Don't take this***

the wrong way but why are you choosing now to message me?

There's a pause. One minute goes by. Then two.

You updated your About Me recently. It says you live in Decatur, IL?

Instinctively I want to tell him that he's wrong. I haven't been on for months. But then I remember that my Facebook is linked to my JustWrite. When I updated my 'About' info on Facebook it must have automatically updated JustWrite without me knowing.

But what's that got to do with him?

As though he can read my mind, a new message pops up that makes me cautious and intrigued at the same time: ***Just thought it was interesting. I live in Decatur, too.***

Sorry to hear that, I type and press enter before I can think twice.

Social media has so many perks but the one thing that drives me crazy is that people can't see your emotions or feelings, whether you're kidding or not. Happy or sad.

Luckily, he seems to know I'm kidding because he replies, *HAHA*

There's another beat of silence. Then another message from him comes through. ***What brought you here?***

This is my hometown. But I came back to take care of my mom.

When he doesn't reply, I quickly type. ***Don't worry. It's nothing too bad. But she can be a lot of work.***

So that's why you haven't published any more chapters then. Mystery solved.

You're really gung-ho on those chapters, aren't you?

Yes and no.

???

Yes because you joined JustWrite around the same time I

did. We were in a lot of group chats with people with the same dreams as ours. They're trying to publish and go further.

How do you know I'm not trying to go further?

Well you haven't been on in months. Kind of telling. Unless you are trying to publish then I'll take back everything I said.

No, you're right. I've put it aside.

So when are you going to pick up where you left off on your SMUT book?

Definition of SMUT: Sexual fiction. Some people give it a negative connotation, but I couldn't care less. It's what I want to write.

With that attitude I'm never sending you another chapter. You're in denial, smut lover.

I take it back. Smut is the best thing in the world.

I smile at my screen and lift my arms above my head for a good long stretch. It's only when I glance out the window that I notice the sun is slowly rising. Holy Shit. How long have we been talking? I glance at the clock: 6:49 a.m.

I just looked at the clock, I type. ***We've been talking for almost five hours.***

That went by fast.

Really fast but I should probably get some sleep.

Good idea. I hear that it's important for people.

So I'll talk to you later?

Silence.

Then, I get his reply: ***You can count on it.***

8

ALL RELATIONSHIPS START out so beautifully.

It's the idea of finding something new and unknown that makes your heart race. It's like the intro to the start of movie: calm and so intriguing that you can't turn away even if you wanted to.

There's no *if* that moment will fade away but *when*.

Still. I can't help but bask in this euphoria. It's absurd, the excitement I'm feeling over talking to a complete stranger. But it's also thrilling. Probably because it's so unlike me to do this. Every time I think that it won't last, that I need to take it slowly, I get swept away in the emotions surfacing inside of me.

Days have gone by since Jackson and I started talking. E-mails and messenger quickly became a hassle so we switched things up and went to our cell phones. There was the smallest warning bell that went off when I gave him my number, but I quickly silenced it. What's the harm in it? It's not like I gave the guy my home address. We text any chance we can get. Even when I'm taking care of Mom, I can't help but furtively glance at my phone. Just in case.

Some people might say Mom isn't running on all eight

cylinders but she's smart enough to notice that something's up with me. Almost instantly she recognized that I seemed happier. At first, I shrugged off her remarks. Told her that there were some good job prospects. Not once did she push for the truth. But sooner than later I would fess up to her.

I drum my fingers on the kitchen table.

"Come on, come on," I say out loud.

When the ping sound comes through I jolt and anxiously type in my passcode. It's from him.

Our conversations have the ability to pull me out of the reality of my life and for a second I forget everything that's happening. I forget that I still haven't heard back from the Credit Union. (At this point I probably won't.) Or had any call backs for substitute teaching.

Tell me your favorite book.

Tell me yours first, I text back.

Why do you need to know mine first?

Cause I need to know your taste in reading.

I'll read anything as long as it allows me to escape the real world, I tell him and that's the truth. In my opinion, people may try but they'll always fail at finding something more magical than reading.

Fair enough. Favorite book? **Levels of Life**.

My reply is instantaneous. ***Julian Barnes. Nice.***

Whew. I was going to say, if you didn't like that book, we could no long be friends, he replies.

Nah, I text back. ***I'm afraid you're stuck with me as a book friend.***

Book friends? Really? I was hoping I'd been promoted to real life friend.

In order to be on that level I have to see you in person.

Maybe I want to see you in person...

My smile fades. I have no idea what to say to that.

I want to meet you, he texts again.

For a second, I waver. We talk online constantly. But meeting in person feels risky. Dangerous. And I know I said this is all thrilling for me but there's a big difference between thrilling and dangerous.

Not yet. I reply. ***But maybe someday soon.***

How soon?

Soon. I hesitate before I type back, ***Are you in a relationship?***

Typing those words makes my toes curl, like I'm an adolescent talking to their crush. But I don't care. This is the most interested I've been in someone or something in a long time. With bated breath I wait for his reply. Time seems to stand still. How many minutes have passed? Two? Three? Why isn't he answering?

Just as my panic starts to escalate, I get a reply. ***No. Last relationship ended two years ago.***

Why? Why? Why? But if I ask that it's only inevitable that he'll aim the question back to me and that's not a road I want to walk down… yet.

You?

No. I'm not in a relationship. I don't offer any more details simply because my relationship history reads like a Who's Who of crap.

I've always been attracted to the unattainable. In layman's terms, I go for the bad boys—the ones I have no business being with. In high school I dated a guy for two years that was no good. He was constantly missing school. Hung out with the potheads and reeked of smoke. But I didn't care. I think I wanted to change him so desperately that I looked past all the bad and tried my hardest to see the good. When we broke up he continued on with his life and I was left heartbroken.

Age made me slightly wiser. My last boyfriend, Pete, was stable both mentally and with his career. But when I moved back home there was no talk of us staying together. We naturally fell apart. I should've been upset but I wasn't; there was too much on my plate. Even now I look back at my high school boyfriend with more nostalgia than I do Pete.

When are you going to send me the rest of your smut book? he asks.

If only you could see me rolling my eyes right now. And for someone who knocks smut books you sure want to know how my little smut book ends.

Just because it's smut doesn't mean it's not interesting.

I smile, feeling victorious, but then my smile slowly fades as I read his next message.

Again, we should meet.

I'll do you one better. We should talk on the phone. You never know, I could have a heavy chain smoker voice.

Somehow, I doubt that.

You're taking a huge risk, I taunt.

I took a huge risk when I messaged you and so far that's turned out to be one of the best decisions I've made in a long time.

Be calm. Be calm. Be calm, I tell myself. But I cling to our conversations like a life raft. And that's just the texts. What will it be like to actually talk to him? I already know in my gut what the decision is. I'm going to talk to him and see where it leads.

Call me any time. I write back.

I wait for regret and maybe something akin to fear but I feel nothing but triumph and elation.

I SHOULD'VE NEVER said the word 'anytime' in our conversation yesterday.

That leaves an open window for him. But I didn't want to say, 'Call me at this exact hour.' That makes me seem high-maintenance and demanding, and I'm not. Yet I've been fidgeting all day. My attention jumps from Mom to looking at the job ads and back to my phone, just in case I've magically missed a call.

My phone stays completely silent the whole day, which does nothing for my mood.

It doesn't help that today is a bad day for Mom. She won't eat much no matter how many times I try to coax her into it. I make her a ham sandwich, even put lettuce and tomato on it. One of her favorites. When I place it on the end table next to her chair in the living room she barely glances at it, just stares at the TV screen with a stoic expression.

Today she did absolutely nothing but make a deeper dent in that chair. The weather didn't help my mood much either. Since this morning it's been snowing. We've had a good five inches and that only means more shoveling for me to do in the morning.

"Mom," I say through gritted teeth. "You have to eat."

"I'm not hungry."

"You're never hungry. That's why you're skin and bones."

"I'm not skin and bones. And I eat toast."

"You can't live on toast for the rest of your life," I argue.

Mom shrugs, like I told her we were out of paper towels.

I turn around and walk back to the kitchen and fight the urge to throw the plate at the wall. I walk over to the kitchen sink and rest my elbows on the counter. I close my eyes and take big deep breaths and try to calm down. Snapping at Mom isn't going to help anything. I think we've been around each other too much. We just need a small break from one another because I'm close to screaming.

I need to keep busy so I clean up the kitchen. I get a load of dirty dishes in the dishwasher and that's a plus. But there's a massive stack of bills on the kitchen counter, and that's been there since well before I arrived. I don't even want to go near that. I go to the refrigerator and grab a trash bag from underneath the sink and clean out the expired food.

By the time I'm done the trash bag is completely full and we're down to nearly nothing. Disgusting. I don't stop working and yet it doesn't matter how much I clean this fucking place it's still a pigsty. I ring out the washcloth and toss it into the sink before I give up and walk back into the living room.

A good hour has passed since my cleaning frenzy. Mom's still in her chair and I've calmed down slightly. We sit in silence and watch as Olivia Benson asks some bruised-up brunette who harmed her. I've seen this one. It's her stepbrother.

I sit back and relax, tucking my hands into the pocket of my hoodie. I doze off at some point. I'm woken up to the sound of a phone ringing. I practically jump off the couch. I look at the clock on the wall. Almost six.

My phone sits right near me on the coffee table yet I dive for it like it's my lifeline. "Hello?" I say, slightly breathless.

"Selah?" A deep voice says on the other end of the line.

Instinctively, my fingers curl around my phone. My eyes slant to the left where Mom stares at me quizzically.

"This is she," I reply, as I make my way out of the living room toward the stairs.

"Hi." The deep voice clears his throat. "This is Jackson."

"How are you?"

"Good, good." He clears his throat again. And the fact that he might be the slightest bit nervous calms me down a bit. "And you?"

"Just finished up dinner and now I'm going to try and successfully fail at finding a job," I tease.

"With positive thinking like that I'm sure you'll get a job in days," he says without missing a beat.

I had many ideas about how our first conversation would go. I even had a Plan B if it was really bad. I'd use Mom as my scapegoat—say that she needed me or I had to take her to some doctor's appointment. There is no need for Plan B.

No need at all.

I should've probably allowed for a Plan C, where the conversation goes so well, so amazingly well, that I'm doing nothing the entire day but talk to the person on the other line. I tell him everything that comes to mind. Why I decided to become a teacher.

"I can't help it. I've always had a spot for kids," I tell him. "I think it's because my mom was a kindergarten teacher. It just seemed natural to follow in her footsteps."

"What about writing?"

"What about it?" I ask.

"When did that passion come along?"

"Probably my early twenties. How about you?"

"Early teens. I started to write these horrid sci-fi novels in middle school. Thought they were amazing."

I smile. "Do you still have them?"

"Unfortunately I do. Sometimes I want to delete them, but I never can."

"I think it's cute you can't get rid of your first manuscripts."

"They're not manuscripts. They're fucking awful. Thank God I never posted them online; once they're online you can never get them back."

I then proceed to tell him about my love/hate relationship with social media.

"Why do you hate it again?"

"Because it's impossible for me to gauge how the other person is reacting to the conversation. I can reply one way and the person can think I'm furious at them. I always send two hundred happy emoticons just so people know I'm not pissed off."

He laughs and the sound does something to me. It's a twist in my gut. There's a beat of silence. But it's goes on for too long because it gives me time to absorb everything. All of sudden, Jackson's name becomes a CD stuck on repeat and all coherent thoughts fade away like tufts of smoke.

Jackson, Jackson, Jackson…

How had he not come into my life sooner?

"We should meet," I blurt.

Shit. Where did that come from? Less than twenty-four hours ago I was the one pumping the breaks on the whole meeting in person idea. But talking to him on the phone has me suddenly thinking differently. If we click so well on the phone, how will we be in person?

"Weren't you the one that was all hesitant for us to meet?" he teases.

"Yeah. But I think we're off to a good start." I pause. "Don't you?"

"Absolutely."

"Good." I smile down at the ground. "Name the time and the place and I'll be there."

10

THERE ARE MANY theories about love.

Some say it can cut you like a knife. Others believe that it's the best feeling you can ever have. But it's not a feeling. It's a choice, whether you know it or not. Whether you like it or not.

All your life people have loved you, Selah. I can imagine that Susie gave you dozens of kisses and hugs when you were a newborn. She probably never let you go as a toddler. And even when you were a kindergartner she probably had a hard time letting you go, even though she knew as a teacher that it was normal to experience the bittersweet feelings rushing through her.

But let us fast forward to what I remember: you on the playground. You're eight years old, standing next to Tyler Addison. You had such a big crush on him. The kids around were singing "K-I-S-S-I-N-G".

And then there was the time you and Sam played a mean game of MASH and you hoped to God that you got that damn mansion, two kids and of course, Dillon. Because you were in sixth grade and you had so moved on from Tyler.

From that first e-mail Jackson sent you, love attacked. And now you were given two choices: continue the conversation or ignore him and go about your life.

We both know what your decision was.

You take your phone with you everywhere. Even when it doesn't ring you glance at the screen on the off chance that you somehow missed a text or call. Sometimes, and you'd be mortified if anybody found this out, you fall asleep clutching your phone. You've even had a few late night talks that ended up with you falling asleep with your phone to your ear like some love-struck high schooler.

Right now you're a walking cliché. And you know it too. I can tell when you think about Jackson because your cheeks turn pink. You feel ridiculous yet you can't help yourself.

What did I tell you, hmm? I knew you'd like my gift. I'd like to say that you can't remember the last time you felt this way but I'd be lying. If you dug deep enough, you'd remember.

But I'm wasting time.

It's been a mere few days since you first started talking to Jackson. The spectacle of the two of you is so sweet, anyone within a mile radius of you and Jackson are liable to get a fucking cavity. No one could ever guess that you've only just started talking. That's how intense things got between the two of you.

I don't mind it; I find it quite fascinating. Gone are the days of you being a Negative Nelly. Jackson is your passport to a whole other world, one where you're allowed to look at your problems in a new light. You're a glass half-full kind of person now.

You haven't found a job, yet you're handling it well. Your savings account is slowly drying up. Yesterday, when you weren't looking, I glanced at your bank account. I give it one month—tops—before you admit defeat and cancel Internet service.

After that it's just a matter of time before creditors start knocking on you door. You moved some money around and wrote down a reminder to cancel the cable. And I could see you thinking to yourself: *Shit. Will the Internet be next?*

But let's be honest, you're in bad times. But not that bad.

It sounds strange but I feel a bit conceited because this is going exactly how I planned. You're starting to look at each new day as a fresh start. I even saw you write a few times this past week. It was nothing major but it was getting to a point where a few words within a week felt like progress. You even sent Jackson a few chapters to read.

Simply put, you were starting to get the spark back in your eyes.

But you're being greedy with my gift. A little too zealous, if I'm being honest. You enjoy my gifts left, right, front and center and you take every single one. Yet you continue not to see me.

But don't worry, whether you like it or not, we're going to meet.

Because I love you so much I feel the need to warn you to slow down, because you've never seen the dark side of love. You've never seen how twisted and malignant it can become. How it can eat you alive from the inside out. How it can drive you completely and utterly insane.

11

THERE'S NO MANUAL on how to handle a depressed person. Better yet your own mom.

Everything I say and do has to be handled delicately, like I'm wearing kid gloves. Not to mention the fact that it is plain bizarre to go through this. All my life Mom has been the caretaker—the matriarch to our small family.

It almost feels like someone has handed me a role and said, "Here you go. Play this character for a bit." It's been long enough and I'm more than ready to give them back the character. I'm done with it. I know the feel of the character—the good and bad sides. In the end, I like being me.

Every day I tread carefully, making sure to have absolutely no expectations. Expectations always result in disappointment and I can't afford that right now.

Today is not one of those days.

"Please come with me!" I beg for the umpteenth time. "You don't even have to change your clothes."

I stare at her lounge pants. They are smeared with the chip

crumbs she's just eaten (but at least she ate!). She hasn't changed in a few days and I'm afraid that if another day goes by a funky smell will follow her whenever she leaves a room.

But right now I'm down to the wire. I have five minutes to get out of the house.

"I'm not going with you, Selah," she replies, not bothering to look away from the TV.

"Yes you are," I insist.

"I've gone with you to your little interview. We've gone grocery shopping together. Not to mention the four or five times that you've had to get gas."

I rub my temples. "Four times."

"Four it is," she continues. "Either way. I would've been perfectly fine at home. But did you listen to me? No. Well, I'm putting my foot down, Selah Kerrington. I'm your Mother, and I'm staying home."

Did you see it? You have to look really closely, but the roles finally, and ever so slowly, were put back in their correct place.

I sigh, like a person who's been wearing shoes that are one size too small and finally steps out of them.

"Are you going to be okay?"

"I. Am. Fine," Mom says slowly. Her eyes never stray from mine and for a second I really believe that she's going to be fine. I see pieces of the old Susie bubbling to the surface.

I push back slowly, feeling myself relent. I sigh loudly. "Thirty minutes. Tops. And then I'll be right back home."

Mom quirks a brow. A gesture that says, *Well? What are you waiting for?*

"I'll be right back. Okay?"

"Okay, honey." Her attention is already back on the screen.

"Do you want anything to eat?"

"No. I had a big lunch."

Since when did a big lunch translate into a handful of Cheetos? I walk toward the front door and snag my coat. I grab the doorknob but at the last second remember that I don't have my purse. I quickly backtrack.

"What are you going to do anyway?" she calls out.

"I'm going to have a quick bite to eat with Sam," I reply as I grab my purse lying on the couch.

"Oh, Sammy," Mom's eyes well up with tears. "I miss her."

Sammy.

Who doesn't miss Sammy?

Samantha Gulick.

Sammy.

Or Sam.

She'll answer to each variation of her name, but I always called her Sam. It's an intimacy reserved for only close friends and family. And me.

Judging from Mom's teary reaction when I announced where I was going I'm genuinely surprised that she didn't change her mind and jump at the chance to go with me. Nonetheless, she stayed home and I left for the lunch date that I've had planned with Sam for the past week.

We decided to me at La Gondola on Water Street. At one o'clock sharp. Not a minute late. God forbid Sam would have to wait. I can see her now, impatiently tapping one heel-clad foot against the floor while she glances at her watch for the umpteenth time.

She's the only person I know who has a watch and actively uses it. Better yet, she's the only person I know who sets her watch ten minutes ahead and the clock in her car five minutes ahead. The reason? She always wants to be prepared. Prepared to be the first at work. Prepared for when traffic hits. Prepared for anything that comes her way.

I always try, or like to be prepared, yet I always end up being the last person out the door. The last person to arrive at a party or lunch.

Today, I'm bound and determined to be on time. More to prove Sam wrong than anything else. Surprisingly, traffic was on my side so I made it across town within ten minutes. My personal best.

Even though lunch breaks are coming to an end, the parking lot is still fairly busy. It's hard to say if Sam is already here because she's probably driving a rental. Still, I hurry out of my car and toward the restaurant, taking the chance of slipping on a patch of black ice and busting my ass.

It'd be so nice to be the one sitting down at the table first and looking impatient. I can imagine myself, drumming my fingernails against the table, irritably glancing at my phone every so often. And then Sam would walk in and I'd give her a look of pure disappointment before I say, "Well, well, well. Look who's late."

It's a pretty image but complete bullshit because the minute I walk through the door I see Sam sitting in a booth in the corner to my right, doing all the things I dreamed of doing. "Holy shit. You're actually on time," she says.

As I make my way toward her, she slides out of the booth seat, leaving behind her grey, lambskin Chloé bag so she can hug me tightly.

She's been my best friend for, well… forever. Mom used to joke that I didn't have one childhood memory that didn't involve Sam. 'You two are attached at the hip!' she'd shout to my retreating back as I ran out the front door, trying to catch up to Sam.

"I can't believe you're actually on time," she repeats, as she pulls away.

"I can go outside and stand there for five minutes if you'd like," I tease.

She just rolls her eyes and sits back down. "Let's not ruin this perfect time, shall we?"

Before I take off my jacket, I give Sam a speculative glance, trying to figure out what brought on this impromptu visit of hers. For most, a scheduled trip isn't considered impromptu. But this is Sam. She has a quota for the amount of times she will visit Decatur and that's twice a year: Christmas and sometime in May. But that was only because we both shared the same birthday month. Hers is the twenty-fifth. Mine is the twenty-first.

A visit so early on in the year? That's virtually unheard of.

She's dressed sharp. A black tweed blazer paired with skinny jeans. A tan Burberry trench is dropped over the back of the seat. Right now, she sticks out like a sore thumb. She belongs in some upscale restaurant, but everyone in Decatur and within a fifty-mile radius knows that La Gondola has the best sub sandwiches. Their bread is to die for. In fact, it was Sam who chose this place to meet up.

"Let me clean this table off for you," a young girl says. She apologizes as she wipes down the table. But she only speaks to Sam. I want to wave my hands in front of her face and say, *Yoo-hoo! You can see me, right?*

Instead, I stay quiet and let Sam work her magic. "It's completely all right," she tells the young girl.

I've always said that Sam has this eerily good ability to portray one thing to the world while being someone completely different. She's small and compact, which instinctively makes people think she needs their help. She has inviting eyes, but that's only so she can draw you in and figure you out.

Essentially she's the exact opposite of me.

Case in point: all throughout our school years, she could look a person up and down, only say a few words to them and have them completely pegged. Most people would call that judgmental. I thought it astute because she wasn't trying to be critical. She just wanted to protect herself and the people she loved most from ever getting hurt.

She uses that same approach in her job.

I wouldn't survive a day doing her job. We both knew that. "You're too sweet, Selah," she once said. "If you had to fire someone, you'd probably have a nervous breakdown and offer them your job."

Kidding or not she was spot on.

"I see nothing in this town has changed," she murmurs as she glances out the window with a critical eye.

She's not the type of person to leave home and think back on her past with nostalgia. The minute she could leave Decatur, she did. The irony is that she didn't stray too far, opting to go to U of I in Urbana- Champaign while I went to K-State in Manhattan, Kansas. But she had tentatively dipped her toes in the waters outside of her hometown, and each year away she became bolder and bolder until, when her college graduation rolled around, she took a few steps back and cannonballed into the water.

She moved to Chicago. (Which, in my opinion, still wasn't terribly far.) Got a job at Bank of America. Married a man named Jason. Climbed the ranks until she had a comfortable job as Vice President of lending. She's living a pretty comfortable life.

When her ten-year high school reunion rolled around and she was sent her invite she told me she'd rather have a lobotomy than go. But what she doesn't realize is that this place will always be the key to her childhood memories. It holds all the laughter and tears. It holds all the conversations we could never have with our parents. It holds arguments with friends. Tailgaiting at football games. Summer nights with the top down, holding our palm out, letting the wind thread through our splayed fingers.

She might love to hate this place but she can't escape it. We can't escape it. There will always be an invisible thread connecting us to this mid-western city.

Sam insists on ordering for the both of us. That's another hidden part of her personality, her willingness to give. She hides it so fucking well. You'd never know that she was always volunteering to pick up the tab. She never misses my birthday or Christmas gift while I'm the one always scrambling to pick out something for her at the last minute.

"So." She gently yet firmly taps both hands on the table like she's getting ready to start a meeting. "How are things?"

I mimic her actions. "Good. How are things with you?"

"I'm being serious, Selah."

I lean back in the booth. "So am I."

"I genuinely want to know how you are."

"And you came all the way from Chicago to ask me that? You could've done that on the phone."

"I could've," she admits. "But you've been acting weird so I thought it was time I came for a visit."

"To the one place you hate," I say deadpan.

Everything she's saying just isn't adding up for me. There has to be a bigger reason as to why she's here.

"Some welcoming this is," she murmurs.

"I don't mean to be a bitch," I speak up quickly. "I'm just familiar with your visiting schedule and now is not that time."

Sam shrugs. She opens her mouth, but our order is called. Sam jumps out of her seat and hurries to the front of the restaurant. Seconds later she's back and hands me my plate. She leans over her plate and dramatically sniffs her food before she groans loudly.

For a few minutes we are silent, the two of us scarfing down our lunch. After half her sub is gone, she takes a long drink and rubs her hands on her napkin.

"I just started the Paleo diet but that little cheat was so worth it," she confesses. "All right. Back to what I was saying—you're concerning me and *that's* why I came for a visit."

"How am I worrying you?" I ask through a mouthful of food.

"You just sound stressed and distracted on the phone."

"Well, I *am* distracted," I admit. "From my job search to dealing with my mom… it's all been hard to juggle."

Sam's brows pucker as she stares at the table, deep in thought. "And you never heard from the Credit Union?"

"Nope. I'm assuming they either found someone else for the job or they're really playing hard to get," I tease, but my joke goes right over her head.

"That's just strange. They should've loved you!" she says.

It was Sam who got me the interview at the Credit Union. She knew a friend who knew a friend who worked there. That person said there was a job opening. That information all trickled down to me and I quickly put in an application.

I shrug helplessly. "Everything went good. At least I thought so."

"Hmm."

"Hmm, what?"

"Nothing. Just strange is all. So have there been *any* job offers?"

"No. Not even substitute teaching jobs."

Sam takes another bite out of her sandwich. "Give it time. The flu season is upon us. I'm sure you'll get some substitute jobs soon."

"Substituting is not bad, but I need something more steady. The bills keep piling up."

Instantly, Sam pounces on my words. "Do you need me to help you with anything?"

Sam considers working on her checkbook, counting out money, doing taxes and spread sheets fun. Any time she can work on her (or someone else's) finances she jumps at the chance. When tax season rolls around I never have to ask her twice if she'll do mine. In fact, she treats the task like it's a gift from me to her.

Yet this time I'm a little more reluctant to take her up on her offer. Things are exponentially worse than they've ever been. I'm afraid she'd go through everything and tell me I was royally fucked and I have enough stress to contend with. So I intend to pretend, just for a bit, that things aren't *that* bad.

"No. I'm good," I say.

Sam squints at me. "Are you sure?"

"Absolutely." I give her a strained smile, which makes her squint even harder at me.

Finally, she gives up on trying to figure out what's wrong and finishes off her sandwich at the same time I do. Before she can put our empty plates on the tray, the young girl comes back. "Ma'am, you want me to take this for you?"

Like before, she only looks directly at Sam.

"Yes, that'd be great," Sam replies.

The girl takes her tray, leaving my empty plate behind.

I stare dumbfounded at it before looking at Sam. I wave my hands over my face. "You can see me right? I'm not a ghost, right?"

Sam laughs. It's an odd sound, probably because she hardly ever laughs. "Yes, I can see you."

"Well, tell it to that girl," I say, who is now back behind the counter happily taking someone else's order.

"Ah, don't worry about it. So," Sam prompts. "What's new with you?"

I've told no one I've been talking to Jackson. At first, I wanted to keep it quiet, just in case things went awry. But now I feel ready to talk about him. Every time I've talked to Sam on the phone, I've had to force myself not to say anything about him. Plus, I needed time to build up immunity against what her or any other person might say about the fact that I'd met him online.

But right now, Sam's here. What better time than the here and now?

Pushing aside my plate I lean in. Sam leans in, too.

"I've met someone," I confess.

She leans back and crosses her arms over her chest. "Ah-ha." Sam smiles with understanding. "So *that's* why you've been so distracted."

"That's why," I agree.

"Well. What are you waiting for? Tell me everything about him!"

My fingers curl around my drink, as if it's a protective barrier. "He's thirty-one. Loves to read and write like me." A broad, yet dreamy smile sweeps over my face and I can't do anything to stop it. "Sam, it's so easy to talk to him. I spend hours on the phone, just talking about everything and nothing all at the same time," I confess.

Sam whistles. "Wow. Sounds intense."

I nod rapidly. "It is. And it should be scary how quickly everything is going, but it's not. With all the bullshit I'm dealing with right now, I need this."

"That's great. Who is he? What's his name? Where did you meet him?" She stops the game of twenty questions to lean in. Her eyes twinkle mischievously. "I need every single detail."

I shift in my seat and take a deep breath. "His name is Jackson and I met him online." And just like that the happy, interested Sam disappears. She looks at me with a mixture of sympathy and sadness, as though I'm a child.

"I know what you're going to say," I rush. "It's dangerous. It's impossible to fall for someone so quickly. Blah, blah, blah. But it's happening."

Sam doesn't say anything and the silence is driving me crazy.

"What are you thinking?" I press.

"I'm thinking," she starts out slowly. "That this isn't a good idea."

"But it is," I say. "I enjoy talking to him."

"Is that what this is about? Talking to someone?" she prods. "You can pick up this magical thing called a cell phone and talk to me until you're blue in the face."

"I'm being serious."

"So am I."

The napkin that was on my lap just a minute ago is now wadded up into a ball, resting in one clinched fist. "You're being dramatic, Sam. I'm not eloping with the guy or anything crazy. We have a lot of things in common."

Sam takes a long sip of her drink before she sits back in her seat. "Like?" her voice is terse.

"I already told you. He's a writer and loves to read."

Sam knows about my pipe dream of being a published author. In fact, she was the first person I expressed my interest in writing to. She was immediately supportive. Always listened to my ideas and never turned down a chance to read chapters of my manuscript. Didn't matter if it was the first, third or fifth draft, she always offered her thoughts.

The problem was that she was biased. We were too close for her to blurt out her honest thoughts.

With Jackson there's a different bond. One that we both understood hinged upon the worlds that we created and the words that described them. It didn't matter how close I was to Sam; she would never comprehend this other, more secretive part of me.

We sit in silence. Alternative rock music plays lightly from the speakers above us. To our right two women bustle in, trying to figure out how many tables they need to move together for their co-worker's baby shower. I'm shamelessly eavesdropping on their conversation, but I don't care. Sam's unnaturally quiet and I'm starting to feel really weird.

"Nothing good can come out of an Internet relationship," she states.

"That's not true. What about that girl from high school? What's her name?"

"Stephanie?" Sam provides.

I snap my finger and point at her. "Yes, Stephanie! Remember how she started talking to a solider that was stationed overseas? Two weeks after we graduated she went off and married him."

Sam frowns. "Where are you going with this?"

"Well, you were so convinced that the marriage would fail within a year and she'd be living with her parents. You even bet me fifty dollars."

"No, I didn't."

"Yes, you did." But that's not the point. Stephanie's once stupid decision in my eyes is now my saving grace. "Anyway," I rush. "She's been married for ten years. Has five kids and seems to love her family!"

"Did you just hear yourself? Five kids. She's probably catatonic from changing dirty diapers and watching cartoons all day."

I've always said that Sam is an assassin of happiness. Just when one good idea or thing pops up in my life she's there, waiting and ready, with her scope set to shoot it to smithereens. And that's why I depend on her so damn much. She's there to get to get rid of anything I don't need in my life. She's there to provide the reality that I desperately need.

Many times I've told her this. But she just shrugs and rolls her eyes. "I'm just trying to protect you. That's all."

Although this time I don't need her protecting. I realize that I'm taking a risk when it comes to Jackson. And I'm okay with that.

In fact, I'm more than okay with that.

"What I'm really trying to say is that everyone thought that her marriage wouldn't make it. We were all against her. And look at her. She's happy. She's in love."

"Are you saying you're in love?" she asks.

At that, I look away. I'd steeled myself against the hard-hitting questions. The ones that make you feel angry, helpless and defensive. I didn't bank on Sam asking such a personal question.

"I think, if I'm given the time, I could love him," I reply.

Sam reaches across the table and places her hand over mine. Her mouth opens but then her phone starts to vibrate.

"Shit." She glances at her watch with a small look of pure panic. "I have to get going."

"To where?"

"I'm going back to Chicago and have a dinner with Jason tonight."

"So you drove three hours just to ask how I am?"

She freezes as she puts on her coat and gives me a smile. "Yes I did. I care about you that much. Aren't you lucky to have me?" she teases.

For now, our argument is done.

"I hate this place."

"Really? I would've never guessed," I respond dryly.

"Seriously, Selah. How can you stay here?"

I tense. "I have to."

"No, you don't." She places a hand on my bicep. "Sell the house and move to Chicago. You can be near me."

The mere thought of moving to Chicago makes me laugh. I went there once to visit Sam and I hated it. It's too busy, too frenetic. Walking down the street made me feel like I was in an incubator. I couldn't wait to go back to my cozy apartment in Kansas City.

"You know what I think of Chicago."

"That was one visit, though. Find a job and really settle down and I think you'd like it."

"So you think moving will magically solve all my problems?"

"No," she admits. "But it'll probably make you feel marginally better."

"Doubtful," I mutter. "The only thing at this point that will make me feel better is getting a job."

Sam sighs and I hate that. It means that she too is running out of options, out of ideas to help and that's never good.

"Call me if you need anything. I mean it, Selah. Anything." She gives me one final hug before she gets into her rental car. I stand by her car and watch her pull out of the parking lot.

I know that Sam's offer will always be on the table, but will I take her up on it? Probably not.

It sounds a bit crazy, but the only person I'm starting to trust is Jackson.

IT'S STILL RAINING when I pull into the driveway. I hurry out of my car, holding my purse over my head even though it's pointless; the rain finds a way to my face and hair. The soles of my shoes squeak across the porch. I grab the house key and unlock the door. I'm out of breath by the time I rush inside.

She's in the exact same spot where I left her. She looks my way and gives me the placating smile. The one she used on me when I was a kid.

See? I'm still here, that smile says. *Didn't I tell you everything would be okay?*

12

THERE ARE BILLIONS of people on earth and yet you chose to talk to Sam.

Don't get me wrong. I understand why you open up to her. But that doesn't mean I have to accept it.

For example: the cashier ringing up all your items right now. She looks good. I understand it can be awkward to open up to a complete stranger. But sometimes strangers are the only people you can trust. They don't know you and the chances of you ever seeing them again are rare. It would be like whispering your words into the cold winter day. You speak, and you see your breath in front of you and watch as it slowly dissolves. It's like it never happened.

It sounds appealing, doesn't it? We both know you won't do it though. So I'll make another, more obvious suggestion: talk to your mom. You're with her almost twenty-four seven. And you know for a fact that she'll listen to you. All Sam is going to do is take all the hard work I've put into finding you the perfect gift and rip it to shreds.

I'm not going to let that happen. I put way too much thought into my present for that to happen.

Besides, Sam's not around enough to know that this is the happiest you've ever been. I see the light back in your eyes. You're starting to see the silver lining. You smile more easily. And you're, dare I say it, starting look a little hopeful.

No, Sam doesn't see any of that.

But I do.

Keep in mind she's only ever here for a few days and the next thing you know she's going back to her fabulous life in the city. Back to her fabulous job where she's the head bitch. Back to where your problems become microscopic.

And when you think about it, that's okay. We're all inherently selfish human beings who focus on our own problems.

I'm the only one that devotes one hundred percent of my time to making sure that you're okay and happy. So much so that I'm starting to feel like your damn therapist. I mark the moments that you are sad and highlight the times you are not. And for what reason? Just so I can make sure that you're okay.

Okay.

Not good. Not great. Just okay.

Okay isn't good enough for Sam. She's the perfect example of a perfectionist. She'd demand that you be great. She'd stick around for bit and then leave.

Would it be wonderful if you were instantly great? Of course. But anything worth having requires work. Lately, I've been reminding myself of that. I'm starting to become exhausted. But trust me, that's not enough for me to give up on you.

No, I'm like a runner who hasn't reached their stride. My legs feel clumsy. My lungs slightly burn. Sweat is starting to pool around the temples. I'm thinking of all the reasons why I should stop. Yet I pull from within myself an inner strength, narrow my eyes and picture the finish line in the distance. Then I catch my second wind and surge forward.

My eyes are narrowed. Looking straight at you.

All I need is to find my stride.

Don't worry, I always do.

13

THIS IS A bad idea.

Maybe the worst I've had in long time. Meeting someone that you've been talking to online? Better yet, for only two weeks? It has all the trimmings of a murder mystery. *Dateline* will run a story of me. I can see the rolling credits so perfectly. Lester Holt solemnly staring at the screen as he says, *Tonight, we turn to Keith Morrison as he shows us the young Selah Kerrington and her tragic ending…*

Thus begins a forty-minute monologue of good ole' Keith interviewing my mom and the few close friends I have. They'll give me a messiah complex, claiming that I had a good heart, lit up the room and loved life. Perhaps they'll roll old videotapes of me as a kid, blowing out candles. Riding my bike for the first time without training wheels. Showing off for Mom by doing a series of cartwheels in the backyard.

Maybe they'll scrounge up some pictures of me growing up. Undoubtedly, they'll list all the hobbies that I excelled at. Cue the B-roll footage of Keith walking down the very block I lived on, telling the viewers that for all my perfect ways I was a very, very lonely woman.

Yet my future TV debut isn't enough to make me turn around and get the hell out of here while I still have a chance. The bottom line is that my newfound friendship with this man has me curious. I want to know more about him and if we'll click in person as well as we do in our conversations.

The saddest part about it is that's not too far off from the truth. I am lonely. I know I should do something about it. In a non-dangerous way I am doing it.

I have friends. I could call them. I know keeping myself locked away with Mom is just making matters worse, but every time I pick up the phone, or go to message someone, I hesitate. Sympathy would ooze from their words. They would give me that sad look. The one that says, *I feel terrible for the predicament you're in but thank God it's not me!*

I don't get that with Jackson and I love it. Not being defined by what's going on in my life feels… refreshing. Like having your head underwater for too long and then reaching the surface. You gasp and suck in all the air you can. And that gasp is the single most important proof that you're alive.

Last night we arranged to meet at a Starbucks off of Mound Road. I deliberately chose a public area, just in case something happens or he turns out to be completely different in person and I need to make a quick and safe getaway.

We agreed to meet at three. My clock reads two fifty-five. I came a few minutes early in the hopes that I would catch an unsuspecting glance at Jackson. With my hands gripping the steering wheel I lean forward and squint at the entrance but I can't tell if he's inside.

Then a thought hits me: *What if he stands me up?* I've been so focused on the potential tragedy of the two of us having no chemistry in person that I never gave being stood up a second thought.

You can always leave, my mind whispers.

Yet my curiosity outweighs the risk of embarrassment. Besides, all I can really think about is that if I do decide not to go inside, I'd potentially look back on this moment years later and think, *What if I did walk inside and meet him? Would things have turned out differently?*

"I can do this. It's just coffee," I say to myself as I open my door. It may be March but that means nothing. In the Midwest the weather is either all or nothing. Winter storms hit with a vengeance. I've heard the tornado sirens go off more than I can count and have experienced heat waves that feel like I'm in the desert. Only fall serves as the smallest buffer from the intense weather.

Yesterday it was a crisp fifty- one degrees. Definitely warm enough to melt away the remnants of past snow and slush. Today it's twenty degrees with the temperature steadily going down. By tomorrow morning we're supposed to have up to six inches of snow.

Welcome to central Illinois.

As soon as I step outside, I instantly feel someone's eyes on me. My heart starts to drum beneath my skin. I tuck my hands into my pockets and hurry toward the building making sure to keep my head ducked down, away from the bitter wind. I sigh with relief when I step inside Starbucks and the warmth greets me. Thankfully, the place is all but empty. One girl looks to be deeply engrossed in studying, with a computer on the table and papers spread out. She doesn't look up when I come in. The other person is a haggard woman with double stroller, trying to take a sip of her coffee while simultaneously feeding an infant and giving the toddler in the stroller pieces of a croissant. She glances my way, a look of envy crossing her face. A look that says: *I was once you.*

I scan the rest of the room. Alarm tingles down my spine as I take a seat facing the door. All I can think of is, *What if he stands me up? He* is the one who wanted to meet. Maybe that's his MO though. Troll social media. Snare a lonely woman, only to humiliate her and never show up.

Or maybe—

Enough with the maybe's, I tell myself. *Get a coffee. Wait thirty minutes and if he still hasn't shown up then leave.*

My chair makes a loud screeching sound as I stand up and walk up to the counter. When I order my drink the girl behind the counter glances at me accusingly, like I'm some loner with nowhere to go and nothing to do. In a way, she's kind of right. If I weren't meeting Jackson today I'd be at home with Mom looking for any job prospects.

As I walk back to my seat, I tell myself that I won't stay here for longer than thirty minutes. I think that's a fair amount of time to wait, plus it won't cause the other patrons to think I'm some pathetic stranger who eats and drinks her coffee alone. Maybe I'm being stubborn about the whole thing; before I left home I told Mom that I've been talking to someone.

"Who?" she'd asked distractedly, her gaze directed on the TV.

"Some guy." I took a long pause. "That I met from the Internet. His name is Jackson."

If I'd said that years ago, Mom's head would've whipped in my direction. She would've looked at me with shock and anger. But that didn't happen. She stared at the TV, watching the QVC lady tell everyone to hurry and place their orders for the brown sweater tunic! Hurry, hurry! The green and black ones have already sold out!

She was giving me the silent treatment. Of that I was sure. And I was also sure that she was banking on me being stood up. I didn't want to give her the satisfaction of being right.

"Trying to get a look without me knowing?" a deep voice asks behind me.

Thank God I wasn't sipping coffee or it would've sprayed out of my mouth. Quickly, I twist around. My left hand curls around the lip of the table but it's only to hide the slight tremor in my hands.

A camera can be a tricky thing. People who aren't particularly beautiful suddenly seem captivating in a photo. Or the petite blonde who does the morning news for WAND, who always looks gorgeous on screen, isn't as flawless in person. Tricky, tricky thing that camera.

Yet for Jackson it's both of those things. He's just as I imagined, but his profile picture didn't reveal how his eyes are a mixture of amber and green. His light brown hair isn't as short and has a stubborn wave to it. I have a feeling that he used to try to tame it with gel but gave up the fight and let it be.

Dressed in a Henley and black pea coat it's still easy to see that he has a lean build. He has on cologne but it's not heavy enough to make me gag. It's just the right amount to make me want to lean in. And lean in I do as he takes off his coat and drapes it across the chair and sits down.

The girl behind the cash register glances my way and I want to flip her the bird and say, *See! I'm not a complete fucking loser.*

"Have you been waiting long?" he asks. His voice sounds deeper in person than it does on the phone.

I shrug. "Not that long."

He glances at my coffee. "Long enough to get a drink."

"It's not as though the place is packed." I smile. He smiles back.

Inside, I'm thinking to myself, *So how does this go?* Because this isn't a normal meet and greet. We've complied hours and hours of phone conversations and thousands of words between the two of us. But never in person. It's like building a house only to tear it back down.

Where do we start?

All the conversation starters that I'd been going over for the past few hours fly out the window, along with my confidence. I clam up and suddenly turn mute.

He's the first one to break the silence: "Never pegged you for a coffee kind of girl."

Veering back, I glance down at my coffee. "Why's that?"

"Because when I talk to you, you always seem so jittery. Like you're moving from one task to the next."

"True. But the only reason I'm able to move from task to task *is* because of coffee. I'm a coffee addict." I take a small sip. "What about you?"

He shrugs before he rests his elbows on the table. "Eh. Not so much."

"If you don't like coffee then why were you okay with meeting at a coffee shop?"

"Because you suggested it. And because it was clear you wanted to meet somewhere where there were witnesses." He laughs at the look on my face. "I don't blame you for choosing a location like this."

"I just don't want to be a *Dateline* statistic," I say defensively, but with a smile.

He quirks a brow but his smile never leaves. "What?"

I go on to tell him about my *Datelin*e spiel, which I realize makes me sounds like I'm prone to conspiracy theories. He has every right to get up and run for the fucking hills but instead he stares at me with general interest, as though what I'm saying has value to him.

It's been a really, really long time since that's happened.

God, that's pathetic.

When I'm done talking, I'm out of breath. Jackson whistles, sits back in his chair and crosses his arms. "That's quite an imagination you have on you."

"You have no idea," I mutter.

"Now I know why you're a writer."

"Aspiring," I correct him. "Completely different from a published author."

"So you think there's a difference?"

"Absolutely," I say.

"I think you're wrong. Published or not. If you've written something, you're a writer. Anyone who tells you different is full of shit."

I find myself leaning in, because Jackson doesn't just speak, he immerses himself into each individual word, pulling you in right along with him. It makes me more comfortable. Very quickly, the silences that linger as we take sips of coffee become almost… cozy.

"So where is it?" he asks.

I frown. "Where's what?"

He rolls his eyes and leans in. Just close enough that I get a whiff on his cologne. "You know what I'm talking about. The next five chapters."

I'm not going to lie, I was kind of hoping he would just forget that late night conversation when I told him he could read some more chapters.

I hesitate and Jackson says, "If it bothers you that bad, you don't have to."

"No, it's not that."

"Then what is it?"

"I hate first drafts," I confess. "I understand that they're the foundation to every story. But they're riddled with so many errors that it almost overwhelms me. I can only imagine what it'd be like if I ever sent it out to an editor."

And because I feel a kinship with Jackson, the last thing I want him to read is a first draft. I want him to read the best version of my manuscript possible. "I need to make more adjustments and—"

"No, no, no," he cuts in. "You said you'd send me the next five chapters. No stalling."

"Do I need to repeat myself?" I ask with a smile. "I hate first drafts."

"Who doesn't? But then there's a second draft. Then a third and possibly a fourth and fifth and—"

"What's your point?"

"My point is that you're a perfectionist. No draft of your book will be good enough."

"That's a fair point. But I think it's less perfectionism and more me being protective. My stories are like babies to me. I want to hold onto them and never let them go, even though I know I should."

"And you should let them go, because you're a great writer."

My heart thumps wildly. "Thank you."

If it weren't so creepy, I think I'd reach across this table and kiss him straight on the lips.

His phone rings, jolting the two of us. He glances down at his screen, sighs, but doesn't answer the phone. It stops ringing. He lifts his eyes to mine. "We've been here for over an hour."

"Hasn't felt like an hour to me," I confess.

His lips kick up into a slow smile. "Me neither."

Nervously, I lick my lips. It doesn't go unnoticed, judging by the way Jackson watches the action. "Maybe… maybe we can meet again soon?" I ask.

His lips slowly curve up into a small smile. "Absolutely."

We stand up at the same time and bundle up for the cold weather waiting for us outside. We throw our drinks away. He holds the door open for me.

The same cold air that hit me when I first arrived does the same thing, but this time I barely feel it.

"Where are you parked?"

I point to the far left corner. "How about you?"

He gestures to the black BMW parked in the first row. I whistle. "Fancy."

"If I told you it's leased would you still call it fancy?" he teases.

"Anything is fancier than my little Volvo."

Jackson places his hand on the small of my back. An innocent gesture but it's enough to make the blood roar through my veins. It makes me smile; whether you're fifteen or fifty everyone wants to feel protected.

And it sounds crazy. And rushed. And borderline ridiculous but I feel safe right at this moment.

14

THERE ARE VERY few places in the world where I feel comfortable.

Places where I can really be myself. I know I'm not the only one who gets anxiety. It hovers around me the second I step outside, before it slips past my skin and settles in my bones. My jaw becomes clinched and every action feels amplified by a thousand. It doesn't matter where I'm going, that feeling never dissipates. I accepted a long, long time ago that this fear would always be a part of me. I don't enjoy having this anxiety, but it does give me a greater appreciation for the places that calm me.

Bookstores are at the top of the list. It doesn't have to be a certain bookstore. I love them all the same. Whenever I step through the front doors, I feel the tension release from my body with every breath I take. My steps become lighter. I can think more clearly. I'm just a happier person all around.

It's the only place in the world where I can time travel. In one aisle I can travel back to 1920 and solve a cold-case thriller. In another I can feel the agony of a widowed, middle-aged woman as she picks up the pieces of her life.

Reading is magic and anyone who tells you differently is either one of two things: insane or illiterate. Everyone has a book meant just for them. Think about it: out there, someone is writing a book just for you. I think that's what I love about bookstores. They offer me thousands of stories to chose from. I'd take all the books home if I could.

When Jackson suggested we go out a second time around, I said yes. We settled for Friday, the nineteenth. He offered to pick me up but I said no; even though our first meeting went amazingly well, I wasn't quite ready for him to know where I live. Maybe next time.

I expected dinner somewhere. Or maybe a movie. You know, all the cliché first and second date locations. I didn't expect our date to be at the bookstore. Second time being with him and he was well on his way to being my favorite person.

"Hey. What are you reading?" Jackson nudges me with his boot.

I look at him from above my book. "It's rude to bother people when they're reading," I whisper.

He smirks and then places his book in his lap. He's leaning against the bookshelf opposite me. His legs are extended in front of him, crossed at the ankles. My leg rubs against his. I gave up thirty minutes ago trying to pull away. His eyes have that glazed over look that people get after sex or drugs. I want to lean forward and frantically ask him if the words on the pages give him a high like they do to me.

I think he would say yes.

We've been here for over an hour. When we walked in, we took our time moving down the rows and rows of books, talking about which stories seemed good. We picked out books that we thought the other should read. I picked out *Transformations* by Anne

Sexton. He said he loved that I didn't pick out the latest Stephen King or Nora Roberts novel.

He chose *The World Before Us* by Aislinn Hunter. I wordlessly made my way through the store and made my way to the H's until I found his book. I plucked it from the shelf and started reading. My ass started getting numb thirty minutes ago but I don't plan on getting up unless I'm forced to; this is the calmest I've been all week.

Before I left to meet Jackson, I told Mom a handful of times that I was going out and that if she needed anything to call me and I would come home as quickly as I could. She shrugged off my words, but I went as far as to write my phone number down and put it on the end table, like she was an elderly woman with dementia.

I thought that action might put my fears to rest, but as I drove to meet Jackson guilt and worry festered inside of me like an infected wound. What if she was gone when I came home? I told myself that I was overreacting but if the past has shown me anything it's that you can never let your guard down. Not even for a second.

"Okay. Books down," Jacksons commands.

I arch my brow but follow his lead. He crosses his arms over his chest. I do the same, which makes him smile.

"If you could meet any author, which one would it be? And," he quickly says before I can speak up, "you can only pick one."

"Oh. You fight dirty, Jackson."

"Answer the question, Selah."

I close the book and place it in my lap, sitting up straight. "Just one?"

He nods.

"Hmm…" I stare up at the ceiling as I think of one good author. Seconds tick by and I still remain silent.

Jackson smirks. "This isn't a life or death question."

"Well to me it is. I can't just pick one."

"Try."

"I am!" I insist. My voice slightly rises, earning a glare from a lady one aisle down from us. Jackson and I wince at the same time. And then we smile at the same time and share a look. My smile slowly fades as my pulse thrums wildly against my wrist. I don't know what's happening between us. This goes beyond sexual attraction or having the same hobbies. It feels like someone's tying an invisible string around my neck, deliberately guiding me forward, whispering in my ear, 'This is where you belong.'

Nervously I clear my throat and stare down at my hands in my lap.

"I'm still waiting for an answer," he says.

I lift my head. "Fine. If I have to pick one—which, by the way, I find completely unfair—I'd have to pick Sylvia Plath."

"Plath!" Jackson smiles knowingly. "I fucking knew it."

"But it must be said that Paullina Simons was a close runner-up. Can't forget Melina Marchetta. Or—"

"You could go all night, couldn't you?" Jackson asks with a bit of awe in his voice.

I blush underneath his scrutiny. "About books? Absolutely. Now it's my turn: if *you* could meet any author, which one would it be?"

When he doesn't answer instantly, I smile broadly. "Ah. It's not as easy as it looks now, is it?"

"It really isn't," he concedes. There's a beat of silence that follows. Then he says, "I have to go with Julian Barnes."

"Barnes! I fucking knew it," I say, repeating his words from earlier.

Again we smile at each other. And again something passes between the two of us. That same feeling flows through me, but it's not as foreign as before. In fact it feels excellent, like the sun warming my skin. I'm not a spontaneous person but if I were I'd kiss him right here, right now, just to see how he responds. Just to see if he's experiencing the same thing I am.

I think he is.

Someone loudly clears their voice. Jackson and I turn our heads to the left at the exact same time and find one of the clerks staring down at us. It's some pimply boy who looks like he'd rather be at home smoking weed with his stoner friends than working here.

"Uh… we're closing," he says dully.

Jackson hops up first and extends a hand toward me. I grab my purse and book and take his hand.

"Well that went fast," I murmur to him as we move toward the cashier.

"It really did."

We wait in line behind a woman who's decided to go on a Liane Moriarty reading binge. Normally I would be impatient, counting down the seconds until I was home and could finish the book that I'd started. But tonight I happily wait by Jackson's side.

Truth be told I don't want tonight to end.

Moriarty's future biggest fan finishes paying and heads to the exit. We step forward and I hand my book to the clerk, a woman in her mid-twenties who's the complete opposite of stoner boy. She looks at the title of my book and something tells me that she does this with every purchase. She smiles up at me as she scans it. "Is this any good?"

"I'm only three chapters in but so far so good." I pull out my wallet to pay and Jackson moves in next to me.

"I got this," he says.

With my elbow resting on the counter, I face him. "You don't have to do that."

"I do." He leans in and says, "Considering I didn't take you out to eat and all."

The cashier stares between the two of us, waiting for our decision. I put my debit card back in my wallet. "Well, thank you for my meal," I say, putting air quotes around the last word. "It's the best meal I've had in a while."

He pays for the book and when the cashier bags the book she hands it to me. Together we walk out of the bookstore, our shoulders rubbing. By now the parking lot is almost completely empty.

"I'm over here," I say, pointing to my car.

"I'll walk you to your car."

"Afraid I'll get jumped in a bookstore parking lot?" I tease.

"You never know who's waiting to pounce," Jackson retorts.

I give him a smile. I want to tell him that I never smile as readily as I have tonight. I want to tell him that lately I have to force my lips to pull up into a smile. In fact I'm certain that if I had to count the amount of times I've smiled tonight I'd fail. Jackson has set a record that I doubt will be broken any time soon.

I press my key fob and the front lights of my car blink once. I put my purse and book in the car and turn back around to face Jackson. "Thanks for the most unexpected date I've ever had," I tell him. It's so cold that my breath appears between the two of us like tufts of smoke.

"I knew you would like this," he gestures behind him.

"I did. It was a well played move on your part."

Jackson tucks his hands into his front pockets and rocks back on his heels. "Maybe I'll think of something even better for our second date."

My lips pull up into a smile. "How can you top the bookstore?"

"Are you doubting my talents?"

"I think I am."

While we've been talking Jackson's been inching towards me in small increments. I look at him through half-shut eyes and watch him arch a brow. He's waiting for the green light. If I give it to him he's taking his shot.

I give him a small nod. I tell myself that I want to wait a bit longer, muddy the waters before I kiss him. But what harm can a single kiss do? If the past has shown me anything it's that first kisses always have a tendency to be awkward and sometimes a bit… sloppy. Doesn't matter how old you are. It's the ones after them that always count.

Yet with Jackson it's different. He tilts his head the right way, doesn't get pushy. I feel the cool surface of the car door behind me. It touches the skin between my shoulder blades. I press myself up on my tiptoes. His hands curl around my waist before they run up my back. He kisses me with an intimacy that comes over time. The kind most people have to work for.

I've never been one for public displays of affection but I forget we're standing in a parking lot where everyone can see us. The only thing I'm aware of is the little distance between our bodies and how I can eat it up. I suck gently on his lower lip. Jackson groans.

I feel a sudden possession over him. I want to stake a claim in what's mine. I want to drag my nails down his back so hard he bleeds. So hard that I leave scars. So hard that any woman after me knows that he belongs to someone else. What I'm feeling becomes so overwhelming that my hands suddenly curl around Jackson's wrists. Gently I push back until our lips are inches apart.

He stares down at me with a slightly dazed expression.

The wind picks up, sending my hair in different directions. Strands cover my eyes. Before I push my hair aside, Jackson reaches up and tucks my hair behind my right ear. And right then I try to pinpoint exactly when I fell in love with him. Was it when he was just now staring down at me or was it earlier, between the bookshelves with thousands of characters and stories waiting for us to pick them up?

I think it was the latter.

I think it will always be the latter.

15

I LOVE WINTER.

I love the atmospheric conditions. And I love the charming aspects of the season. Like standing in front of a window late at night, watching the snowfall, a cup of hot chocolate in your hand. Or, as a child bundled up to the hilt, walking around like the Michelin man, throwing snowballs and making snow angels.

But doing real life activities? Say, dragging your garbage container down the driveway? Not so pretty.

It's only half an inch of snow but it feels like twelve feet. Both of my hands are curled around the blue container unit. They feel like icicles but that's simply because I had to take off my gloves because they gave me no traction. The snow has been shoveled and salt has been scattered so many times on the driveway that a nasty, hard brown slush has formed, causing the wheels to get stuck every other minute. It's really, really starting to piss me the hell off and ruin the start of a good day.

After days of coaxing Mom, she finally relented to meeting Jackson. It felt like a victory of epic proportions. There is no way around this meeting. It has to happen.

We had our third date mere days after our second. It was at a restaurant in downtown Decatur. It wasn't as creative as the bookstore, but at this point I think I'd enjoy doing anything with this man. We spent the whole dinner pouring our hearts out to each other.

In texts I had given him the Cliffs Notes version of my mom, but during that third date I told him just how depressed Mom was. He listened the entire time with those big, honest eyes of his and never said a word. It's like he knew of the frustration and worry building inside me, needing to come out.

When I was done pouring my heart out, he reached across the table and linked his fingers with mine.

And now he's coming over in less than forty minutes. Because Mom's a recluse we are going to have lunch at home. I refuse to have any expectations for the meeting. At least that's what I tell myself. There's a picture in my head though, on constant repeat, of things going bad. Of a lunch filled with awkward coughs and silences. Maybe I'm just so used to things going wrong that I've become a perpetual pessimist. You never know. They might actually get along.

The wheel gets stuck on a small but stubborn piece of ice, making the garbage can jerk to a halt. I let go of the handlebar. "Stupid piece of shit." For good measure I kick the garbage can.

"Need help?"

The deep voice behind me makes me raise my shoulders to my ears in surprise. Noah. Of course it'd be him. I slowly turn and see him standing there. If it weren't for his rosy cheeks you wouldn't know he's been outside. He's holding a shovel that I wouldn't mind borrowing and bashing my garbage can with.

"Nope," I breathe out. "I'm fine."

Yet my words mean nothing because he drops his shovel,

walks over, and helps push the garbage can down the driveway. I'm not all *I am woman here me roar* but having his help does make everything go faster.

When we reach the end of my driveway he dusts his hands off and smiles. This happy-go-lucky act grates on my nerves. He acts like an F-5 tornado could blow through here and instead of taking cover he'd drive after it—just to capture its beauty. For the millionth time, I wonder one thing: what is he like behind closed doors? Because it's a known fact that everyone, including me, is a different person the minute the doors close and the blinds are shut. In the end we're all made up of secrets.

I'm dying to expose him, just so I can magnify everything he wants to hide from the world. In plain sight I've yet to catch him being anything other than a perfect citizen. Tricia stares at him with a half-glazed, 'I want to jump your bones' expression. In the past week Noah has shoveled her driveway and poured salt on her sidewalk twice. If I were handing out Boy Scout Awards he'd win the Good Citizenship badge. Yet for all his wonderful doings the small, still voice in my head tells me not to trust him. I feel partially bad, but it feels good following my gut.

"What are your plans for today?" he asks.

I shrug as I look around our cul de sac. Some driveways are shoveled (Noah probably did them) but some aren't, so they have that pure innocent look that untouched snow always seems to convey. Reminds me of white glitter. Pretty soon the snow will drift drown, wrapping around all the homes like blankets. For some reason that gives me a cozy feeling.

"I don't know," I finally reply. "Probably watch *Dr. Zhivago* with my Mom."

Technically, it's not a lie. Mom watches that show just as much as HSN and *Law and Order: SVU*. I just didn't think it was any of his business that Jackson was coming over. My relationship with

Jackson is so fragile that I protect it with everything I have. And besides, I owe Noah nothing.

"*Dr. Zhivago*, eh?" He takes off his left glove and wipes the sweat from his brow. "I used to watch that all the time with my Aunt Abby."

"Who's choice was it?" I find myself asking, shocked at the teasing tone in my voice.

"Mine," he says deadpan.

I smile and for a millisecond I understand the allure to this man, what Tricia (and every other woman in Wildwood) finds so appealing. I look toward her house and automatically see the blinds close. Who's the weirdo now, bitch?

He relents, a slow smile creeping on his face. "It was my aunt's choice."

"I can't think of many boys that'd choose to watch *Dr. Zhivago* with their aunt."

"Neither can I but I was raised by her so I really didn't have much of a choice."

In spite of myself I lean closer. "Really?"

While I may be interested and nosy about his past, it's obvious that it's the last thing that he wants to talk about. He closes up quicker than I can blink. The wall that goes up between us is stronger than the frigid air and it's enough for me to take a step back.

"Well, thanks for helping with the garbage can but I should be going," I tell him, slowly backing away.

Noah's gaze is impenetrable and intense. No, intense isn't the right word. More like coercive. I wonder if this is a rare side of him that most people never truly see.

"Have a good day," he calls out.

I give him a courtesy wave as I hurry toward the front door. Quickly, I stomp the snow off my boots on the doormat. There's urgency in my actions. Like Hell is nipping at my heels. Like I have a target on my back. When the front door slams behind me, I lean heavily against it, knowing that there's a good chance I just overreacted.

Not even one glove off and I hear, "So how was your talk with Noah?"

I look up and see Mom standing at the living room doorway.

"Every day I beg you to get up and move around and you refuse, yet you somehow found your way to the window just now?" I reply as I walk past Mom.

Mom arches a brow and patiently waits for me to answer.

"We talked. Like neighbors." I line my wet boots up against the wall and hang up my coat. "I've had more stimulating conversation with a cashier at Target, so calm down."

"But you hate Noah," she points out.

"I don't hate him. Hate is a really strong word," I say as I walk past her. Coffee sounds perfect right about now. "I just don't trust him. Talking to him once doesn't mean that I changed my mind."

Sure enough, I have to make a fresh batch of coffee and while I wait I lean against the counter. It's starting to look really messy in here again. I don't know how that's possible. Yesterday I took out the trash and cleaned what I could to make the house look halfway decent for today.

"What happened here?"

Mom raises both hands. "Wasn't me."

"Then who? We have Casper the Friendly Ghost living in our midst?"

Again, Mom shrugs.

"So," I start out slowly, ready to change the subject. "Are you ready to meet Jackson?"

A minute ago when I walked through the door her eyes had life in them. Her cheeks were flushed. She looked so happy. Now her smile is gone. She crosses her arms. "Oh. You're still wanting to do that?" She says it like I've asked her to go skydiving. I'd like to say it doesn't hurt, that she doesn't mean it. But that's a lie.

"Of course. I really like him."

"Nothing can come out of it, Selah, my dear."

My eyes narrow. "How do you know?"

"I'm your Mom. I know everything."

The coffee finishes brewing. I twist away from her and pour myself a cup. "You've been saying that for so long I'm beginning to think that's your go-to saying."

"This time you need to really listen to me."

"I promise to think about it," I say gently. "Until then, he'll be over in a few minutes. Are you sure you don't want to…" My voice fades as I take in Mom's appearance. You know how over the course of time people can become nose-blind to a certain scent? Well, I'm immune to Mom's… aroma. I never flinch at her greasy hair, foul breath and dirty clothes.

Jackson is not immune, though. I'll be honest, if the roles were reversed and I were meeting his mom and she was in the state my mom's in, I'd do a U-turn and walk right out the front door.

"Do I want to do what?" Mom prods.

"Take a quick shower?" I suggest gently.

"I can't."

The 'I can't' excuse has been used before and it's something I will never understand. I've heard that people with depression sometimes find the task of taking care of themselves monumental tasks, that they just lose interest. I know this is something that she can't help but I still find myself getting incredibly frustrated.

"Maybe you should cancel this little get together if you're so embarrassed of me," Mom says, her voice hopeful.

"It's not a get together," I reply, irritably. "This is really important to me."

Mom's eyes soften. "If I could clean myself up for you, I would. But I can't." She drops her face into her hands. "I just can't." Her voice cracks.

A breakdown is not what either one of us needs right now. Instantly, I'm by her side, my arm wrapped around her slender shoulder. "Mom, it's okay," I lie. "Don't worry about it."

Some people might say that it's bad what I'm doing, lying to Mom like this. But put yourself in my position. Watch someone you love wither away ever so slowly. Would you make them suffer worse by telling them to get their shit together or put a soothing balm on their pain?

My choice will always be the latter.

"Let's go into the living room," I say, as we move out of the messy kitchen, past the filthy dining room that's stacked with nothing but bills.

It takes a few minutes to get Mom calmed down. Luckily, there's an episode of *SVU* on (shocker) and soon she's back to her normal self.

Right when I think I've put the fire out, the doorbell rings.

I'd spent so much time getting Mom settled in that I completely lost track of time. Funny how that happens. When you're desperate for it to move forward, a noose wraps itself around your ankles and drags you backwards but the moment you turn your back, the moment you become distracted, it speeds back up.

"Everything will be okay," I say aloud as I open up the front door. Without a jacket I feel the frigid air slam into me, and it almost makes me take a step back.

Jackson stands in front of me, bundled up with his arms crossed. He gives me a half smile that shows me that even he's little nervous over this awkward meeting.

"You ready for this?" I question as I take a step back for

him to walk through.

He lifts a brow. "Are you trying to scare me?" he counters.

"No. I'm just trying to prepare you for my mom," I reply in a hushed voice.

Jackson laughs and takes off his jacket and beanie. "I'm sure she's not that bad."

"Oh, you have no idea," I mutter. I take his coat and hat and put them on the coat rack.

Side by side we walk through the small foyer and into the living room.

"Mom," I say with more bravado than I feel. She lifts her head. "This is Jackson. Jackson this is my mom, Susan Kerrington."

Jackson steps forward and gives her a firm handshake. "Nice to meet you," he says, making steady eye contact.

"You too." Mom gestures to the couch. "Please. Sit down."

At the last second, I grab the wadded up blanket he's about to sit on and toss it aside. I sit right next to him, my legs bobbing up and down. Jackson lays a hand on my knee to calm me down.

Mom tracks the movement but says nothing.

"It's great to finally meet you, Ms. Kerrington."

In a perfect world, Mom would say, 'Please. Call me Susie.' But this situation is the direct opposite of perfect. The tension is so thick you can cut it with a knife.

He tries again: "So Selah told me you'd planned on watching *Dr. Zhivago* today."

"Oh, yes." Mom smiles. "I do love that movie and today is the perfect day to watch it. I'm surprised you're even out in this weather."

"They have the roads pretty much cleared up. Besides I wouldn't miss the chance to meet Selah's mom. She's said a lot of amazing things about you."

Well played, Jackson. Well played.

Mom flourishes over these words, like a wilted flower that's been neglected. They idly chat for a bit and then Jackson asks what she does.

"I'm a teacher."

Jackson's brows rise in feigned interest. I already told him this but it's obvious he's attempting to make the conversation run smoothly. "Oh yeah? What grade?"

"Kindergarten."

Jackson whistles. "Good on you. I watched one of my nieces once and it was completely exhausting."

"It can be tiresome," Mom admits. "But so rewarding. To tell you the truth, I'm thinking about retiring."

"What?" I say at the same time Jackson goes, "Really?"

What the hell is she talking about?

"This past year has been very difficult for me," she continues. "I realize that I'm not a twenty-five-year old fresh out of college."

She graces Jackson with another smile. Where's the woman who was so insistent on not meeting him? Hm? Nothing she's saying or doing is making any sense whatsoever.

For the rest of the conversation I remain quiet and carefully watch Mom. Jackson smoothly talks to her and the longer they speak, the deeper she falls under his spell.

A few minutes later Mom yawns and scoots forward in her chair. "Jackson, it's been lovely talking to you, but I'm exhausted. I'm going to take a nap."

Jackson stands up the same time as Mom and steps aside for her to walk past him. "It was nice meeting you," he says.

She stops briefly beside him and pats his shoulder. "You too."

I watch her walk up the stairs, still dumbfounded by Mom's confusing statements. She can get disoriented sometimes, but never has she had been that bad. Is it Alzheimer's? My gut tells me no, but who am I say what's going on in that mind of hers. Either way it's concerning as hell.

Jackson moves closer to me. I tuck my hands into the back pockets of my jeans and tilt my head back to meet his gaze. "Thank you for being so great," I say softly.

He tugs at the hem of my shirt and guides me closer until I'm flush against him. Both of his hands cup my face, his fingers slightly threading through my hair. He tilts my head back. Just because I want to be closer to him, to this feeling he gives me, I wrap my arms around his waist.

"Everything was fine. I don't know why you were worried."

Yet everything isn't fine. Something is off with Mom. It wasn't like she was telling a bold-face lie. At one point she did think of retirement. But that moment had come and gone.

About an hour later I walk Jackson to the door. Before he leaves he turns around and gives me one last kiss. When he pulls back I take a deep shuddering breath. "Call me later, okay?"

"Absolutely," he replies before he turns and walks out the door.

I shut the door behind him and sigh loudly because I know that instead of enjoying a moment alone I need to talk to Mom. I walk up the stairs toward her room. I knock once and open the door. Mom's lying in bed but instead of taking a nap she's watching TV. Her face is a blank slate. Emotionless.

"Well, that was strange," I say.

"It wasn't strange. It was wrong." She tightens the belt around her waist. "Wrong, wrong, wrong."

"Wrong how? That you lied to him?"

"I didn't lie to him!"

"You told him that you were thinking about retiring."

Mom stares at me like I'm delirious. "I said no such thing."

Am I losing it? Have I been cooped up in this house so much that I'm now imaging things? That's the first thing that dances through my head but I know what I heard.

I walk deeper into the room. "Mom. I know what I heard."

"Well, you heard wrong. Do you hear me? Wrong, wrong, wrong."

I wave my hand in the air. "Stop saying the word wrong," I say impatiently.

Mom suddenly becomes silent.

Crossing my arms, I walk closer to her bed. She flicks her gaze to mine and for a brief second, looks at me with pity.

"You're acting crazy, you know that, right?" I whisper. Mom looks momentarily hurt but I continue. "You acted strange for no reason today." I point a shaking finger at her. "I'm trying to be happy, trying to find love, you're trying to ruin that."

She could scream. She could yell. She could react in many ways. But instead, she leans forward and smiles softly. "Selah, you shouldn't worry so much about me. Worry about your own well-being. You have it all wrong. Wrong, wrong, wrong."

16

OUR FILMING PERMITS for outside shots were finally approved a few days ago.

You'd think in a podunk city like this they'd be accepted the second we filed them, but I think everyone in Decatur was getting a kick out of bigshots being on their home turf. This was just their way of showing their power. The exterior shots of the house were done yesterday and tomorrow we'll film where the body was found.

All the small (and large) pieces that go into creating just one episode can sometimes make my blood boil, and now we're down to the wire. This is always my favorite part. I never know why. Confidence grows. I know just the right questions for the interviewer to ask to get the reaction I'm searching for.

Unfortunately, we aren't going to get that reaction out of Selah's Aunt Ruby. She's sixty-one, eight years older than Susie. Ruby doesn't fit the bossy older sibling mold, judging by how timid she is around the production crew. She never married and has no kids. She's lived in Blue Mound (a small town thirty minutes away from Decatur) for over fifty years. In a way, her sister's children were her children. She spoiled them rotten and was there for them when Susie just didn't understand them. (Ruby's words, not mine.)

Her hair is completely gray and coated with so much hairspray you could throw a baseball at it and it would ricochet off. Laugh lines curve around her lips. Crows feet indent the skin around her eyes. She wears bright pink lipstick and refused to let the makeup artist change it, although she did cave and allow her dark blue eye shadow to be replaced with a subtler shade. Blue veins are prominent in her skinny, arthritic hands. They shake as they lay limply in her lap.

She looks prim and proper, probably has her best Alfred Dunner outfit on, but so earnest. She smiles at every person on set. By the end of the day everyone is calling her Aunt Ruby. She basks in all the attention.

"Aunt Ruby, this is amazing," I say with a bit of awe.

"It's not too much?"

I glance at the stack of photo albums on the table and back at Ruby. "It's not too much. You've given us plenty of pictures to chose from."

A week ago I called Ruby and asked if she would be willing to bring some photos along of Susie and Selah to this interview. She readily agreed. I never thought she would bring *so* many. Out of all the people we're interviewing, I'm most interested in Ruby because she knew both Susie and Selah. It's a two-for-one special with her. But I want to tread lightly, simply because she looks like such a sweet old lady.

"What time do you think this interview will be finished?" she asks.

"Not sure. It all depends on you. Why?"

"Well, there's a Hometown Buffett not too far from here and if I go after five I get my senior citizen discount."

I try to keep a straight face but Ruby makes it really, really hard. "We'll get you to your buffet meal. I promise."

Her blue eyes widen in delight, revealing that once upon a time she wasn't this old lady whose only friends were her cats.

"Thank you." She bends down and digs through her purse before she finally fishes out her wallet, loaded with coupons. She pulls one out of the stack and peers carefully at it before she tries to hand it my way. "If you want to go I think I have coupon."

"No, thanks. I'm all right."

Thankfully, a production assistant tells me we're ready. A crewman is holding a clapperboard, signaling we're seconds from the cameras rolling.

And, snap.

"Ruby, what is your relation to Susie and Selah Kerrington?"

Aunt Ruby remembers what I told her about not staring at the camera and keeps eye contact with me. "I'm Susie's older sister and Selah's aunt."

"Take us back to the beginning; how would you describe Susie?"

Aunt Ruby sighs wistfully. "Oh, she was a gentle soul. Our Mom always said that she'd never met a stranger that she didn't like. Everyone gravitated toward her. Growing up, I worried for her."

"Why was that?"

"I didn't want people to take advantage of her."

"So, you were the protective older sister," I remark.

Aunt Ruby sits up straighter in her chair. "Absolutely. I had to be."

"As you grew older, did you still feel the need to watch over your sister?"

"No, not as much," Aunt Ruby concedes slowly.

I look down at my notes. "And then there's Selah. How was your relationship with her?"

"As far as aunt and niece relationships go, I'd say we were pretty close. We saw each other several times a year." She gets a faraway look in her eyes. "She was a very shy kid. Always let other people do the talking." "So she was a lot like her mom?"

"Oh, no. She was… cautious. It took a while for her to warm up. She became more closed off after that awful tragedy."

Even though I know what tragedy she's referring to, I lean in closer; this is news that the viewers, the one that haven't researched Selah and her entire family for hours on end, will by dying to hear.

"What tragedy?"

Aunt Ruby looks down at the ground. She laces her fingers together. "The passing of her dad." Nervously, she licks her lips before she continues. "It was a normal day. Susie said he got up for work, made some coffee. An hour later, when she got up, she saw that his car keys and wallet were on the kitchen table. She asked Selah to go into the garage and see if her Dad's car was still there." Aunt Ruby takes a deep breath. "When she went out there, she found her dad. He'd shot himself in the head."

"That's tragic," I say after a beat of silence.

Aunt Ruby nods. "It really was. Robert was a good man. Him taking his own life just seemed unfathomable."

"Death is always hard but to find your dad in such a way must have been really horrific for her."

"Oh, you have no idea. She was closed off and withdrawn. Susie and I were really worried about her for such a long time. During her youth, she acted out. Hung out with the wrong kids. Dated older boys she had no business being with."

"Over time she grew out of this dark period?" I asked, checking my notes.

"Thankfully, she did. But, like I said, I really wondered if she'd ever recover."

"What was your impression of Selah and her mother's relationship?"

A shaky sigh escapes Ruby's mouth. "It was rocky."

"How so?" I ask gently.

"They were like most mothers and daughters. They could be really close but at times they were almost too close. Susie gave Selah everything. That girl could get away with anything she wanted."

"Some people might think that you're alluding that Selah was deceiving or spoiled by her mom."

Aunt Ruby kicks back her head and laughs. "No, no. She wasn't deceiving. Spoiled?" She shrugs. "Possibly. But deceiving? No."

"My next question is going to be difficult but I'm going to ask it: when they found the body, what went through your mind?"

Tears well up in Aunt Ruby's eyes. "I don't remember much. I just sank to my knees. My world stopped. I've felt grief like this before but I will never get used to it. I hope to never feel it again."

I take a deep breath. "And cut."

Within seconds people around us start moving around the set, but Aunt Ruby and I sit completely still. Tears stream down her cheeks. I motion a production assistant to find a Kleenex. She hurries to the kitchen and rushes out with a paper towel. I take it from her and hand it to Aunt Ruby.

With shaking hands she grabs hold of it and dabs at her eyes. "I'm sorry. This is embarrassing."

"Don't be. I know this was really hard for you." I stand up from my chair and pat her on the shoulder. "I'm really proud of you. Thank you."

"Everyone has a side in this story, an opinion of what they thought really happened." She stands up and moves toward the living room. I follow behind her, my curiosity getting the best of me. She stops in front of the fireplace and grabs a glass picture frame on the mantel. She brushes her wrinkled fingers across the faces in the photo before she looks up at me, her eyes a brilliant shade of blue. "I think it's important that I get my side out. If I didn't, I'd be failing my family."

I stare down at the smiling faces and my heart speeds up because the next person I want to interview—no, *have* to—is in this photo. The only problem is, I didn't know if they'll say yes.

17

"IT'S THE BOYFRIEND. It's always the boyfriend who kills!"

"Can we turn this?" I reach for the remote.

"No, Selah." She swats my hand away. "It is just getting good."

No. It isn't. Mom has watched every single episode of *Law and Order: SVU*. Twice. And no, I'm not kidding. I wish I were.

There are very few things I miss about living on my own. But one is the ability to watch what I want when I want. Another is the freedom to walk around in my own space and not worry about anyone else. Those seem like selfish things, but I can't help it. It's hard to live on your own for almost ten years, then move back into your childhood home where there's a whole different way of living.

"Tell you what, when the show's ten minutes from ending we'll turn it back and you can see if your boyfriend theory is correct."

Mom snorts. "Of course it's correct. It's always correct. Sure, they mix it up a bit and make the villain the least person you expect but that doesn't happen very often."

I sigh loudly and keep my mouth shut. We've had many conversations about this theory of hers. Spent hours dissecting each episode. Which is just sad. It crosses the border of Patheticville and enters Pitifulville. Population? Two.

The confines of the house are starting to drive me crazy. I swear these walls can talk. And you know what they're saying? "Get out. Get out. Get out." A few days ago it started out as a whisper but now it's a scream.

It's not that I don't want to go out, I do. It's just I've never been a particularly outgoing person. I'm more than happy to spend my time at home reading or writing but it makes me feel removed from reality. When I venture outside I get a dull headache from the sunlight beaming down on me. The fresh air assaults me, revealing that the house is stuffed up and I should probably open up a few windows.

But I never do. The blinds stay shut. Whenever they're open I become paranoid. My skin tingles with awareness and my daily activities become altered. I feel like an actress putting on a show for some unknown audience. *You're ridiculous,* my mind whispers. And it's right. I am being ridiculous.

There's always Sam to lean on. But there's only so much I can tell her before I start to feel like an emotional vampire, slowly sucking the life out of her. And friendships shouldn't be like that. Talking with a friend should make you both feel energized and just plain ole' happy. Sam doesn't feel happy when she ends a conversation with me. Of that, I'm certain.

And I have Jackson. How he makes me feel is enough to get me through each day. At least I think so. Lately, our conversations have become fewer and fewer. There's a small wall that's ever so slowly building between us and I don't know why. I partially blame that for how I'm feeling.

Today we're having lunch. I've been looking forward to it for the past few days. I plan on asking why he's being so distant, but I don't know how. We're still in the beginnings of a relationship and the last thing I want him to think is that I'm nagging him.

"Are you going to hole yourself up in the house again all day?" Mom asks.

"No. Jackson is picking me up. We're going to have lunch."

Body language can tell you so much more than words. Right now Mom is as stiff as a board. She's quiet for a few seconds before she says, "You're still seeing that boy?"

My eyes slant in her direction. "His name is Jackson. And don't call him a boy. Makes me sound like one of those creepy teachers who sleeps around with one of her students. Besides, you seemed pretty chummy with him when he came over here two days ago."

Mom's lips flatten into a thin line, but the subject isn't remotely close to being over with. She obviously has something to say and I want it out in the open; otherwise her feelings will just fester inside of her until she explodes.

"Mom, you're clearly thinking something. So just say it."

With a heavy sigh, Mom sits up and shocks me by turning off the TV. She twists around in her seat to face me. "I was nice to him because I have manners, Selah. I wasn't raised in a barn and neither were you. But if you must know the truth, then here it is: I'm not happy about your relationship with *Jackson*." She puts extra emphasis on his name.

"And why not?"

"Because it's unhealthy."

I laugh darkly. "How can you possibly know our relationship is unhealthy? You've met him once."

She gives me a condescending smile and says, "Trust me. I know."

"You really don't."

Of course I knew the risk of meeting someone online. But fortunately, things didn't go bad for me. I always expected that the biggest uncertainty with Jackson would be meeting him in person and discovering whether or not we had chemistry. We had that, so I thought we were in the clear. I didn't expect my mom to be so upset about it.

"If you get to know him, you'll see what I see."

She leans back into her chair and groans dramatically as she adjusts herself. "Selah, I just want to help you. And this whole thing with Jackson just screams wrong." The last thing I want to do is grab a ticket onto the 'wrong, wrong, wrong' train again.

Suddenly, the doorbell rings. I jump up so fast I resemble a puppet—all loose limbs and jerky movements as I rush to the door and swing it wide open. I have a smile waiting and ready for him, but it fades the second I see him. Jackson looks like he's seconds away from vomiting in the shrubs.

Instantly I step forward, ignoring the cold wind that cuts through my paper-thin sweater. "Hey. Are you okay?" I ask.

He leans over, his fingers curled around his knees. He holds up one shaking hand and smiles faintly. "I'm good."

"Don't take this the wrong way, but you look like shit."

"Thank you, Selah." There's an edge to his words. Not razor-sharp but acute enough to make me take a step back.

Glancing into the house, I quietly shut the door and take a small step forward. "If you're sick, maybe you should go home and get some rest," I offer.

"No," he rushes out. His hand shoots out and grabs my wrist. "I'm fine. I promise. Let's go eat, all right?" Another smile but he never lets go of my hand.

I look at him and back at his fingers. "You're hurting me."

He glances down at his fingers and instantly drops my hand. My fingertips start to tingle as the blood rushes back into my hand. I take in Jackson, dissecting him as I would an insect. His face is clammy. There's no way in hell that he's in any condition to go eat, let alone drive.

"Why don't we just sit here for a second? If you feel better in a few minutes then we can go eat?"

"It's freezing out."

"Some cool air might be good for you."

He nods and sits down on the first porch step. I sit right next to him, resisting the urge to go back inside and get my coat. We stay quiet for a few minutes. But this isn't a comfortable silence. It's filled with unspoken questions and answers and tension.

"Want to tell me what's wrong?" I finally ask.

Jackson drags his hands through his hair and takes a deep breath before he looks over at me. "If I tell you then you'll never speak to me again."

I look him straight in the eye. "That's not true. We've only known each other for a brief amount of time and I already feel like I can tell you anything. Hell, I already have," I say with a half-smile before I continue. "So don't worry about it. Whatever it is, I won't judge."

I want to shake him for his silence, yet simultaneously cover my hands with my ears. Because I have a feeling that what he's going to tell me is a big reason he's been so distant with me.

"What I say could change everything between us."

Then he opens his mouth and tells me everything.

18

THE THIRD PERSON we interview is named Donald Warrick.

Everyone calls him Donnie.

He's lean, bordering on skinny. He's dressed in jeans and a blue dress shirt but from the way he tugs at the collar every few minutes it's apparent that he doesn't wear it very often, if ever.

His brown hair is shoulder length. He face is sprinkled with freckles across the cheeks and nose—which hardly makes him intimidating, and his pocked-marked scars reveal a case of stubborn acne in his youth. He has a five o'clock shadow and dark circles beneath his eyes that make it look like he hasn't slept in days. Without question we needed the makeup artist to get rid of them. His fingernails are chewed to the quick.

He seems amicable, looking around the room and the cameras with a bit of awe. The conference room is set up a bit differently today. We placed a rented table between the two chairs. His interview is important but not crucial to the episode. It will help give the viewers a more in-depth look at the story.

Donnie drums his fingers on the table. If I've learned one

thing in my eighteen years at this job it's that you can't always predict the person being interviewed. Sometimes they're completely eager to tell you everything they know and then some. But then there are the shy ones. You have to pry the answers out of them. And you can't forget about the hostile, defensive ones. They treat the process like you're invading their privacy even though they agreed to the interview.

Suffice it to say, Donnie seems like the first category. Like Claribelle, minus all the makeup and wardrobe fuss.

"So how does this go?" he asks me.

I give him the whole spiel and he listens, but the longer I talk the more he tugs on his collar.

"How does that sound to you?" I ask.

Donnie shrugs, as though it's of no concern to him. "Fine, fine." He swallows and leans in. "But you're not gonna, like… pry into my business, right?"

There's a touch of fear in his eyes and I wonder how many and how strong the skeletons are in his closet.

"Nope," I reply. "This is only about Jackson and your relationship with him."

Donnie visibly relaxes. "Great, great."

"We're just about ready. All right?"

"Yeah, totally."

We go through a sound check and then like all the other interviews, we dive straight into the questions.

"So, Donnie, how long did you know Jackson?"

Donnie shrugs a shoulder. "Ahh… maybe two years?"

"Did you consider him your friend?"

"Yeah. I mean… we didn't share each other's deep and darkest secrets."

"Did he ever talk about Selah to you?"

"He vaguely mentioned her, but that was it. He made it seem

like they weren't too serious."

"There've been conflicting opinions about the whole tragedy. Some say Selah enabled him and that Jackson—"

Donnie snorts. "Let me cut you off right there. I liked the guy. He was great. But Selah didn't enable him to do nothing."

I nod my head like I'm his therapist calmly listening to everything the patient has to say. This is the fascinating part of my job, watching the interview come alive. My silence, which should deter Donnie, only spurs him on.

'The truth is he was doing drugs before Selah, and he was doing them while he was seeing her."

"What kind of drugs?"

Donnie looks away, just for a second, and it's crystal clear that Jackson wasn't the only one who's had multiple encounters with drugs.

"He was addicted to meth. Actually, he was addicted to any drug out there."

"A lot of people watching this, Donnie, are going to ask themselves if that ever concerned you."

"Not really."

I don't bat an eye as I ask the next question. "Is drug use what you two had in common?"

"No, no, no," Donnie quickly says. "He was having a hard time. Family issues, was all he said. I knew some people who could help him out and the rest is history."

"Do you regret that decision?"

Donnie places his elbows on the table. He turns slightly away and rubs at his chin. Out of all the questions I ask, I can tell this is the one that's going to pull out raw emotion.

He straightens and takes a deep breath. "Of course I regret it. But I didn't make him do what he did. And I didn't force him have a relationship with Selah Kerrington."

19

DIDN'T I TELL you that there's a dark side to love?

Well, you're getting ready to experience that and you don't even realize it. Yet.

But you will. Your heart will pain you like never before. It will be pulled back very slowly. Dissected. Raw and exposed. You're going to ask yourself why you put yourself through this pain. You have to ask yourself if Jackson is worth that pain.

Any discerning eye can tell it's about to happen. The way you look down at your phone with a mixture of fear and happiness. Happiness because you want to talk to Jackson. And fear because you don't know what he's going to say or do.

Since your last conversation there have been two relapses. Yet you still believe that you have the power to turn him around.

Newsflash: you can't save him on your own. No matter how hard you want to, Selah. It doesn't work that way. Only he has the power to save himself. He has to want it more than anything. Not you.

I suppose you're expecting me to say that this isn't part of my gift. But it is. Not every gift is good and pure and filled with happiness. Some gifts are dark to the core, but wrapped in a pretty package.

Please don't be afraid. I don't want to scare you. I'm just keeping the lines of communication open. I think it's vital that we always tell the truth to each other. I just want you to be cautious, not afraid, because I have a plethora of gifts for you.

Some good. And some… indescribable.

If I have to persuade you to take them like I did in the beginning, I will. But something tells me that you've fallen so deep I have to do nothing but snap my fingers and I have your attention.

You'll take my presents whether you like them or not.

20

LIFE WITH MOM hasn't always been easy.

To the outside world she was the sweet teacher Susie who loved and nurtured their children's ravenous minds. And at home her ravenous depression came out to play. She wasn't exactly a monster to live with but she did have really bad days. We never ever, ever talked about her bad moments. To talk about them would shed light on them and to shed light on them would make them real.

Yet there was one time—one single time—when Mom drank too much pinot grigio and told me in a voice so quiet I had to lean in to hear it, 'I hope you never have to deal with a mind like mine.' The next morning it was like the conversation never happened.

It took me years to adjust to her mood swings. She could be calm and soft-spoken one moment, and unhinged and mercurial the next. With eyes that never stopped moving she'd ramble about nonsensical things. You could tell she had a point at the beginning of her tangents, but by the end of the conversation she'd be ranting about how they only had two lanes open at the grocery store—or some other random thing.

Who she was at home was contradictory to the person everyone knew and loved, but she was my mother. I couldn't just stop taking care of her because she had some good and bad days. There was no set schedule to them, just hints here and there to let me know that atrocious days were on their way and they'd be here to stay. It's kind of like squatters: they have no title or lease, and certainly make no payments to take occupancy in your life… but dammit, when they come they're here for the long haul.

The only difference between now and then is that the squatters come more often than they used to.

February has faded into March and those bad days refuse to leave. Snow is starting to slowly melt, revealing the muddy, patchy grass underneath. Parking lots still have giant mounds of snow pushed off to the side from snowplows. It'll be a good week until they completely thaw out.

The temperature sometimes reaches the high forties, which is enough for some kids to run outside without coats, like it's in the mid-sixties or something. But like everyone else, they're just so tired of winter, and desperate to hold onto any vestiges of spring, no matter how fleeting.

Today is going to be in the forties again. I change out of my typical sweats and slip on some black slacks and a white blouse. Before I go downstairs I run a brush through my hair, put some makeup on and brush my teeth. And then I do something unexpected. Something I haven't done in weeks. I sit down at the dining room table and start to attack the pile of bills. There are a few pre-approved credit card offers, one automated mail from a local insurance agency, and a postcard from Mom's dentist with a 'friendly reminder' that she's due for a cleaning.

"Yeah right," I snort.

I can just imagine the dentist sticking his hands in Mom's

mouth and her flying off the wall. Besides, money is dwindling. Fast. At this point I don't think we could afford even a simple teeth cleaning.

But I got a substitute-teaching job today (thank you, God, for the random flu bug going around!) so there will be the smallest bit of money coming in soon. But I'm going to be honest: I don't know if it's going to be enough; it is brutal. Late notices here. Late notices there. After a while I give up and start writing down all the bills that have late notices and all the ones that don't.

And then there are Jackson's problems. I've been taking his issues on as my own and now they're piling up on my shoulders like the bills in front of me. The weight is starting to become unbearable and I don't know how much more I can take. Emotionally, I'm running on empty.

"Good morning," she says.

I'm trying to keep a good attitude around her but it is damn near impossible; we live in a 1,900 square-foot home. For two people that should be an ample amount of room. But add in our combined 13,000 square feet of personality and the house suddenly feels like an incubator. It's like trying to fit eight pounds of sausage into a five-pound bag.

It's starting to drive me crazy.

Suffice it to say, I was more than relieved to get the call informing me that a local school needed a substitute teacher. I have to get a break from Mom. I can feel something dark and crazed brewing inside of me. I felt restless and part of me is just begging to blame Mom.

"Good morning," I grit out.

She sits down across from me. As always, she's clutching her cup between her hands.

The silence lingering around us feels suffocating.

"Did you sleep well?" I ask.

She shrugs and I'm close to pulling out my hair. I really am; a person can only put up with so much. I'm at my wit's end. I take a sip of my coffee and watch her above the rim of my cup. When I place it back on the table, I mimic her actions and clutch it with both hands. Instantly my hands feel warm and I wonder if she did this very thing when she was in the psych ward.

When I signed her out all those weeks ago, I obsessed over how she was treated there. It would keep me up at my night. It tortured me because I wanted to see and experience every moment through her eyes. Just so I could know that she wasn't harmed. I always thought there'd be no match to the helplessness I felt during that time.

I was wrong. Completely and irrevocably wrong.

Over and over my mind tells me that I should've been there more. I should've grabbed her arm before she slipped off the ledge and fell into the deep ravine of depression. I may be with her now but I feel like no more than a small boulder, trying to hold her up from completely falling.

The clock in the dining room ticks, magnifying the silence.

I drop my pen and look at her. "Can I ask you a question?"

"Of course."

"Were you… treated okay when you went away?"

Went away. Phrasing it like that makes it seem like Mom went on a cruise or something. But there's no perfect way to ask someone about their time in a psych ward.

She looks down at the table. "I suppose."

That's not the answer I want to hear at all. I lean forward. "What do you mean by that?"

"It's a terrible place, Selah. A terrible, terrible place. It's where people are at their most fragile." She looks back down at the table. And I want to shake her and scream, *Why didn't you tell me you were suffering so much? I could've intervened! I could've saved you!*

Her eyes lift, as though she can read my mind.

"You know the hospital smell?" she asks.

I swallow and just thinking about it, the disinfectant and bleach, makes my nose scrunch up. "Who doesn't?"

"I would rather inhale that stench every day for the rest of my life than smell what I did there. It was a mixture of sweat and fear."

"Were the doctors nice to you? What about the nurses?"

"Well, enough. I guess. But they didn't bother me."

"What did, then?"

"The woman I had to share a room with talked to herself constantly and when she wasn't doing that she made the strangest keening noise, as if she wanted to scream but didn't have the strength to."

Goosebumps appear on my arms.

"You're not going back there again," I say firmly. And I mean it.

"No one can predict the future, Selah," she sighs.

"True," I reply as I stand up from my seat. I dump the remains of my coffee in the sink. "But one can be determined."

Mom stares straight ahead. "You know it's up to you to keep me out of that place, right?" She has said that before and it always makes my stomach dip in fear. Like she knows something I don't.

"Are you going to be okay while I'm gone?" I ask.

She rolls her eyes. "Of course, Selah."

"Well, can you blame me for asking? Especially after what you just said."

"Oh, I'll be fine."

For a moment, everything in our relationship seems fine. For the time being that is. So I grab my purse from the table and give her a kiss on the head. "See you later, okay?"

"Okay."

I'm so distracted putting on my coat that I walk straight into a solid wall of male as I walk out the door. I veer back and hit the door and see Noah Harrison standing in front of me. He reaches out to right me, but I shrug him off.

"Sorry," he says in that deep voice. "Didn't mean to scare you."

"No worries." I adjust my purse strap. "I wasn't paying attention."

He holds out a stack of mail, a rubber band holding the pile together. "The mailman brought over your mail yesterday. Said that your mailbox was full."

"He could've put it on our porch," I remark.

Noah nudges his head to the right, directly at the stack of newspapers and mail near the door. Shit. How long has that been there?

"I should check the mailbox more often." Awkwardly, I reach out and grab the envelopes in his hands. "Thank you for bringing it over."

I try to avoid any hand contact whatsoever, but I graze his fingers. The touch gives me a slight jolt.

I look down and notice his dog. What's his name again? Duke, isn't it? He sniffs around my yard, slowly edging toward me. Noah gently tugs on his leash.

"Duke, no."

"He's fine." I bend down and pet him. Like his owner, he's too friendly for his own good. The only difference is Duke's sweet on instinct. Animals have no motives. They just want to be fed and loved. And this golden retriever is no exception. I can't help the small smile that creeps onto my face as Duke kisses it. Noah tugs on his leash once again. This time Duke obediently retreats back to Noah's side like a loyal doggie.

"Sorry about that. He gets a little excited when he meets new people."

"No worries." Even though I'm supposed to be going to work, I take a step back toward the house—a friendly yet obvious sign that the conversation is over with. The gesture flies directly over Noah's head. He tucks one hand into his jeans like he has all the time in the world.

"Are you enjoying the day?" he asks.

"Today, sure. But that's only because I have a job to go to. Ask me tomorrow. My answer might change," I say. He raises both brows, but doesn't say a word.

I'm not good with awkward silences. I either laugh nervously or keep talking. This time, it's the latter. "It's just me and my mom living here. She retired a year ago. Someone has to make a living."

"What'd she retire from?"

"She was a kindergarten teacher."

"And what did you do before you moved back home?"

"Second grade teacher." I take a step closer. "What's that little smile for?"

He raises a surrendering hand in the air. "Just think that it's interesting you more or less followed in your mom's footsteps."

"Oh."

Another awkward silence.

"Have you lived in Decatur for awhile?" I ask him.

"No. I previously lived in New York."

"You chose Decatur, IL over New York." I cross my arms and let that sink in. "The rows and rows of soy beans just became too irresistible?"

He tilts his head back and laughs. "No. I have family here. Remember my Aunt Abby?"

Vaguely, I remember him talking about her during our last conversation. I find myself nodding.

"Growing up we lived in New York but when I left for college she moved back home to be with her family. She died a few years ago but I've just been curious as to where she grew up."

"Spoiler alert: it's a dull, dull Midwestern state," I say dryly.

"It's not that bad. But I get what you're saying."

"So what do you do?" I find myself asking.

"I'm a journalist for the *Herald and Review*," he supplies.

Huh. That's not what I imagined but his strange work schedule now makes sense.

"Ohhhh…" I draw out. "So that must be why you work from home."

"Do you watch my every move?" he teases.

"Yes," I reply bluntly.

"So what did you think I did?"

"I don't know." I sigh as I think of an answer. "You're friendly. Yet a little too friendly. So maybe a car salesman?"

I know I'm being a bitch. I seemed to have left my filter inside the house. I think I'm deliberately testing the waters with Noah to see how he'll react.

Noah quirks a brow. "I don't know whether to be flattered or insulted."

Right now, I don't know either so I don't say a word.

"I feel like I'm being interviewed," he says. "Do you want to know where I graduated college? Perhaps you want to see my birth certificate?"

"No, no," I reply. But inside I'm saying, *Yes, yes.*

"Graduated from Northwestern, majoring in journalism. And my birth certificate is probably in some filing cabinet inside my house. Give me a second and I think I'll be able to find it," he says.

There's a second. A small, minuscule second where we both smile at the same time. And my perception of him shifts. Just for a second. And I concede that maybe he isn't that terrible guy I pictured in my mind.

Noah clears his throat and tugs on Duke's leash. "Well. I

should probably take this guy inside. I'll see you later."

"Yeah. See you around," I say to his retreating back.

I watch him walk back to his house. Going up the front steps he stops to unhook Duke's leash and grabs the paper on the second step. He tucks it underneath one arm and goes inside.

All right. So the man might not be a serial killer. Or a man with psychopathic tendencies like I first painted him out to be. But there is something off. I just don't have enough time to think about it.

Quickly, I hurry inside the house to drop off the mail. It lands on another pile on the dining room table.

"Wondered when you'd be back," Mom says.

I stop short at the living room entryway. "Why?"

Her gaze stays rooted on the TV. Unfortunately, today there is a *Law and Order: SVU* marathon on. Fortunately, I don't have to hang around and watch it. "Because you left your phone here." She nudges her head in the direction of the end table.

Sure enough there it is. I check my phone and see I have a few missed calls. For a second, my pulse jumps. But I take a deep breath when I see when they're from Sam.

"Why didn't you tell me Sam called?" I ask Mom.

She shrugs. Mom may miss Sam being around, but she knows how Sam feels about her, too.

"I really have to go or I'm going to be late."

Mom just nods.

Now that I'm standing here, with my full winter gear, I notice that it's really cold inside the house. "Have you been messing with the thermostat?" I ask Mom.

"Now why would I mess with it?"

I remember, years and years ago, when she was going through 'the change' as she called it, she would have the thermostat set so low you could practically see your own breath while sleeping.

This cold is way worse.

Walking out into the hallway, I peer at the thermostat and my heart sinks. It's clearly set at seventy-two degrees. That means either the thermostat is broken or the heater has decided that now would be a great time to stop working. I would assume the electricity has been turned off but then how would Mom be watching her beloved show? In time I'm sure that will be shut off, too. I shudder to think what Mom will be like without television.

With a hearty thwack, I hit the thermostat and turn back toward the front door. "The stupid thermostat is broken," I call out. "If it gets really bad just bundle up, okay?"

All I hear is a light, "Mmm-hmm."

As I'm walking out the front door, I distractedly text Sam back: ***Sorry I missed ur call. I have a teaching job. Call u later?***

Her reply comes within seconds with makes me think she's in between meetings or she's been waiting for me to call her back: ***That's what you said last time. Is everything okay?***

Everything is great. Talk soon!

I make it to my car and throw my purse into the passenger seat. Luckily the car is nice and toasty, instantly warming me up. Before I put the car into reverse I text one more person.

How are you?

Lately, I've been talking to Jackson multiple times a day. When I made that promise to help him, I meant it. I just had no fucking idea how hard it'd be. The honest truth is that I had no idea what I was getting myself into. I've never been an addict or dealt with one and I wanted to go about this the right way, not treating Jackson with kid gloves. He deserves better than that.

But I also want him to remain clean because that night at my house, with his eyes half dead and his skin clammy still makes my blood run cold. Because even though he looked sick, there was this hunger in his eyes that showed me he'd do almost anything for his next high.

Anything.

My phone rings in my hands, jolting me slightly. I see it's Jackson and quickly press answer. "Hello?"

"Can I see you? I really need you right now! Where are you?"

"At home. Getting ready to leave for a teaching job."

"I need to see you. Right now." His voice sounds jittery. Shaky and disjointed. Like he's out of sorts.

I pause for a second and take a deep breath. I know I shouldn't. I know I need this job, but I made a promise to be there for Jackson whenever he needed me. I sigh and stare at the garage door in front of me.

"Where are you?"

"The Starbucks where we first met."

After that, he hangs up.

WHEN I WALK into Starbucks, I instantly see Jackson. He's sitting near the front register, tapping his hands against the counter, loudly, to a beat that no one else can hear. His left knee rapidly bounces up and down. His lips are briskly moving, as if he's having a conversation with someone. There's just one problem: no one is around him.

There are a few people—a cashier, some businessman on his cell phone waiting for his coffee—that give him curious glances.

With a deep breath, I take a step forward and lay a hand on his shoulder. He jumps in response. It's only been a week since he opened up to me about his problems but it feels like so much has changed.

"Selah!" His hands cage my head and he kisses me deeply.

At night, away from prying eyes and with your guard down,

this kind of kiss would arguably be an amazing kiss. But right now, in front of everyone inside and outside of this Starbucks, it's just sloppy. Sloppy and all wrong. Completely bad timing.

With my hands on his chest, I push back and try to keep my face impassive. "Jackson, what's wrong?"

He looks oblivious to my rejection. "So I was reading a book last night," he says. There's a dramatic pause.

"Okay…." I draw out. "What book?"

He takes a deep breath. "*Of Mice and Men.*"

At first, I think he's joking. My lips turn up at the corners, but he's staring at me so intensely that my smile fades. He's being serious right now.

"So there I was. Reading the book. I didn't sleep until I was finished."

"And?"

"And the book fucking sucks!" he explodes.

I flinch slightly but he doesn't notice.

"And so I'm reading the story, rooting for Lennie. Poor Lennie who plods along while it's obvious people think he's one big fucking joke. He makes a mistake. On accident, of course, and what happens? George fucking shoots him at the end!"

That has to be about the worst synopsis of *Of Mice and Men* I've ever heard. There are so many questions running through my mind but the biggest one is for a man who claims to love *War and Peace* by the one and only Leo Tolstoy, why hasn't he read *Of Mice and Men* before? Wasn't it on his high school English syllabus? It seems almost sacrilegious not to have read it. Like not reading *Charlotte's Web* in elementary school.

"A lot of people consider *Of Mice and Men* a work of art," I say quietly.

Jackson snorts. "Fuck Steinbeck!"

At this point, Jackson earns the attention of the people around us. I reach out. "Jack, why don't you take a deep breath. Okay? It's just a book."

"Just a book?" He narrows his eyes. "Just a book? Just a fucking book? God you don't get it."

The only thing I'm getting right now is that he's ridiculously angry over a high school novel that shouldn't evoke a reaction like this. He's on an adrenaline rush… and all I can think of is drugs. Cocaine, specifically. I can't prove it, but it's pretty obvious.

"Look," I start out slowly. "I'm all for books. You know how I love them. But I think you're reading way, *waayy* too much into it."

Jackson leans in until our lips are inches apart. "I thought you loved words as much as I did?" he whispers.

How can I ask him if he's on something without making him go off on another tirade? I can't. But I have to know. I hesitate for one second and then ask, "Jackson, did you take something?"

He pushes away and laughs darkly. "Did I take something," he repeats before he shoots me a dirty look. "Real nice, Selah. Real fucking nice."

I grab his arm and force him to look at me. "Can you blame me for asking? You're acting… erratic," I hiss.

Jackson's lips kick up in small grin. "That's rich, coming from someone who has a crazy-ass Mom."

I veer back, almost as though he's physically slapped me.

Instantly, he sits up straighter. His smile fades. "Selah. Wait. I'm sorry. That was a fucked-up thing to say."

"It was," I reply. My heart's racing, ready to explode out of my chest because I'm seeing a side of Jackson that I've never seen before. And it's not a good one.

Jackson drags all ten fingers through his hair and takes a deep breath. "Look. I might've taken something today."

My face falls. "Oh, Jackson."

"But I just had a shitty day yesterday." He looks at me with those big, blameless eyes. "I lost my job."

"I'm sorry," I reply. And I mean it. I know the fear of not knowing what comes next after being let go. Hell, I'm still dealing with that fear as we speak.

His shoulders slouch. "I've worked at Caterpillar for six years. It was a good paying job." He pinches the bridge of his nose. "I knew they were laying people off I just didn't think I'd be one of them."

I gently rub his back. "I'm sure you'll find another job quickly."

He snorts. I slowly pull away from him. "You and I both know that's bullshit. I mean, look at you. You've been out there searching for a job how long?"

I swallow. "Two months."

Jackson arches a brow. "Two months," he repeats. "You have a good resume and yet no one will hire you. Let's face it: it's not looking promising for the both of us."

"I know you're upset right now but using isn't going to make anything better."

"Yes, Dr. Phil. Anything else you need to say to me?"

This is the main reason why I didn't want to confront him—I knew he wouldn't see me as the good guy. I had a feeling he would lash out and I was right. I reach out and grab onto Jackson's bicep, making sure I have his full attention.

"When you came over to my house and told me about your drug addiction, I didn't judge you. I listened to you and promised that I would help you, in any way possible. And now you're being a complete asshole when I'm just trying to help."

Jackson stares at me with stony silence.

"I care for you. And I don't want anything bad to happen to you." I take a deep breath. "Promise me that you'll stop using."

Again, he says nothing. My grip around his arm tightens.

"Promise me, Jackson," I say.

His jaw works, but he doesn't say anything.

"Jackson," I press. "Promise me."

He wraps an arm around me. Gives me a kiss on the forehead and guides my head toward his chest. "I promise. I promise."

21

LAST NIGHT I dreamed I was drowning in a sea of blood.

I kept trying to swim to the surface but something in the water kept pulling me back down. The few times I made it to the top, I could see Mom and Jackson standing on a beach. Frothy, red waves splashed against their feet but they didn't seem to notice. Jackson stood there, arms crossed over his chest, a look of remorse on his face. Mom's arms were behind her back as she stood there piously, looking at me with pity instead of worry. Yet she was crying. Her blood red tears trailed down her cheeks.

Neither one attempted to help me.

Further and further I slipped into the blood-filled ocean, until the metallic scent filled my nostrils and absorbed my entire body. The water turned a murky blue but I could see my hand in front of me. I continued to try and break free from whatever was holding onto me. When I looked down I saw two hands wrapped around my ankles. There was no body attached to those hands.

I screamed. Blood bubbles floated in front of me.

This is it, I thought to myself. *I'm going to die and no one will ever find my body*. I started to hyperventilate. which only made me flail about.

I couldn't breathe.

I couldn't breathe.

I kicked at the hands holding onto my ankles. And I heard an unrecognizable voice say, "Let me help you, Selah."

If I could speak I'd tell that person that they weren't helping me. They were hurting me in every way possible.

The fight slowly left my body. My chin dipped to my chest, but my eyes? They remained open, filled with unmistakable fear. I stared at the dark mass beneath me, hoping that the last thing I saw was the very thing that was killing me.

Instead, those hands pulled me further down. Gradually, I slipped out of consciousness, but by that point I didn't care. I didn't care that I was going to die. I didn't care that I was leaving Mom and Jackson and Sam behind. I didn't care that they didn't help. I just wanted this insufferable pain to end.

My body became numb and then—

With a loud gasp I wake up. My heart is pounding so hard my entire body shakes. My hands curl around my neck as I reflexively swallow and gasp. Swallow and gasp.

Clearly it was just a dream. But it felt so real that for the first few seconds I'm still gasping for air. Dazed, I look down: my sheets are pushed down around my legs. My oversized sleep shirt is drenched in sweat. My skin is clammy. I can still smell the body wash I used last night before I went to bed, but I feel filthy, like I'm actually covered in blood but I can't see it.

The look on Jackson and Mom's face gives me chills. They both became two strangers that I didn't know. I know that I'm reading into the dream but I can't stop the goosebumps that cover my arms.

I roll out of bed and walk quietly down the hall toward Mom's bedroom. I see the light from the TV peeking out from beneath her door. That should make me feel at ease but I have to see her. I need the physical proof. I gently open her door. Her love for HSN and *SUV* are strictly confined to daytime. At night, it's either the Hallmark channel or Nick at Nite. Right now *I Love Lucy* is playing. I sneak closer to her bed and when I see her lying asleep on her left side I finally take a deep breath.

See? I tell myself. *It was all just a dream. Your mom would never do anything to hurt you.*

My heart is pounding so hard that sleep is completely out of the question. So I slip into bed next to her. Me, Selah Kerrington, thirty-year-old woman, is sleeping in her mom's bed like a little girl who just saw the fucking boogieman. But it's not the boogieman I saw. What I saw felt akin to déja vu, it felt like I had experienced that dream in real time. The thought makes me shudder.

Mom doesn't stir as I get comfortable and watch TV. For the next three hours I lie awake. It's only when the sun rises that my eyelids become heavy and I slip into a deep, dreamless sleep.

22

I TRY NOT to count the good days against the bad.

There are times when the bad days take over, stacking themselves one on top of the other until it feels like a fortress has been built around me. To combat the overwhelming feeling I hold on to the good moments.

Lately that's been working. I've started to become optimistic. I'm playing a dangerous game with my emotions, but I deserve to feel happiness roaring through my veins. I deserve this.

So does my mom.

I think my optimistic approach has been rubbing off on her. She's helped tackle some of the bills with me. Together, we might get the never-ending pile under control. She's even cooked us dinner a few times. She's starting to act like the fun-loving, eccentric mom that I grew up with.

Today I have another substitute teaching job, and I wake up to the sound of my alarm. I'm dressed and walking down the stairs by 6:12. Not bad. I start the coffeemaker and inhale the deep rich scent. I grab a bagel and pop it in the toaster.

While I wait for my breakfast, I walk to the calendar hanging on the wall and cross off yesterday's date. March 5th. I drum my fingers on the counter, wondering whether I should fuel up before I leave South Shores or wait until after school. I decide to leave early and fuel up, but that means I have to leave now if I'm going to make it on time.

I pour my coffee in a to-go cup and quickly smear some cream cheese onto the bagel before wrapping it in a paper towel. I hook my hand through my purse straps, then grab my food and coffee and walk out of the kitchen toward the foyer. Because of Mom's recent behavior, I've become more comfortable leaving her at home. But I still make it a habit to check on her before I leave.

"Mom?" I shout up the stairs. "I'm leaving. I'm teaching in Warrensburg so I might get home a little later than I usually do. Okay?"

Silence.

"Mom?"

More silence.

"Oh, for Pete's sake," I mutter to myself as I place my bagel, coffee and purse on the small end table in the front room. I hurry up the stairs, and make a left toward Mom's room.

Sometimes she stays up the entire night. She'll watch TV, color in one of those adult coloring books, or catch up on reading. But her late-night activities make her sleep well into the afternoon and you have to practically shout to wake her up.

I knock on her door once before I walk in.

Per her usual, the TV is on. The blinds are shut, giving the room a cave-like vibe. I turn on the light, expecting to see Mom softly snoring, but her bed is empty. The sheets have been pulled back and I can still see the indentation of her head on the pillow.

"Mom? You in here?"

Silence.

The first inklings of worry start to course through me. Forgetting about my substitute-teaching job, I leave the master bedroom and search every single room in the house.

She's nowhere to be found.

Standing in the middle of the foyer, I look around and feel panic take hold of my heart. "Take a deep breath, Selah," I tell myself. "Just breathe." I try to follow my own suggestion but miserably fail.

I stalk toward the kitchen where the back door is. I open it up, ignoring the cold air. Our backyard is covered in snow, making it look like a winter wonderland. The wind lightly picks up snowflakes that swirl in the air and go up and over our fence. With the exception of animal footprints, there are no other footprints. And no sight of Mom. If anyone were out in weather like this not properly dressed, they'd get hypothermia pretty damn quick.

I slam the door. The black hinges on the porch door creak loudly behind me as I hurry to the front door.

"Mom?" I inch out of the house.

It's then that I realize she's really gone. I don't have proof and I've hardly been looking for her long but it's a feeling in my gut. Something is very, very wrong. My vision starts to blur. There's an acid taste in my mouth. I always worry that Mom will once again wander off. It's one of my biggest fears but lately she's been so great. I lowered my defenses.

This is my entire fault.

"Mom?" I ask a little louder, but my voice is hoarse.

Hurrying inside, I grab my car keys hoping that maybe she fell asleep in the backseat or something bizarre. I don't care how crazy it seemed, I'd gladly accept any other option running through my head.

She's not in my car. Or the garage. If I could tear apart the house, rip the walls down, I would.

She's nowhere.

It gets harder and harder to breath, I think I'm going to vomit because that gut feeling won't go away.

Just then I see Noah walk out his front door. He gives me a friendly wave as he walks to his car. I don't wave back. Instead, I hurry over to his driveway.

"Have you seen my mom?"

He unlocks his car and frowns at me. "No, I haven't. Why?"

"She's gone."

"What do you mean gone?" he repeats slowly.

"Gone! She's nowhere to be found!" I half shout.

"Calm down," Noah says in a soothing tone. He walks around the car and stands in front of me. His hands curl around my bicep. "Why do you think she's gone?"

"Because she's not in the house and she's been known to wander the streets."

"And have you searched the streets?"

"No!" I say impatiently. Frantically, I look around the cul de sac, hoping that she'll magically appear. Noah's fingers dig into my flesh, making me wince. But I don't tell him to let me go because the pain keeps me wide awake and alert.

"She's done this twice before," I admit, my voice shaking. "A third time and they'll involuntarily commit her. I can't let that happen. I can't."

Noah lets go of me and I cross my arms over my chest. "Let's look around the neighborhood first before we panic," he says calmly.

He opens up the passenger car door and waits for me to get in. My distrust of Noah is still alive and well, but at least he's on my side, willing to help me out. And right now I need all the help I can get.

FOR THE NEXT two hours we search Wildwood for Mom, but come up short. Noah has the heat on full blast but nothing can warm the frigid cold that's swallowed up my marrow. Very slowly, it's spreading through my bones until I can feel nothing.

It's apparent that Noah wants to give up the search. He keeps drumming his fingers against the steering wheel and looking out his window with idle eyes like I'm asking him to search for a garage sale or something.

Yet the fact that he is helping me stands for something.

Eventually, we broaden our search to South Shores shopping area. I text Jackson multiple times to tell him what's going on.

Hey! I need to talk to you ASAP!

No reply.

Five minutes later.

I'm with Noah. We can't find my Mom. I don't know what to do.

Nothing.

"Earlier, you mentioned that she's done this twice before… Is she on any medication that she should be taking but isn't?"

"No," I lie, trying but failing to keep the defensiveness out of my tone.

"Hey, now…" He momentarily holds his hands up in surrender before he drops them back to the steering wheel. "There's nothing wrong with medication. I just didn't know if there's something else to the story that I don't know." He glances at me searchingly. "Because if there is, it stays between you and me. I won't tell a soul."

Never, ever trust someone to hold your secrets, my mind whispers. Yet I still hesitate because Noah's here, helping me search, and that means a lot. Reaching across the console he pats my hand. I expect him to pull away but he lays it there for a few seconds longer than necessary. I don't say a word because for a second I feel comfort that I haven't felt in hours. Maybe days.

Toward the end of the day, I tell Noah to park outside of Kroger. Maybe someone inside or leaving the grocery store saw her. I ask over twenty people. Not one person saw her. Something starts to break inside of me. Something important and vital. My sanity? Nothing is making sense anymore.

"She's going to come home," I say aloud, just to fill the silence.

Noah doesn't reply.

Even though we're canvassing, I feel like we're wasting time. Short of calling the police, I don't know what else to do. I can't exactly call the police because my fear is that they'll find her. They'll find her and take her away from me. From her home. They'll do one better than St. Mary's and lock her up in an insane asylum. I know they will. With the exception of Noah, I can't ask the neighbors. I'm too afraid that any questions I ask, they'll repeat to the police.

My phone vibrates. I jump slightly at the sound. My heart pounds as I look at the screen. My shoulders slump down when I see that it's Sam.

"You just don't get it," I whisper to the screen as I press the decline button.

PART II

23

IF YOU FEEL like it's been forever since we've been together you're right.

We measure the time differently. For you, it's been days. Four, to be exact. I watch as you cross off the days and longingly stare at the calendar.

For me it's felt like years but that's only because I've been tirelessly working on a way for us to be together. Not in brief fleeting moments like before, but forever.

So when you think I'm playing games with you, just know that I'm not. I ache. I rage. I scream out for you, too.

There are times when I watch you and I have to fight the urge to give in. To reach out and give you another present. Yet I dig deep. I find a sliver of determination I didn't know existed because it's for the best that we remain apart. For now. Until I find a way for us to be one.

Trust me. It's better this way.

Right now, I watch as you pace the floor of your living room. You've been doing this for hours yet you can't seem to stop. All your thoughts are focused on your mom. Abruptly you stop and drag your hands through your hair and pull. You pull as hard as humanly possible. You want to feel pain. You want a distraction from the hell that is your life.

Close the damn curtains, I want to tell you. *People might be watching you.*

But I don't. See, this is what I'm trying to show you. You need me. You need me to protect you. To show you right from wrong. To reward you and make you feel good.

I've been holding you up, slowly ushering you forward. It's time that you take a few steps forward all by yourself.

24

THERE ARE SO many rooms in this house and I know each one of them by heart.

I know that the guest bedroom has a creaky floorboard. I once pulled it up and decided to grab an empty Folgers can and put some treasure in it. At the age of ten it sounded like an amazing idea. I told Sam about it and she surprisingly agreed and brought over some of her treasures. I think that Folgers can is there to this day.

I know that the wallpaper in the dining room has been peeling in the upper right-hand corner for the past two years. It's barely discernible to most people but it drives me crazy.

I have a huge quilted rug in the middle of my room but that's only because I decided to paint a chair white when I was a freshman in high school. I stood up to go to the bathroom and tripped over the bucket of paint. It went everywhere and I was too chicken shit to tell Mom. So I put a rug over it. She found about it, of course—years later when we were able to laugh about it.

I know that there's a small crack in the master bedroom

window from a storm. Instead of getting the damn windowpane replaced we used duct tape. Sometimes, when the wind picks up, it whistles through the crack, making the house creak in protest.

I know so much about this house but the crazy part is that these walls know so much more, and if I were silent—as still as a mouse—I could here them whispering.

They talk about me. About Mom. They talk about our good and bad moments. Dissect them as though I'm not even here. I want to rage at them, scream at the top of my lungs that I'm still here. I can hear everything they're saying, but I'm too afraid that they're going to say something of value about Mom and I'll miss it.

But they say nothing of value.

It's too late, you dumb girl, the walls whisper.

I pace the hallway and moan. "You don't know that. You know nothing."

It's too late. It's too late. It's too late.

I bite down hard on my lip. I taste blood but I don't let up. I'm talking to myself but it feels… good. Because I'm slowly going crazy not knowing where Mom is or having any answers. All I have are questions: what if someone has found her? What if they've hurt her? What if Mom left on her own free will?

If I went to the police and reported her missing they'd probably laugh in my face because she's a grown woman. Yet she's not thinking clearly. She's a woman who's not of sound mind. That should count for something, right?

Bile rises in my throat. I run upstairs while the house whispers, *It's too late, you dumb girl.*

"Shut up!" I scream.

My words are met with silence. I walk into my room, intent on calling the police and getting help one way or the other. I pick up the phone, but when it asks for my passcode I pause. I toss the phone on my bed and start to pace. I can't do it.

Take your medicine, says a voice in my head. *It will help you think clearly.*

"Why is this happening?" I groan in frustration as I grab my hair at the roots and pull.

I walk into the bathroom and stare at myself in the mirror. Flecks of toothpaste sprinkle the lower portion of the mirror, but I don't care. I lean in, stare closely at myself. I'm scared out of mind and it shows. My eyes are wild with fear. My face is pale, making the dark circles underneath my eyes prominent. It doesn't help that I'm exhausted. I can't keep going on like this.

Before I can think twice I open up the medicine cabinet. The only thing that's organized in this damn house is this cabinet. All of Mom's medicine is neatly lined up, with the labels facing forward.

This isn't the smartest thing I've done. In fact, if doctors could see me now they'd be cringing before telling me about the dangers of self- medicating. Addictive, they might say. Or perhaps dangerous. They'd be correct on all fronts. But it beats drinking myself into oblivion.

It's one little pill. How can it hurt?

In paranoia I glance around the room, like the walls have eyes. I feel like I'm living a version of *The Truman Show.* Wouldn't that be a trip—I go through this whole ordeal only to find out that it was set up this way, staged for the viewers?

That's not an option. But taking a pill just might be.

"Fuck it," I mutter before I toss a pill into my mouth and swallow it down.

I cross my fingers that it kicks in fast and walk back to my bedroom. My body feels so heavy. It hurts to walk, to even function, but my mind won't turn off. It's the most infuriating feeling in the world.

I lie on my bed and stare up at the ceiling, watching the fan blades slowly move. Within thirty minutes, I'm knocked out.

I'M SO FOCUSED on finding Mom that it's becoming increasingly difficult to function like a normal human being. It's been days since she went missing.

Yesterday I once again canvassed all of Wildwood, walked around calling out her name like I was searching for my missing dog instead of my adult mother. When I came up empty-handed I searched half of South Shores. I drove around Kroger's parking lot, peering at every single person: moms pushing shopping carts, older ladies slowly shuffling to the handicapped parking.

I drove slowly across the bridge, gazing at the railings. A chill went through me. Mom was confused a lot of the time, but she wasn't suicidal. At least I didn't think so. I kept driving around until my gaslight went on and then I turned around. It felt like a betrayal, driving back home.

I sleep in small intervals. An hour here. An hour there. At night I pace the house and keep all the lights on, as if they're a bat signal that Mom will see and then she'll realize that it's time to come home.

Simple tasks like going outside to get the mail feel like a marathon. I have to pump myself up. Take deep breaths. I think my heart is ready to collapse. In fact, I'm sure of it. I don't know how much more I can take.

It's early in the morning and I'm not tired. Sleep eludes me. My heartbeat has slowly faded throughout the night. Staccato rhythm fades.

And fades.

And fades.

I expect it to stop altogether when the sun rises. I almost pray for it.

But the sun is up, doing its job.

What exactly is *my* job in life? Not so long ago, I would say it was taking care of my mom. Now, I don't know.

Other times, I get the strangest feeling in my body. It's exhausted, begging for much needed sleep. Yet my heart pounds and my mind races a mile a minute. And my thoughts? They're scattered and make no sense. One second I'm thinking about Mom and all the ways I should look for her and the next I'm mentally compiling a list of all the things I need to clean up in the house.

Sometimes they're so grandiose I feel like I can conquer the world. I get this incredible surge of energy but that feeling only lasts for an hour. Two at the most. And then I crash. Hard.

And when I do, it's a black, dreamless sleep.

25

IT'S BEEN SAID that the first seventy-two hours in a missing person's case are crucial.

Credit cards can be traced. Evidence hasn't been washed away by rainfall or snow. If the media picks up on the story then the missing person's case will reach more people. Your loved ones picture will appear on TV's in thousands of living rooms. And the witnesses, if there are any, still have the events fresh in their memory. They can remember if they saw a white van driving around the neighborhood. Or a mysterious stranger who didn't make eye contact walking down their street.

I can't help but ask myself: would Mom's missing person's case be considered high profile?

I remember when I was a kid and I would leave the grocery store with Mom and we'd pass a bulletin board with all the missing children, from local all the way to Chicago. Mom would always stop and scan the faces and names. Sometimes she said nothing and other times she would put a protective arm around me and gesture to the board. "This is why I never let you leave my sight for a second. There are bad, bad people everywhere."

Never in a million years did I think her words would be ringing in my ears twenty plus years later to haunt me. Never did I think I'd be calling the police to say my mother was missing. I was afraid that if I called the authorities they'd find her and lock her away in a loony bin. She didn't belong there.

It was Noah who talked me into it. Noah who dialed 911. And Noah who handed me the phone.

"They'll take her away," I blurted out. "They'll put her in an insane asylum but at this point I'll take it. I just want her to be okay."

I don't know why I said the words out loud, probably more for my benefit than anything else. Noah stood beside me wordlessly. I hesitated for a second but then I pictured her lifeless, dead. Her body rotting and nothing but bones. It made me want to double over in pain.

I closed my eyes and forced the image out of my head, and then made the call that I knew I'd regret.

"You know what you need to do, right?" he'd said earlier this afternoon.

I stared at him, stubborn. I've discovered that if you look someone in the eye long enough, if you shed your armor and reveal all your tragedies, they can't bear it and quickly look away. But Noah resolutely stared back at me. If anything he leaned in, like he found my sadness fascinating.

"I know what I need to do," I finally said.

So I did and here they are.

The sky's been a slate gray all day. Dark clouds seem to be coming toward me, threatening to swallow up the sky whole. It has all the makings of a good thunderstorm. Yet when the cops arrive, the clouds start to part. Ever so slowly. And the sun peeks out like it's playing a game of hide and seek.

I know I said earlier that the rain was starting to get old but at this moment I want thunder. Lightening. Rain. I want it all to match how I'm feeling inside. I want to know something, even something as big as Mother Nature, is on my side. And every time the thunder strikes it'd be saying: *Hey, Selah. The world is a fucked-up place. I'll rage right alongside you.*

There are only two police cars. They don't pull up with lights flashing or sirens screaming. Nonetheless, neighbors filter out of their houses. Nosy Tracy boldly stands on her front porch. Thanks to her everyone and their dog will know that the police are here. But for once that might work in my favor. The quicker the news spreads that Mom is missing, the faster she can be found.

Right?

Right.

"You don't have to stay here," I tell Noah as the cops walk toward the front door.

"I'm not leaving."

To be honest, his presence has been… soothing and shocking all at the same time. In my mind I had built this image of him based on nothing but my own imagination. Maybe he's not such a bad guy at all.

When I step outside, I come face to face with a portly man with a perpetual line of sweat around his graying hairline. There's a younger officer next to him. He's tall and skinny with an eagerness about him that even I can tell screams, *newbie*. This doesn't sit well with me. New translates into inexperienced. And inexperienced means mistakes. I can't afford mistakes. I'm starting to realize that every minute I naively refused to call the cops and report Mom missing was a mistake on my part.

I've lost so much time.

"Ma'am, Officer Cooper," says the portly man.

"Selah Kerrington."

He holds his hand out to shake. It's sweaty and I discreetly wipe the sweat off on the side of my jeans.

We go through introductions, which just seem tedious. Instead of coming inside all four of us stand outside.

The pudgy one is the first to begin asking questions. They start out harmless. Full name. Date of birth. Height. How about her weight? Can't forget eye color. After that he went on to ask more pointed questions. When did I notice she was missing? When was she last seen?

"March 6th… I think?" I say. "My brain is a little foggy on the exact date."

The officers share a look that I want to punch off their smug faces. "So it took you almost six days to report your mother missing?"

"Look, it's happened before and I just thought she would show up and—"

"Wait," the newbie interjects. "Has she left before?"

"Yes, but—"

Suddenly, they both become interested. I can't stand the neighbors openly staring at me so I invite the officers to come inside. How many times?" the portly one asks.

Shit. Why did I say that? They're going to read into that—it sounds like Mom chooses to come and go as she pleases. Even I know there's no crime for an adult to up and leave their house.

"How many times, miss?" the older officer prods.

"Two times," I finally admit.

"And did she come back home?" the newbie asks.

"No. She was taken to the hospital and put on seventy- two hour watch."

"I see."

"And before you ask, I've already called DMH and St. Mary's. Neither hospital could give out patient information. But if she were there right now, I should've gotten a call from one of the doctors taking care of her, and there've been no calls.

The older officer looks to Noah, as to verify what I'm saying. When Noah nods, the officer turns back to me.

"We can file a report but we need the most recent photo of your mom…" his words fade away as he takes in the state of the house. Sure, to someone new it might look messy. But I've been here long enough to know where Mom stores most of her belongings, and the pictures are in the spare bedroom upstairs and in the dining room.

"Wait one second." I hurry to the dining room, leaving Noah with the officers.

I go straight to a box shoved against the wall labeled TEACHING and thumb through dozens of class pictures that show Mom standing next to her small students, proud and tall, or sitting on a chair, her students flanking her. None of those are close-up photos, though. I find one of her in her last year of teaching; it's with her student on the last day of school. She's kneeling, one arm wrapped around a boy's shoulder while he gave a toothy grin.

I snatch the photo from the stack and rush out into the foyer. "Here!" I say triumphantly.

Newbie takes the photo and scans it. Portly starts to ask me questions: did she have an abusive spouse? Was she in financial trouble? I think they call those push factors—things that would force someone to leave of their own accord.

I answer each question as best as I can. There's no time to think over the last question carefully because I can hear my phone ringing in the other room.

"Hold on for one second."

I leave the officers with Noah again and run toward the direction of the ringing. It's coming from the kitchen. I swear if this is a call from Mom and I miss it, I'm going to lose it. By the time I get there the ringing has stopped. When I check the screen, I see that it's a missed call from Sam.

She's called almost every day and I keep forgetting to call her back. I shoot her a quick text, knowing that I'm a lousy friend for not answering her calls. ***Busy. Promise to call back.***

You better. Or I'm coming to visit this weekend. I'm concerned about you.

I place my phone face down on the kitchen table and walk back into the foyer, only to see the officers leaving. Newbie turns towards me right before Noah closes the door. "Ma'am we'll immediately get to work on filing a case report. You should hear from us within a day."

I stare at him, feeling a bit shell-shocked. Noah closes the door behind Newbie and gives me a weak smile.

"What did they say to you?"

"Pretty much the same thing they said to you. Filing a case report. Asked me a handful of questions."

I cross my arms "That's it?"

"That's it." He gives me a once over. "You were expecting more, weren't you?"

"Of course I was! I thought that they would start canvassing the area. Asking the neighbors, putting up fliers. Like they did for that little girl who disappeared over a month ago!"

"But your mom's not a nine-year old little girl who was snatched from the playground. She's a grown adult," Noah points out.

"She's been missing for days, though."

"In their eyes it hasn't been that long."

Suddenly I turn around and throw my hands up in the air. "So. That's it? I give up and wait?"

"No one said that."

"But that's how you make it sound."

Noah approaches me very slowly. His hands curl around my arms as he lowers his head so our eyes are level. "Look, I'll help you keep searching for your mom. That hasn't changed. All right?"

With a shaky breath I nod.

"What did you mean earlier about you being okay with your mom being put in an insane asylum?" he asks.

Gently, I extract myself out of his grasp. I'd been so worked up I forgot I said a word about Mom's past stints. I sigh, debating whether I should tell him the truth or not.

The truth prevails.

"In early January, the neighbors called the cops on my mom a few times for roaming the streets." I stare at a picture of Mom with Aunt Ruby when they were children. "They said she was scaring the children. She's been in and out of St. Mary's and that's what brought me back home. I had to look out for her. Protect her. The doctor told me that if the cops were called on her again they were going to admit her into DMH."

"Like, the hospital?"

"No, like Decatur Manor Healthcare."

His eyes light up with understanding. "A place for the mentally ill."

"Yes."

"And that's why you were hesitant to call the police."

I take a deep breath. "Yes. But you've talked to my mom. You understand that she can't go there, right? She has her struggles but she's not crazy."

Noah becomes silent.

"She's not crazy," I insist a little bit louder this time.

"It's okay. It's okay. I believe you," Noah says softly.

He opens his arms up to me and because Jackson won't answer me, because I feel so alone, I go willingly.

I believe that there are levels of affection, so impossible to discern you'd miss them if you blinked. But if you catch them they can be revelatory. People think sex is complicated but affection is the thing that's dynamic and oh-so confusing. With a friendly kiss on the cheek there's a healthy distance between your bodies. But with a passionate kiss, for example, you can't get enough of that person. Hands are everywhere. You are ravenous.

The hug between Noah and I starts out friendly. Meant to comfort and console, but in that moment when both of us should pull away, we don't. There's a small step forward and I feel Noah tighten his grasp. His hands are splayed directly below my shoulder blades, making my skin prickle. And I'm no better, slowly and hesitantly curling my hands around his waist.

I hate myself. Hate that I need this affection more than anything.

See? Levels of affection. To know them is to love them. And to love them is to hate them.

26

I'VE ALWAYS FOUND the color of blood a fascinating thing.

Two things happen when people see it: some jump into action, grabbing towels, rubbing alcohol. Or, in more dangerous situations, they call 911 for help. Others stare at it, transfixed by the color, the metallic scent.

I'm the latter.

Blood gives you life. It courses through your veins and lets you cry those endless tears for your mom. It allows your wild imagination to think of all the sick ways your mom could possibly be dead. You know it's demented that you think that way. But you're only human and you're trying to protect yourself from the worst possible outcome.

You've always been a heavy bleeder. I remember a time when you were in Home Economics in high school and you became too impatient opening a box of pasta. You used a steak knife and cut your left middle finger. (Look down, right now, at your hands and you'll see the small scar near the knuckle.) Blood was everywhere. You'd think you'd lost a limb.

I remember I froze. I couldn't move. I just stood by and watched the blood pool over the cut before it trailed down your skin and dropped to the floor. The teacher jumped into action. Students stepped back and some moved in to help clean all the blood up. After a few minutes, it was cleaned up. It was just a minor nick.

You might not know this but your mom is a bleeder, too. It could be for a multitude of reasons, from fragile blood cells to something deeper like cirrhosis, but it's something that you two have in common.

It's not the only thing you have in common. You become easily depressed for days. But if I told you that you wouldn't believe me.

Right now you are too focused on finding her. You put in calls to the police, but they won't answer you. You rack your brain thinking of your last moments with her.

You're searching too hard. Just look around you; I keep trying to show you the clues. Blood has the ability to stain fabric and seep into porous material. There may be no visible traces of blood but it's there.

It's always there.

So lift your head. Stand up. Let that blood flow and listen carefully to the walls. They'll start to whisper to you and if you're lucky those whispers will transform into screams. You'll hear the honesty and truth that you need.

All because of the color of blood.

27

MY DREAMS ARE smeared with the image of Jackson.

It always starts out sweet. The two of us together and so happy, surrounded by people. But then he starts to distance himself, like a car slowly moving in reverse. I cling to him even though I know it's desperate because all I can think of is how happy he makes me and I can't lose that when I have nothing else.

But he keeps moving farther and farther away. He becomes a small, black in a dot in a sea of people.

"Fuck you," I say. At least I think I do. But he never turns my way. It feels as if someone has my heart in their hand and is squeezing it as hard as they can. "Look at what you're doing to me!" I shout at him.

He hears my words. Feels my pain. I know he does. But he just shakes his head and laughs as if I'm making a joke. Then he starts to speak and even though he's so far away, I still hear his words as if he's whispering them directly into my ear.

"I'm sorry," he says.

I want to feel sad for him. But I can't.

I want to be angry with him. But I can't.

I run after him to get answers. I start to catch up to him. I reach out for him and just when I go to grab ahold of his arm, I wake up.

It takes me a while to realize that it's all a dream and I'm in my room with the TV. A sitcom is the only thing keeping me company. I stare at the screen and watch as the show goes to commercial. Light from the screen flashes across the room.

After a minute or two I calm down and grab my phone. I type in my passcode and pull up Jackson's phone number. I hesitate before I press call. I can't remember the last text or call I've received from Jackson. It's been at least a week. Not once has he called back. Why?

Is he okay? Did he get into a wreck and now he's laid out on the side of the road, injured? Or is it something more simplistic, something that I just simply refuse to believe? Like, he just doesn't want to be with me anymore.

To anyone outside of the relationship, I'm sure the signs of him breaking up with me were there. He'd been distant. Snippy. But he was trying to stay clean and just lost his job—factors that would stress anyone out.

Never did I think he would completely cut off all ties of communication. It seems like a coward's way out of a relationship. And Jackson never seemed like someone to end a relationship like that. My conversations with Sam and Mom come rushing back to me. Maybe they were right. What did I really know about him?

"Fuck it," I mutter and press call. It rings once before a female, automated voice says, "We're sorry; you have reached a number that has been disconnected or is no longer in service. If you feel you have reached this recording in error, please check the number and try your call again."

I hold the phone away from my head and frown down at the

screen. The message starts over. I quickly hang up then re-dial Jackson's number and just like before the automated voice comes back on.

He purposely turned his phone off.

"What an asshole," I whisper to no one.

I force myself out of bed and walk down the stairs with only my misery to keep me company. At this time of night the house is eerily quiet. I can hear the grandfather clock ticking in the dining room. The sound of the fridge in the kitchen. I know it sounds crazy but I feel eyes on me. I want to run back up the stairs and hide in my bed like a fucking four-year old but I continue forward because the pain of being ignored by Jackson outweighs my childish fears.

Without a second thought I start to rummage through the pantry until I find what I'm looking for. I grab a glass from the cabinet and a Coke from the fridge. I pour myself a shot of Svedka. I kick it back and chase the burn with some Coke but my lips still pucker.

Give it up, my mind hisses. *There's a reason his phone is turned off.*

My heart says differently. It tells me that can't possibly be the reason. Jackson was someone good. Someone I had a true connection with. Kismet, some people would call it. Yet look at me now. I'm relentlessly contacting a person who has no desire to speak with me. If Jackson did want to talk to me, he would've told me that he changed his phone number. He would make an effort.

"Screw him," I say out loud. I pour myself another drink and raise my shot glass in the air and invisibly toast myself.

I look at the clock on the oven. Eleven. I'd only been in bed close to an hour, but if dreams of Jackson are the only thing waiting for me in my sleep then I'd rather stay up all night. I take another shot, feeling the warm liquid travel down my throat.

I walk out of the kitchen and move toward the living room; the house is too quiet. I need the TV on. I find the remote and see that a sitcom is playing. I slowly lower myself onto the couch and numbly watch the show. It used to bother me how Mom would just sit here day in and day out and do nothing. But now I miss her presence so acutely it's like a gaping wound, open to the elements, begging to be closed shut.

I hear a loud sound coming from outside. I twist around and peek through the blinds and see that Noah's garage door is open. Light spills out, illuminating the patches of ice on the concrete.

What is he doing outside at this time of night?

My curiosity gets the best of me. I stand up and slip on my jacket, step outside, then quietly shut the front door behind me. The sky is nothing but a blanket of stars. I take my time walking toward Noah's house, making sure to avoid any ice. I exhale and notice the way my breath appears inches in front of me like fine mist.

Everyone on the cul de sac is indoors for the night. Lights are off and cars are parked in garages. In a few of the second-story windows I can see the glow of TV's flashing every few seconds. I've been filled with anxiety and sadness all day, but knowing that there's someone up at this hour, that I'm not alone, makes me calm down.

When I step onto Noah's driveway he finally lifts his head from his workstation. He has on a Carhartt jacket and there's a black beanie on his head. Day-old stubble covers his face. He looks a good ole farm boy. I know he's anything but. There's a radio on the rough wooden counter behind him, softly crooning the latest country song.

I tuck my hands in my coat and take a tentative step closer.

"What are you doing up?" he asks, surprised to see me.

"Uh… it's eleven o'clock at night. Not *that* late. Besides, I could ask you the same question."

Noah smirks. "I was working on an article and had writer's block. I needed to clear my head so I came out here."

"I've heard of people taking bubble baths to relax. Or reading right before they go to bed. But carpentry? Not so much."

Noah shrugs and blows the sawdust off the smooth layer of wood. It scatters onto the table. "I fell in love with carpentry in high school when I had to take workshop during my sophomore year. There's something gratifying about using my hands to build something. Makes me feel useful and accomplished." He looks my way. "Ever felt that way?"

My mind instantly replays the years of teaching and all the children I'd met. There were rough days. But the good far outweighed the bad. Nothing was more gratifying that watching a child blossom underneath my tutelage. I look him in the eye and nod. "Yes. I have." I walk slowly around the piece placed on a waist-high narrow wooden table. "So… what's this?"

"A bench." He takes off his work gloves, puts them in his back pocket and arches a brow at me. "You've heard of a bench before, haven't you?" he asks teasingly.

"Of course. I just never pegged you as someone who made them."

"Well, I do."

"So you're a journalist by day and moonlight as a carpenter. What's next? You're a chef at a five-star restaurant?"

"Nope."

"Pity. I was starting to think you were a jack-of-all-trades."

Noah walks around the worktable and grabs a tape measure. "What brings you here, Selah?"

"I couldn't sleep. Looked out the front window and saw you were out here."

"You sure do look out that front window of yours a lot," he

replies as he turns back to the bench and measures its front right leg.

I shrug. "What can I say? My life is miserable and I'm desperately searching for company." I try to smile. I really do, but I can feel my lips slightly quivering because my words aren't a total lie. I am miserable, but I'm more than that. I am terrified. I am scared. I am alone.

Noah stares at me for a long second. His sharp green eyes betray nothing. Finally, he clears his throat and gestures to a patio chair placed in front of some unopened boxes. "Sit. You can keep me company."

"Are you sure?"

"Positive."

"Where's Duke?"

"Inside. Not being a good guard dog. Obviously."

I stand up. "Look, if I'm being a pain in the ass, I can leave."

"No, no, no. I'm just kidding. Sit down."

Because I'm lonely as all get out, I sit back down. At least that's what I tell myself. Noah gets back to work and for the longest time I just watch him methodically working on the bench, only stopping to make measurements. His dark brows slant low over his eyes. His lips form a thin line. I watch as his tongue snakes out to lick his lips. My stomach twists at the action.

I veer back and cross my arms over my stomach. Mom's gone and I don't know if she's coming back. The same can be said for Jackson, and yet here I am staring at Noah like a starving woman. What the hell is wrong with me?

I swallow loudly. "You're really good," I say out of nowhere.

He lifts his head and grins. Another twist in my gut. "You seem shocked," he says.

"I guess I am," I reply.

Noah gives me his full attention. He leans against the counter and gives me a once over. "I know you're lonely but what really brought you here?"

"Didn't you just answer your own question? I'm lonely."

"Yes, but you were lonely when I moved in and this is your first visit."

A sarcastic retort is on the tip of my tongue but at the last second I say, "My boyfriend Jackson isn't answering my calls. I'm concerned."

He frowns and stands to his full height. I tilt my head back slightly. I forgot how tall he is. "Your boyfriend Jackson," he repeats slowly.

I nod anxiously and sit on the edge of my seat. "Yes. We've been dating for a short while."

"How long is a short while?"

"I don't know. Maybe a month."

"And he's stopped answering your calls?" He gives me a look that says, *That doesn't sound good.*

"It sounds bad. I know that. But it's completely unlike him."

"So your mom goes missing and now your boyfriend."

He's stating the facts but they still sting against my fresh wounds. "I don't know if he's missing."

"Then confront him. Go to his place." I hesitate and Noah sighs. "Where did you meet this guy, Selah?"

"Online," I say through gritted teeth.

"You're a smart girl. I never pegged you as an online dater."

"I didn't plan on meeting someone online. It just happened."

"So you've never been to his place?"

I nod.

"But you have seen him in person?"

I nod. "Of course. He's been here a few times."

At that, Noah looks skeptical. "Really?"

"Yes, really," I snap.

Noah is silent for a long moment, staring down at the garage floor. "Is there any other way for you to contact him?" he asks quietly.

"No, there's…" I start to say, but then I stop short because that's a lie. I never checked JustWrite. My eyes widen. "We met on a writing site. I haven't checked there!"

"Even if you do go on there and contact him, do you really want to stay with someone who's ignoring you?" Noah says. There's the golden question. One that I've been thinking about constantly. "If he's not talking to you, Selah, then perhaps you should let it be. It's his loss."

I try to read his face, but his head's down, focused on the bench in front of him.

I go to say thank you when I notice that his left hand is bleeding. Alarm sweeps through me. I stand up and move next to him. "Hey. You're bleeding."

He glances down at his hand. The blood is now dripping onto the garage floor. He doesn't look shocked to see it. Just slightly annoyed.

"Shit." He snatches a roll of paper towels and wraps a few pieces around his palm.

"What happened?"

He gestures to the wooden chair to our left. "Probably just cut my finger on some wood and I didn't even notice."

I grab the paper towels from the paint-stained wooden counter and clean up the drops of blood on the cement floor. I have a flash of my nightmare—the one where I drown in a sea of blood with Jackson and Mom watching. The very thought of it makes me shiver.

Noah bends down next to me and helps me clean up. We make quick work of cleaning up the mess. I stand slowly, looking at Noah from the corner of my eye. In spite of our little tête-à-tête about Jackson, I'm glad I came over. He has helped me search for Mom. He encouraged me to call the police. And now he's keeping me company when two people I love the most have disappeared.

I've been very wrong about him. Would a serial killer act like this? Possibly, but highly doubtful. Is he a sociopath? Once again, highly doubtful. He's just someone that I grossly misjudged. It's on the tip of my tongue to apologize. At the last second I close my mouth so the words don't escape.

"Why are you looking at me like that?" he asks quizzically.

Quickly, I duck my head. "I'm not looking at you in any way."

"Yes, you were. You looked like you didn't completely hate being in my presence."

At that, I lift my eyes and meet his gaze. His face is inches away. I want to lean forward and…

God, what am I thinking?

It's the alcohol. That's it, I tell myself. The racing of my pulse says otherwise. I've never experienced a love triangle: I'll leave that to teenage TV shows or the books lining my shelves. Yet here I am feeling something for Noah while I ache for Jackson. If my heart could speak I'm sure it would say. *This is fucked up. What are you doing to me?*

And my reply would be: *I don't know. I don't know.*

I stand up, wadding the paper towels into a big ball, envisioning that it's my heart I'm crushing. "I'll throw these away." I turn toward the door that leads into the house when Noah jumps in my way.

He smiles thinly at me. "You don't have to do that. I have a garbage can in here."

"What are you hiding there?" I say teasingly.

"Nothing. Trust me, there's nothing in there."

"Okay," I draw out slowly.

Noah extends a hand for the paper towels. I hand them over

and watch him hurry over to the almost-full trashcan next to his workstation. I scan the counter and notice the tools lying out: hammer, nail puller, utility knife, chalk line, circular saw. And other items I didn't know.

Noah looks over his shoulder at me. "Have you heard anything from the detectives?"

It's been only two days since I reported Mom missing. I know that I should give them time but I don't know how to do that. How can anyone do that when their loved one is missing? The not knowing feels like someone is slowly plunging a knife into your chest.

"I've called that older detective," I reply.

"And?"

"I keep getting voicemail."

"I'm sure he'll call you back soon."

"I know he thinks Mom just left of her own free will."

"How do you know that?"

I cross my arms over my chest. "I could just tell by the look in his eyes."

Noah turns his back to me and starts to put away some of his tools. "You never know. He might be working on her case as we speak."

I walk over to him and watch him carefully. He refuses to meet my gaze. "I hope so; I'm sick with worry. All I can keep thinking about is whether she's okay."

Noah finally turns and fully faces me. He places a hand on my shoulder. "You have to think positively."

All I can do is nod; I can feel the tears threatening to drop from my eyes. There's a second where I wait for his comforting hand to move away from my shoulder. But it stays puts and as the seconds pass so does the friend zone that I thought we've been in.

I stay perfectly still underneath his touch and stare back boldly at him. I don't know where this is going but I'm curious to find out. So I wait and my heart flutters wildly in my chest like butterfly wings. Noah's thumb brushes against the edge of my throat. The action is so soft, so quick, that for a second I think I imagined it in my head. But the blood coursing through my veins doesn't lie. Neither does my body as it subtly shifts closer to him.

Out of the corner of my eye I see my house and the living room lights and it's like a bucket of cold water has been dumped over my head. I should be home. I don't have my phone with me and what if Mom calls? If I missed it, I'd never forgive myself.

Very slowly I take a step back. The cold air instantly greets me, making me regret my decision. But it has to be done.

"I should be getting back," I say quietly.

Noah's hand drops heavily to his side. He nods. "All right."

I take a small step back because I want to stay and I want his warm hands around me. "Thank you for keeping me company."

One more step back.

"You can come over anytime."

"I might take you up on your offer," I tell him.

I say those words at the same time my heart is shouting violently inside my chest, *Don't do it! We're barely surviving Jackson's absence. If you think you can survive Noah, then you're sorely mistaken.*

I swallow loudly because I know my heart is right. "Good night," I say to Noah.

"Sweet dreams," he replies.

At that I smirk and turn around and walk back to my house. The back of my neck tingles and I know Noah is watching me the whole time. When I reach the front door I turn back around and sure enough, he's still looking at me. I wave at him. He waves back.

I close the door behind me, flip the lock and walk into the living room. And even though the blinds are closed I swear I can still feel Noah's gaze on me.

28

MOM WASN'T ALWAYS a messy person.

Growing up she kept a pretty clean house. Items were allowed to be out of place. And the dishes didn't always have to be washed the second you were done with a meal. If the bed wasn't made first thing in the morning it wasn't the end of the world. She was normal.

She started to let things go downhill when I left for college. Every single time I'd come home for a visit, I'd see more things in the house. Items that she had no business buying—like baby diapers, or twenty cans of Spaghetti O's.

"You never know when someone might come over with a baby, Selah." Or, "You know how easily snowed-in we get in the winter, Selah. I'm just stocking up on canned goods!"

The excuses were endless.

"It's empty nest syndrome," Sam once told me. "She's trying to compensate for you leaving and shopping is her only comfort."

I always defended her, but now, as I stand in her room, I realize that Sam probably had a valid point.

Maybe the key to finding Mom is hidden in her belongings. But where? In her room, the king-sized bed is headquarters central. She'd eat in bed. Sleep in bed. Read in bed. Watch TV in bed. And if she could've figured out a way to bathe in bed she would've done it.

There are bookshelves to my left. I run my fingers along the spines. A heavy layer of dust coats my fingertips. I pull out a few of her favorite books and flip through them, hoping to find a secret document that might reveal new information about her. But all I find is a photo of me on my eighth birthday. It's of Sam and me. I'm proudly standing in front of my cake. Sam and I have our arms wrapped around each other. Other kids move around in the background.

I put the photo on the bookshelf and move to the other side of the room toward the mountain of clothes so high it covers the windows. I start throwing the clothes behind me. And when I find nothing, I move to her end table. I open the drawer. There's a pad of paper, some pens, batteries, chapstick, bobby pins. Basically nothing of interest.

For the next few minutes I move around the room. I go through every drawer. I look under the bed. I even pull back the mattress and still come up empty-handed. With my hands on my hips, I take a deep breath and look at the mess I've made. From the corner of my eye I see the door to the walk-in closet is half open. I do a double take and hurry toward it.

I open the door wide and flip on the light. It's a complete disaster in here. The rods holding her clothes bow in the middle—one item away from completely collapsing. The top shelves are filled with boxes of shoes that probably still have the tags on them. I step deeper into the closet, trying to ignore how claustrophobic I feel in here. I rifle through the hangers, kicking the piles of shoes that lay on the floor.

I'm close to giving up when I hear a whirring noise. Holding my breath, I focus on where the noise is coming from. It's in the closet; that much I know, but where?

I pull apart the hangers to touch the surface of the wall and that's when I see the small child-sized desk shoved up against the wall. An overheated computer modem is whirring. But that's not what has my attention. It's the lone computer screen showing four black-and-white images from a security camera. One is directed at the front door. Another by the garage. The other two are aimed at the backyard near the gate and the back door.

My heart races as I bend down to peer closer to the screen. When did Mom have this installed? And why didn't she tell me?

"Surprise!" someone shouts.

Startled, I stand up suddenly. Someone is inside the house. The voice sounds familiar. My first thought instantly goes to Mom. I run out of the room and hurry down the stairs, my heart pounding in my ears. But my hope is short-lived when I see that it's Sam. I freeze in my tracks.

"How did you get in?"

"You have the spare key in the same place it's been in for the past twelve years."

"Oh," I mumble.

She takes off her tan trench coat to reveal a black wool blazer offset with a white turtleneck. "Well, I try to avoid Decatur like the plague but someone—" she pointedly looks my way, "won't answer their phone."

"No one's called me," I argue.

"Yes, I have," Sam replies patiently, before she snatches my phone sitting in my lap. She groans as she stares at the screen. "Yep. Just as I thought. You have the damn thing on silent." She tosses the phone and leans against the doorway, slowly scanning the living room. Her mouth slowly parts. Not much longer and she'll start to resemble a codfish.

"What?" I ask a bit defensively.

Sam holds her hands in the air. "Nothing, nothing!"

I scoot over on the couch, pick up the empty bag of Doritos and flick away the crumbs before I pat the seat for Sam to sit in. She doesn't move from the doorway.

"So you came all the way from Chicago because I didn't answer a few phone calls?" I ask as I grab some of the fast food wrappers scattered about and head to the kitchen.

Sam follows behind me.

It's not uncommon for Sam and I to go a few days, hell, weeks, without talking. It's a given that when we do talk we instantly pick up where we left off and typically spend a good two hours talking about everything that we've missed out on. But traveling for hours—one-way—because we haven't said a word to the other? That's never happened.

Something is up.

When we enter the kitchen I practically groan because I forgot to take the trash out so now it's overflowing and I probably don't have any trash bags beneath the sink. If Sam thought the living room was messy she's going to love the kitchen.

I walk toward the trashcan and shove down as much of the trash as I can with the wrappers. It works. For now.

"Oh, God." Sam screws up her face and plugs her nose. "What is that smell?"

"What smell? I don't smell anything."

Her blue eyes swing in my direction. "That's because you're nose-blind to the stench. Seriously, Selah. This place is a disaster."

If I step back and really look at things, I can see Sam's point.

The house is a fucking mess.

I've devoted so much time to searching for Mom and Jackson that making sure the dishes are done, the trash is taken out, or the clothes are washed hasn't been a top priority. A stack of dirty plates in the fridge heavily leans to the left, resembling a Jenga tower seconds away from collapsing. The floor hasn't been swept in… shit. How long has it been? I should know that. Countertops are caked with breadcrumbs, spilled coffee grounds, and eggshells. The only open areas at the kitchen table are directly in front of my and Mom's chair

And now that Sam's mentioned it there is a smelly miasma lingering around the overflowing garbage can. Disgust at my own laziness sweeps over me. How did I let it get this way? I'm starting to act like Mom.

"I know it's been really bad but I've been busy," I murmur.

Sam kicks at the trash bag next to the back door. "Doing what?"

"Well, for starters, trying to find a new job."

She's my best friend. I should explain to her what's going on with Mom. But at the same time, I know *how* she feels about Mom. Plus, Sam isn't one for the sympathetic talks and hugs. For a long time Sam has thought that Mom should live with my Aunt Ruby.

"She's lonely, Selah," she'd told me while I was in college. I'd waved off her words but now I see how right Sam was.

"And since the job part isn't panning out so well I'm trying to keep my head above water," I say. Sam remains in the kitchen doorway. I roll my eyes and point to Mom's seat. "Come on. Sit."

She hesitates and glances at the chair with abject horror. Finally, she gives in, but not before she takes off her jacket, folds it in half and uses it as a makeshift cushion.

"Bit dramatic, don't you think?"

"No offense, but I wouldn't be surprised if you have an influx of mice and gnats." She picks up a bill from one of the stacks and opens it up. "You're living like one of those people on *Hoarders*. All you need is a village of stray cats and you're golden."

I snatch the bill out of her hands. It's a final notice for my car. If I don't pay the outstanding late fees in addition to the actual car payment they'll repo the car. Even though it's terrible, part of me believes that it's not *that* terrible. It could be worse. It could be the electricity being turned off or the bank taking the house and short-selling it. If that didn't work it'd go into foreclosure and then Mom and I would be homeless.

When I think like this, I can feel the weight of my stress start to balance. I can regroup and close my eyes and when I do I can step back from my ever-growing problems. I can keep my focus ahead and try to tackle one issue at a time. This exercise has been working for a while now. But lately it's getting harder and harder.

"Where's that one book I made for you?" Sam asks.

"What one book?" I reply, using air quotes.

She waves a hand in the air. "The finance notebook where you can keep track of everything that's coming into your account and everything going out."

"Uhh…" I rack my brain trying to think of the 'finance book' Sam's referring to. When I first moved back home and explained my stress in trying to find a job, Sam happily volunteered to help me keep track of my finances. At the time it sounded really good. Made me feel like I had the upper hand on everything. But things just continued to slide downward. God only knows where that book is.

Sam impatiently taps her fingernails against the dirty table. "See-Lah," she draws out my name in annoyance. "Don't tell me you lost it."

"I lost it," I tell her point blank.

"Damnit. You said you would use it."

"Yeah. Well. I had other pressing matters," I retort.

Sam closes her eyes and stares up at the ceiling for a few seconds before she rocks her head back and forth, like she has a nasty kink in her neck. A few seconds later she drops her head into her hands, looking more human than I've seen her in well… ever.

It's eerie.

"This is why I don't like visiting. I turn into a raging bitch," she admits, her voice heavy with defeat.

"It's fine." I want to reach out and comfort her but I know that'll just make it worse.

Sam's head shoots up. Her eyes are bloodshot and her perfect blonde locks are a mess from dragging her hands through them. "It's not fine. None of this—" she gesticulates at our surroundings, "is okay." Her hands fall heavily onto the table. She takes a deep breath. "I really worry about you. I hate that you're living like this. You tell me that everything's okay but clearly it's not. Can you at least admit that maybe you're in over your head?"

My fingers curl around the coffee cup in front of me. I have no plans to drink it considering it's probably been out for a few days, but it keeps my hands busy. I can squeeze that damn cup as hard as I want.

"Promise me you'll think about moving closer to me. I'm really worried about you," Sam says softly.

"I promise," I say through gritted teeth.

"Don't just say it to get me off your back. Really mean it."

"I'm a grown adult, Sam."

"Really? Okay, then. What's today's date?"

"Uhh…" I pause, frantically trying to think of the last time I looked at a calendar. Quickly, I glance at the calendar near the fridge. But that's useless because the last date that was marked off was March 6th and I know that can't possibly be it.

Sam gets up, walks to the calendar, and stabs a finger on a date in the middle of the month. "March. It's March 16th." She drops her hands and sighs. "This is no way for a person to live." She stares at me like I'm a child who's done something wrong, and you want to be mad at them but you just can't because they don't know better. "How about we get out of here? Go shopping and get some fresh air. Hmm?"

I narrow my eyes at her. "What kind of shopping?"

"Grocery shopping. We'll go to the Kroger down the road."

When I say nothing, she quickly speaks up. "I promise that's all we'll do. Groceries and come back."

"And nothing else?"

"Nothing else."

Once again, I take in the squalor that I've been living in. How did it get like this? Sure as hell didn't happen overnight. Everything in life usually takes work, and so did this monstrosity. But it was the kind of thing that you didn't want anyone else seeing. The kind of thing that pulled out all your internal baggage and made it external. God, I'm a fucking mess.

Sam's right. I do need a break from all of this. I sigh and stand up. "Sure. Let's go."

The relief on Sam's face is palpable. For a second I feel good because I know I'm responsible for that.

AT ONE IN the afternoon the grocery store is relatively empty. It's filled with moms with Bjorns strapped to their chest, or others telling their younger kids for the twentieth time to keep their hands on the cart. A few elderly people are scattered throughout the store, quietly taking their time.

All is well and peaceful. There's even some nice alternative music playing from the speakers above us, but I feel like I bird trapped in a cage.

According to Sam, the store is a 'fucking sauna' and she takes her jacket off, placing it right next to her purse, where you'd put a toddler or a car seat. As for me, I keep my sweatshirt on and cross my arms tightly over my chest.

"When's the last time you went to the grocery store?" Sam asks as she pushes the cart down the sugar and cake mix aisle.

I shrug, my gaze furtively moving around the aisle, taking in all the stocked goods. Is it me or is the space slowly getting smaller and smaller?

"Se?" Sam has stopped in the middle of the aisle, twisting around to look at me.

"Uhh…" I grasp for an answer. "It's been awhile."

"So I figure we'll just stock you up on all the generic things until we figure out your living situation."

"My living situation?" I groan. "Not this again."

She drops a container of peanut butter, then jelly, into the cart. "It's a conversation that's not going to go away."

Quickly, I catch up to her. "The house is fine," I say with a smile.

"From the outside, maybe. But it's like a shirt that's bursting at the seams. It's going to pop and then everyone will see what you've been living in and I don't want that. I know you definitely don't want that either."

We turn into the next aisle and pass an elderly woman. She gives me a small smile. Her eyes linger on me too long. Why is she starring at me? Can she tell how messed up I am right now? Is she going to talk to her friends and tell them about the damaged woman she saw at the supermarket? I bet she is. She looks like the type of person who would do that. She'll give them a play by play. Describe how I look. Compared to Sam I am a fucking disaster. I knew this little shopping trip was going to be a mess.

My hands start to shake. I dig my nails into my palms. I move one foot in front of the other, but my feet feel weighed down. It's starting to feel really, really hot in here. Do they have the heat blasting? I'd take my sweatshirt off but I don't have anything on underneath.

Beads of sweat start to form around my temple as Sam continues to move down each aisle. She's oblivious to my little breakdown. Everyone is. Other than the sweat on my forehead I know my outward appearance gives nothing away, but inside my mind there's a riot. Alarm bells are going off. Screaming voices are telling me to go home. My heart is pounding so furiously I think I'm seconds away from having a heart attack. Still, I continue to walk behind Sam.

Finally, she says four glorious words: "I think I'm done."

I practically sag against the cart with relief.

We make our way to the front of the store. I glance to my right and that's when I see it. Or shall I say, him. It's out of the corner of my eye, but I'd recognize that profile anywhere.

Jackson.

Son of a bitch. Bastard. Asshole. Think of every name in the book and I'm calling him that.

But there's also a part of me that's happy to see him.

I grab Sam's arm, not taking my eyes of Jackson. "Hold on one second. I forgot something in the deli section."

"What? Selah, come back!"

But I take off, not bothering to excuse myself back through the crowd of people waiting to be checked out. All I see is Jackson. His head is bent as he takes in the sandwiches the deli has to offer. He's carrying a basket in his left hand. It's filled with a few little items. Bachelor food items, I call them. He's wearing a brown leather jacket that I've never seen on him but I know it's him. I'd recognize his brown hair anywhere. Or the cut of his shoulders.

"Jackson," I call out.

He doesn't turn around but that's okay. I've been told many

times that I have a soft-spoken voice. Maybe he didn't hear me. I raise my voice.

"Jackson!"

Still, he doesn't turn my way. I'm so close that I can reach out and touch him. There's a beaming smile on my face—waiting and ready. It fades the second the man turns around.

This isn't Jackson.

For a moment I'm in shock. Embarrassment steals my voice and I stand there in complete silence. The man arches a brow. "I'm sorry. Do we know each other?"

It's not Jackson. Why did I think it was Jackson?

"I'm sorry." I take a step back, then another and another and tip over the display of freshly baked croissants and sugar cookies. Everyone, and I mean everyone, stares at me. I'm still staring at the Jackson wannabe.

"You were Jackson," I finally manage to get out.

He frowns and appears afraid to come any closer. "No. My name is John."

"Jackson," I plead.

Just say the fucking name and I'm good, I think to myself. *Say his name. Just so I know I'm not crazy.*

"No, ma'am."

The seconds tick by and I take in the man's features. His hair's too dark. Eyes too blue. He really isn't my Jackson.

The man looks around like he's searching for someone, or possibly for help. It's then that I really look around and see Sam rushing over, her face beet-red with embarrassment. Now that I think about it, everyone looks embarrassed on my behalf.

Jumping up, I dust my pants off, rejecting Sam's outstretched hand. "Everyone just stare at the crazy person!" I yell

There's complete silence in the store. I swear, even the radio is silent.

"I know what you're all fucking thinking. And you." I point to the older woman I'd passed down one of the aisles. "I saw the way you judged me. I knew what you were thinking and I know you're going to talk about me. I know what you're all about!"

"Ma'am, I'm going to have to ask you to leave." I twist around and see a man with a name badge that reads 'Eddie. Assistant Manager' standing behind me.

I turn to Sam. She gives the guy an apologetic smile. "Of course we'll leave. I promise we'll pay for this mess."

While Sam offers up apology after apology, the crowd slowly filters away. Even the man who I wanted so desperately to be Jackson hurries to the self-checkout lane. He doesn't bother to glance my way. Not that I blame him.

I stand there awkwardly while Sam pays for our groceries.

Her lips are compressed into a tight line as we hurry out of Kroger. We make it to her rental car and together we put the groceries in the trunk. When we're done I slam the car door shut and sit in the passenger seat. She takes the cart back and a few seconds later slams the driver side door.

We sit there in uncomfortable silence. I'm shaken by my actions. By what I thought I saw. And Sam is just mortified. I can feel the anger coming off of her in waves. Should I apologize? Yes, but I don't know where to start or how to explain where my brain is right now.

I don't think anyone will understand.

"Selah. The hell was that about?"

I drop my hands into my lap and turn to look at her. "I saw him."

She looks confused. "Saw who?"

"Jackson." My voice breaks at the end of his name.

Her face falls a bit. She sags against her seat and drops her hands heavily into her lap. "You didn't see him," she says dully.

"Yes I did. But when I went over to talk to him, he disappeared and—"

"Selah," she cuts in. "Are you hearing yourself right now? No one just disappears into thin air. It was someone else the whole time. You just wanted it to be Jackson. That's all."

Her words hold some weight but I still can't get the fleeting image of Jackson's back out of my head. The back of the skull, haircut, shoulders were all the same. I stare straight ahead and place my shaking hands on my lap.

"Why can't you just believe me?"

"I'll start to believe you when you start making sense."

"You make me sound crazy."

"I'm not making you sound anything. You're doing a pretty good job of that yourself."

"Why are you being such a bitch?" I snap.

She throws her hands up in the air like she's giving up. "I'm not being a bitch. I'm just trying to figure you out."

"I don't need you to figure me out, I just need you to believe what I'm trying to tell you."

I've been looking out my window but suddenly I duck. My arms wrap beneath my thighs as I turn my head and look expectantly at Sam.

"What are you doing?" She looks around in alarm. And she should. "What's wrong?"

"Is she there?" I whisper.

Sam frowns. "Is who there?"

"That old lady from inside the grocery store? I just saw her get into her car. She looked right at me."

"So?"

"So," I say pointedly. "She's been following me around for the past two days."

Sam tilts her head to the side and gives me a strange look.

"What are talking about? No, she hasn't."

The more I think about it the more I know it's true. I've seen that woman around Wildwood and I've been feeling someone watching me. It's her. It has to be. Sam hasn't been around enough to know that. And I'm just too tired to explain that, or anything, to her at this point.

Sam rests an elbow on the armrests and tentatively asks, "Have you been taking your meds?"

I mimic her actions, just to piss her off. "No, I haven't," I pronounce slowly.

"You need to. It's not an option."

"Of course it's an option. It's my body. My decision. My life."

"But when you don't take your meds you stop acting like yourself."

"Enough, Sam!" I yell loud enough to make her jump.

I take a deep cleansing breath and itch at my neck. The old lady might be gone but I still feel fidgety. Sam's eyes aren't the only ones on me.

It's then that I realize that Sam's right. There is something wrong with me. But how can I explain to her that there's a war in my mind? It's me against paranoia, fear and madness. Together they form a trifecta that's hell-bent on controlling how many times my heart beats. They snatch my thoughts, normal thoughts, and warp them at such odd angles there's no way to smooth them out. I don't know how to fight back. Or where to take cover. I just want to escape and make it out alive.

Crossing my arms over my mid-section, I lean my forehead against the cool glass of the window. I exhale loudly and watch fog appear on the window. "Just take me home. Please."

"Selah, I'm really concerned about you."

"I know. You've told me that already," I say, watching as I fog up the window.

She puts the rental into reverse and looks at me, a sad expression written across her face. "I just want you to be all right."

"Mmm-hmm," is my reply.

Sam pulls out into traffic and drives us back to the house.

I breathe onto the glass one more time and write into the heavy mist, HELP ME.

LATER ON, HOURS after Sam has dropped me off, I finally get the courage to step back into Mom's room.

I'd fallen asleep while the sun was still up. I vaguely remember Sam tapping me on the shoulder, saying she was sorry for everything. I think I told her I was sorry too. She mentioned that she was going to try and clean things up and then she would leave.

I wake up at 9 p.m. to an eerily silent house. It makes goose bumps break out across my skin. I instantly turn on the TV before I get out of bed. I grab my robe and walk downstairs. It's obvious that Sam tried to clean up. Blankets are folded in the living room and draped over the couch. All fast food bags, empty soda cans and coffee mugs are gone from the coffee table. Magazines are neatly stacked.

In the kitchen it's the same: counters are cleaned off (as much as they can be), the trash is taken out, and the sink has been washed down. All the dirty plates, utensils and mugs are in the running dishwater.

"Thank you, Sammy," I say quietly.

My stomach rumbles but I bypass the fridge and go to the cupboard and find my stash of Svedka exactly where I'd left it. I take one shot and ignore the taste. And instantly take another. I take two more and walk back upstairs.

When I enter Mom's room, I take a deep breath and turn on the light. I'm not a glutton for punishment; I just need more answers. Everything is just as I left it. The clothes are still scattered about the room and the bed is still unmade. I turn on the TV and start to make my way toward the closet. Earlier in the day I'd made sure to close the closet door. I can see the glow of the multiple screens underneath the crack of the door.

A shudder racks through my body and I open the door. The three computer monitors are still on. I lean in closer to get a better look. I was outside just hours ago and it was snowy and bitterly cold. But judging from these pictures it's windy and rainy outside. Clearly the cameras stopped taping a while ago. I just don't know when because the date on the upper right hand corner reads 03/04/2000.

I doubt it was recording in 2000. More like Mom, or whoever set this surveillance up for her, forgot to set the date. The only thing that *was* set is the time. I kneel in front of the computer screen and slowly move the mouse around. I have no idea how to work a surveillance video. Is it like a regular one that lets you stop, fast-forward or rewind?

There's a keyboard in front of me but I don't know what it's for. I lean closer to the modem-like equipment that the computer screen is resting on. To the right is the power button and to the left is a slew of other buttons. In the middle is rewind, fast forward and pause.

I press fast forward. The seconds and minutes tick by at rapid speed. Placing my chin in my palm, I avidly watch all four screens as best as I can. At this pace the tree limbs move quickly. Leaves don't skip, but run across the sidewalk. I notice a stray cat hanging around the front hedges. Our next-door neighbor comes home late. Another walks her dog and doesn't clean up his poop. The mailman delivers some more overdue bills. Most of the action is in the front of the house. So I keep my gaze on cameras one and two.

And it's there that I notice something strange at 22:45.

I watch as a man walks up to my front porch. To slow it down, I quickly press play and lean in. He has a hoodie on and his head is bent, making it impossible to tell who he is. He pounds on the door and then looks over his shoulder. He waits for a few seconds before he disappears out of sight of the camera.

My heart pounds in my ears as I pray that the guy has given up and walked away. He emerges onto camera three in the backyard and my heart sinks. He's either impervious to the motion sensor lights or just really stupid, because he takes his time and casually walks through the backyard. He opens the back gate and walks toward the patio. He appears on camera four. At this point I'm shaking with fury that a complete stranger is on Mom's property when he has no business being there.

"No, no, no," I whisper to the screen.

Here I have it: proof that someone broke into Mom's house. Before I can see what happens next the screen cuts out to static.

29

YESTERDAY WE BOTH were at the bookstore at the same time.

You just didn't notice. The people roaming the aisles didn't give you a second look. If they did, they would've realized that there was something wrong with you.

You walked down countless aisles, alternating between picking up a book to read the synopsis on the back or blindly staring down at the floor. This continued for thirty minutes straight. You couldn't focus to save your life and it was starting to make you feel sick to your stomach; you loved reading. It was a passion of yours but now that's another thing being stolen.

First your Mom. Then Jackson. Now the words.

What's next?

Then you saw a lady who, from behind, looked identical to your Mom. God, that woke you up pretty damn quick, didn't it? You looked around to make sure no one was watching you—and I have to say, I was really proud of how circumspect you were before you trailed behind her.

You kept a healthy distance. Your heart was practically beating out of your chest as you tried to talk yourself into saying something to her. You felt stupid because all this time you've been searching for your mom and here she's been. At a bookstore just miles away.

Your cheeks turned red. Is it because you were embarrassed that you didn't try hard enough? Once the lady ventured toward the checkout line you realized that you needed to spring into action before she tried to leave again. So you tapped her on the shoulder and when she turned around you felt the crushing weight of disappointment. It was so powerful that your knees almost buckled.

Of course she wasn't your mom.

You gave her a weak 'sorry' and told her that you thought she was someone else. Before she could reply you quickly walked away. You didn't want some stranger to see you cry.

Stranger.

You're starting to really hate that word. Strangers are everywhere you go, and all you want are your Mom and Jackson.

Is that too much to ask? You want to rage to the world.

If you asked me I'd tell you no, it isn't, and then I'd tell you that all is not lost because for a few blissful seconds as you followed that woman around, you were the former version of yourself. You were happy and hopeful. It looked like your heart was pieced back together again. And you know what? It was a beautiful sight.

Lately, I've been giving you a lot of thought. Scratch that. You're all I think about. I've been trying to figure out where and when everything went wrong. There's not one single moment, more like a collective group of them that piled on top of one other. Those moments gave you sadness and pain. Sometimes happiness. You could combine them all together and they still wouldn't compare to your depression.

Until you, I'd never really had much experience with her. She always seemed like a formidable opponent, but one that could easily be beaten.

I was so wrong.

Depression leaves claw marks on everyone she touches. Deep wounds that leave jagged scars. You couldn't see her but I did. Yesterday as you stood there surrounded by books, she crept up on you very slowly. Her body touched yours the same time her elbows rested on your shoulders. She threaded her fingers through your hair and you visibly shivered. Her hands curled around your skull and when she had a solid grip her fingernails turned into talons and sank into your flesh. She filled your mind with dark venom. It coursed through your veins and I was certain that if I cut you open your blood would be black.

You started to feel helpless to the worthlessness you were feeling. Depression started to smile. But she wasn't done; your heart hadn't been touched yet, and that's what she really wanted. You started to shake. Tears started to pool in your eyes. Then I watched in fascination as your hands curled into fists. You took a step forward. Depression screamed as she lost her grip. She was so fucking close to stealing your soul. So close.

But you won this round.

Once again you made me proud.

You walked out of that bookstore, even though you didn't want to. You walked to your car even though you didn't have any destination. You put the car in drive and headed in the direction of home even though you didn't want to, because memories of your mother were waiting there.

Well, if you think where you live is bad, you should see the space I occupy. I know no one here. It's small and dark. The windows are so small, I can barely see outside, and when I do there's nothing but darkness. The rooms are so empty that when I talk all that echoes back at me is my own voice. Where I live would drive any sane person crazy.

Why do that to yourself? you ask.

Good question.

The answer is: I do it for you. Especially right now, when you're so vulnerable. Jackson is gone just when you need him the most. And your mom is nowhere to be found. You are so, so lost you don't know which way is up or down. You're getting no sleep so there are bags under your eyes.

There's no fucking way I'm leaving now. You need me so much more than you know. You're desperate, afraid. The worst part is that you're so terrified of being alone that you're clinging to anything that comes your way.

Remember this: you're a pretty fucking smart girl so don't make a dumb choice by being oblivious. Please open your eyes so you can see the storm on the horizon. The clouds are rolling in. Bolts of lightning are starting to strike.

You know what it is? Time. And it's bearing down on you. It wants to devour you. You have to take cover.

Shit. Now you're starting to cry. Please don't. Wipe away those tears; you're starting to hurt me.

If I give you another present, will you try to be happy again? I know I can't be harsh with you, but I'm quickly running out of ideas.

If you're scared just imagine how I feel.

But please, don't be greedy with this gift; it's all I've got. After this there is nothing left.

30

"I STILL DON'T understand how I can possibly contribute to… all this."

"You knew Selah before she came back home," I reply. "It's imperative that you describe her last few days in Kansas City. It will show another side of her that no one else knew about."

Meghan squirms awkwardly in her seat as she soaks in my words. It's evident she doesn't want to be here but at the same time she agreed to the interview so she clearly has something to say.

Meghan licks her lips. "I'm telling you up front: I don't want to put Selah in a bad light."

The crew and I get it: she's Team Selah. Meghan Bure is the principal of the last school that Selah taught at in Kansas City, Kansas. I contacted her through the school website, expecting to hear back from her but I never did. I finally gave up and called the school. I got her secretary and after calling her numerous times, Meghan called me back. Initially, she was cold but polite. You could hear in her tone there was no way in hell she'd agree to an interview in any capacity. It was only when I told her that the world needed to see the many facets of Selah's life that she finally gave me the okay.

Meghan had family in Springfield, IL so they would make a weekend trip out of the whole thing. When she stepped into the room I was initially shocked because her voice on the phone was strong and confident. In person, she's mousy and lean. It looks like she belongs in a library, alphabetically putting books away. Her golden hair is pin straight and pulled halfway up. Save some chapstick, her face is completely bare of makeup. She's wearing a blue sundress and a white cardigan, as though she knew that the hotel would be too cold for her delicate self. She reminds me of Miss Honey from Matilda—a movie that my daughter loves.

"Can you promise me that you won't edit me in a bad light?" Meghan asks. "I don't want to upset Selah's family."

"I promise," I say for the billionth time. Both the crew and I are starting to get restless. We've been at this for an hour and every time we ask a question that's even remotely incriminating for Selah, she stiffens up. "I respect your feelings about Selah, but at the same time we want to give the viewers an honest portrayal."

She mules over my reply for a moment before she finally nods.

Before she can change her mind, we take twenty. The clapperboard snaps. The camera focuses on Meghan.

"Would you say that you had a good relationship with Selah?" I ask.

"Outside of school? I suppose. There were a few times we'd have coffee together. But we weren't incredibly close."

"How was she as a teacher?"

Meghan faintly smiles and looks down at the floor. "With the kids? She was wonderful. She was only there for three years but she made a lasting impact on the kids. Students from previous years would always drop by her room and say hi. I think she was definitely more comfortable with the students than with the adults.

Around me and fellow teachers she would turn shy and keep to herself. It took her a long time to come out of her shell."

"She sounds like an amazing teacher."

"She was," Meghan agrees. "And I would've loved to keep her as a teacher at Notre Dame de Sion, but things started to become strange."

"How so?"

Meghan takes a deep breath. "Selah was sometimes incredibly depressed. It started getting worse around November. She'd eat lunch in her room. Hardly spoke to the teachers, became very distant. This went on for months. She lost a lot of weight and when I asked her about it, she just laughed. Said that she'd hardly lost anything. She was lying. I knew it."

Meghan leans forward in her seat. "In fact, the teachers and I were thinking about staging an intervention, but—"

"So what else did she do that you found alarming?" I cut in quickly; Meghan's getting off track.

"She would flip like a coin. One moment she'd be energetic and have all these amazing ideas and field trips that she wanted to take her class on. And she'd talk real fast. So fast you could barely make sense of what she was saying. And then, on several occasions I would find her crying at her desk during free time. Last December I decided it was time we had a talk."

"What did that talk entail?"

"I never got the chance. During Christmas break she said she was moving back to her hometown. Something about going home to clear her head."

"So that's it? She just up and quit?"

"Yep."

"In your personal opinion, what was wrong with Selah?"

Meghan hesitates. "I'm not entirely sure. It's obvious she was depressed, though to what degree it's hard to say. I tried to keep in contact with her but her phone was turned off. It was through another teacher that I found out she'd officially moved back home. When I heard the devastating news… my heart broke. It had me thinking that I could've done something to help her. Maybe I could've encouraged her to see a doctor and then she would've stayed in Kansas City. And…" her voice slowly fades away.

I give her a sympathetic smile. "I don't think there was a thing that anyone could've done to stop what was about to happen."

"Really?" Meghan asks, her voice a bit desperate. "Because I think about it all the time."

I motion for cut and Meghan sags in her chair as if she's just finished a marathon. "Was I okay?"

"You did good. We might ask you some more questions but—"

Meghan sits up straight. "What kind of questions?"

"Don't worry. They're standard questions: your name, age, things like that."

She nods with relief but I notice that the she's looking a little pale.

"Do you want some water before we start filming again?"

"No, I'm fine."

She doesn't look fine. Her hands are curled tightly around the armrests and her left leg is bobbing up and down.

"Hey. Are you okay?" I ask.

Meghan's mouth opens and closes before she finally says, "I could've helped her. I know it. And I know we weren't incredibly close but she would've listened. She was crying out for help, and I didn't do a thing." Meghan looks at me, her eyes a bit wild. "She haunts me. I know it sound impossible but it's true. All of this could've been stopped."

31

"IT'S GONNA BE another rainy one out there, Liz."

"I know! I wasn't sure if I should travel to work by car or boat," teases the female radio personality.

"Oh, shut up," I say to the radio and quickly change the station.

I flick my windshield wipers to the highest level possible. My fingers tighten on the steering wheel. For me, there's nothing better than a good rainstorm, but even this idiosyncratic bout of thunderstorms is starting to become tiresome to me.

According to the forecast, there will be a small lull. Long enough for some of the roads to clear up and the sun to timidly peak out of the sky. But then it's supposed to start back up again, and so will the long blue streak that runs across the TV, listing the counties with flash flood warnings. Which is almost every one from here to Springfield.

There's still time for me to stock up on what I need in case it gets really bad. But first I have something more pressing to do.

I drive toward the police department intent on talking to

someone about the video surveillance equipment I found in Mom's closet. I've tried numerous times to call the detective who came out to the house a week ago but he wasn't picking up. It's now March 19th and I think that I deserve some sort of update. I'm on the verge of a nervous breakdown if I don't get answers about Mom and Jackson.

I'm going to make sure someone sees that man in the video. More than anything I need validation; up until now, everyone, including Noah, thinks that Mom left on her own accord. There was obviously foul play involved and surely that video proves it. My gut twists at the thought. All I can think about are the what if's. It's driving me insane.

I park my car outside the police department, double-check my purse to make sure that I have the disc with the video surveillance on it and open my car door. I put my purse over my head and run toward the front door.

My knowledge of police stations stems from *Law and Order*. I expect to see people bustling in and out the door, the phone ringing off the hook. But it's not like that. It's quieter than I pictured. A few officers work behind desks and the phone does ring but for the most part it looks like an office—if everyone in an office carried guns.

A man behind the front desk lifts his head the second I walk through the door.

"Can I help you?" he asks dully, like the last thing he wants to hear is what I have to say.

I rush forward. "I need to speak with…" It takes me a second to remember the older detective's name. "Tim."

"Tim who?" he replies.

Shit. I can't remember what his last name was. My mouth opens and closes. Then, out of the corner of my eye I see just the man I'm looking for.

"Hey! You!" I shout. "Tim!"

He turns around frowning. When he sees it's me his face slightly relaxes. "Ms. Kerrington. Why am I not surprised to see you here?"

I hurry toward him. "Maybe it's because you haven't answered any of my calls."

He hurries his pace down the hall. Little does this motherfucker know, I plan on stalking him until he looks at the video. He gestures to the load of paperwork in his hands.

"As you can see we're very busy here." He walks around a desk and dramatically lets the stack of paperwork heavily fall onto the desk before he sits down.

"Well, I've been busy too." I drop the disc onto his desk.

He frowns and leans forward in his chair. "What's this?"

"Footage from a home surveillance camera that my mom had set up in her closet." I quickly sit down on one of the chairs across from his desk. "It shows a man walking up to the front door. When no one answers he walks around the back and approaches the back door." I gesture to the disc. "Go ahead. Look at it."

Tim stares at me for a long moment before he drags a hand over his face and sighs. "Sure, Ms. Kerrington. Let's have a look. Shall we?"

He pops the disc in and I smirk; I know he's humoring me but in a few seconds I'll have the last laugh. The image of the man appears. I've stared over and over at and it still gives me chills.

My eyes volley between the computer screen and the detective's face. He stares intently at the screen and watches the man with the scrutiny that I was longing for. Hope starts to blossom in my chest. Perhaps he's going to realize that I was telling the truth after all and start taking me seriously. Perhaps he'll launch a full investigation and search for Mom.

The video cuts out and I sit up straight in my chair. The

detective hands the disc over. He's quiet for a few seconds before he looks me in the eye.

"Do you know what I see?" I arch a brow and wait for him to continue. "I see a suspicious man trying break in and then the footage cutting out."

"So you suspect foul play with my mother?" I ask anxiously.

"I didn't say that."

And just like that my hope disappears. I stare at him, my disappointment surely written all over my face.

"He's not caught breaking in."

"But… but he's trespassing!" I say, but even I know my argument sounds weak.

The officer leans back in his chair and links his fingers behind his head. His pot belly spills over his pants. The buttons on his shirt strain to remain intact. "True, but do you know how many people trespass onto property that's not theirs on a daily basis?"

"No," I say quietly.

"Too many to count." He sits forward in his chair and looks me in the eye. His face softens. "Ms. Kerrington, I think it's in your best interest to let this go."

"How can you say that? My mom's missing!"

"You don't know that and some video of a guy trespassing doesn't prove that."

"So that's it?"

I'm so angry I can't think straight. I want to jump across the desk and choke the life out of him.

"For now I'm afraid so. Now if you don't mind I need to get back to more pressing issues."

I can't believe it. He's really giving up on Mom before her investigation ever had a chance to begin. If it were one of his own family members missing I bet he would feel differently.

I slowly stand up, my gaze rooted to the disc. I place it back on the desk. "You should keep this; I've made more copies. I know you don't believe that something happened to my mom, but you're wrong." I tap the disc with my index finger. "This video is proof. If I have to search for her all by myself I will. I'm not giving up."

My eyes remain locked on his. I wait for him to reply but he stays quiet.

Fuck him and fuck his silence.

I turn around and walk back to my car.

I'M STILL SEETHING when I park my car outside of a Wal-Mart. I pull up my hood before I get out of the car. The rain feels like cold, heavy needles hitting against my skin. I squint and run like everyone else toward the store.

There are two Wal-Marts around Decatur. I go to the one near Mt. Zion. Today it's a madhouse because when there's a flash warning for anything in the Midwest people flip out and stock their shelves with everything you can think of. As for me I'm a woman on a mission, bypassing the rows and rows of food and crowds of irritable people.

While I drove here I started to formulate a solid plan for how to search for Mom. I'll put out fliers, asking random strangers if they've seen her. I'll staple the 'Missing' fliers onto poles. I'll search in the woods around Wildwood. I'll swallow my pride and knock on every door in Wildwood and ask if they've seen Mom.

And I won't quit until I get more answers—I know they're out there. I found the video footage out of nowhere. Imagine what else is waiting for me. I tell myself that it's going to be okay because at least I have Jackson. It takes me a few seconds to remember that I don't.

Two days ago I took Noah's advice and logged onto JustWrite and sent Jackson a message. I haven't gotten a reply. I might get a terse 'Fuck off,' in reply but at least then I'll know he's alive. Any reply is better than silence.

I place five bottles of Svedka into my basket. A man lingering in the aisle glances down at it. "Rough day?" he asks with a smile.

"Oh you have no idea," I reply straight-faced.

I walk toward the front of the store and groan. Six lanes are open and each one has a long line. I choose the one closest to me and wait. After awhile the basket starts to make my arm ache. I set it down in front of me and cross my arms over my chest. My skin starts to tingle. I feel slightly woozy. I try to ignore the people around me, but that's pretty damn hard to do when the store is packed.

Get out. Right now, I tell myself. But then I'd have to go out again later and get the alcohol. I'm already out now. I just need to suck it up and deal with the crowds.

"No one is going to hurt you," I whisper to myself. "You're okay."

I repeat that a few times over and take a few deep breaths. After a few seconds I feel a bit better. I lift my head and see the people in line to my left, a man and woman, staring at me like I have two heads. I fight the urge to flip them off and all but sigh with relief when it's finally my turn to check out.

"Hello!" the cashier chirps.

"Hi," I say back.

"Is there no end in sight to this weather?" the cashier happily asks me. According to her badge her name is Steph.

I blink rapidly, trying to think of how I should reply. It's like normal, everyday conversations have become impossible for me. All I can do is nod.

Her smile fades and she goes silent as she scans all my precious Svedka.

"That'll be one hundred and fifteen dollars," Steph says without any trace of her previous smile.

I pull out one of my credit cards that isn't completely maxed out and insert it into machine. As I type in my pin I look at Steph and all but snarl at her. Hasn't she seen someone purchase alcohol before?

Quickly she looks away and busies herself with straightening up the magazine rack to her left.

I grab my receipt and bags and hurry to the exit. It's still pouring down rain as I run back to my car. It's only when I'm in the safety of my vehicle that I take a deep breath. I have a plan. And a plan is better than nothing.

I can do this on my own if I have to.

NOW THAT I'M finally home and I've consumed a half a bottle of Svedka, I feel great. Music blasts from the speakers of the living room sound system—Frank Sinatra crooning *have yourself a merry little Christmas*. I don't even care that it's not Christmas. I feel amazing right now.

I take another swig of Svedka. About an hour ago the shots I was taking started to lose their effect so I've been drinking straight out of the bottle. It tastes like water.

Stumbling down the hall, I follow the trail of Frank's voice, the Svedka loosely dangling in my left hand.

When I reach the living room I see Mom sitting in her chair. But instead of her usual uniform of a ratty robe and slippers, her long hair is pushed back with a headband and she's wearing a long green skirt with a black tank top. She always wore that outfit on uncharacteristically hot days at school.

Damn alcohol has dulled my senses so much that I'm not even shocked to see her. It's as though I've been expecting her. As if we've both been expecting this meeting for a while now.

I point an accusing finger at her and slur, "Glad you decided to finally show up."

She rolls her eyes, but says nothing. But she doesn't have to say a word for me to know what she's thinking. She doesn't like me drinking this much.

"If you were in my situation wouldn't you be a little… down, too?" I say aloud.

She doesn't say a word.

I continue, "From the beginning, this year took a big shit on me and it's been nothing but bad news. Forgive me if I want to take a bit of a break."

Again with the silence. She, like everyone else, probably just thinks I'm depressed.

"There's a misconception about depression. People think that it suddenly consumes your life, but it doesn't. Are you listening to me? It's a monster hidden behind one singular action. You don't notice the clouds slowly blocking the light because just for a second you get to think. You think you can beat it, this heaviness pressing you down. You think that you can find yourself. Even if I saw the signs beforehand I don't know if I would've been strong enough to stop it."

I stare down at the ground. When I lift my head, I see Jackson sitting on the couch, right next to Mom. He's dressed in jeans, a black Henley and a brown jacket. He's freshly shaven, hair windblown, like he just came in front outdoors. He looks so real. Like I can reach out and touch him.

I don't.

The three of us stare at each other in mock silence. No one seems to be inclined to say the first word. I've been hearing the walls talk for days. It's time for me to do the talking for once.

"What are you two—the judge and the jury?" I ask with a slow smile. I raise my hands, palms facing up and laugh. "I admit it. I drank half this bottle, but don't arrest me. I didn't drink and drive. That's gotta stand for something, right?"

Neither one says a word. They share a look and it sends me over the edge. They have the audacity to judge me when I've been trying so hard to keep things together?

"Fuck you both!" I scream at the top of my lungs.

If there were another bottle near me I would throw it at the two of them. Deep down I love them, but right now I hate them. They continue to stare down at me, like I'm a filthy, dirty person for drinking. But not once do they say anything.

Two can play at that game.

I grab my MacBook and open it up to my latest manuscript. My hands fly across the keyboard as I type away. They say drinking does so many bad things, but for me it creates magic. My inhibitions are lowered and the things I want to type but normally am too afraid to come out of me. A new world comes alive. And it's one that doesn't judge or hurt me. One filled with people that don't leave me or gawk at me.

I lift my eyes away from the keyboard and peer above the screen to see that Jackson and Mom are still there. Still looking.

"God! Stop staring at me!"

Yet they continue.

Silence drives people crazy.

Typically, it's my weapon of choice.

Tired of a conversation? Silence.

Sad? Silence.

Angry? Silence.

Hurt? Silence.

Silence.

Silence.

Silence.

But now I'm on the receiving end of that silence and you know what? It aches. Like poison slowly taking over my veins. Frank's crooning voice suddenly isn't enough to fill the silence. I lift my eyes once more and see them staring. I've had enough.

Slamming my laptop, I stand up. "You won't leave the room, so I will," I announce loudly. I stomp through the hallway, feeling triumphant in my departure. "Assholes," I mutter to myself.

But as I enter the kitchen I see Mom and Jackson sitting at the kitchen table, expectantly waiting for me.

"Shit!" I scream. I'm so startled my laptop slips from my fingers, slamming onto the ground with a loud thunk. I stumble back, my spine painfully hitting the doorframe. "How did you get here?" Shakily, I point behind me. "You were just back there."

Neither one blinks. Neither one says a word.

The shaking spreads from my hands through my whole body. I take a shaky breath and grab my laptop before turning back around and rushing toward the stairs, not bothering to turn off the Christmas music.

"They weren't there," I say. "They weren't there. It was all in my mind."

I continue up the stairs, making sure to stomp my way up. I don't know why, but the sound of my own feet reverberating throughout the hall makes me feel better. Right now, what I need to do is go to bed. It's been a long day and I hardly got any sleep last night. My mind needs a break, that's all this is.

But when I enter my room, there they are again. Mom and Jackson. The two of them sitting on my bed.

I hit the wall and slowly slide down until my butt hits the floor.

I don't know what's happening and why it's happening to me. I can't look at them. I can't be in the same room with them, but no matter how hard I try to escape them, they just keep following me.

"Just leave me alone. Leave me alone," I moan. "Leave me alone."

I should know better. Things never go my way that easily because, of course, they stay. The three of us sit there in the room. I refuse to sit on the bed next to them. So I lean against the wall.

My eyes grow as heavy as my heart and finally sleep grabs hold of me and pulls me down.

32

THE NEXT MORNING I wake up in the upstairs bathroom with no clue as to how I got there.

I wretch into the toilet and rest my head on the seat.

Shame.

That's what follows people after a night of heavy drinking, right?

Shame at what you said. Or what you didn't say.

Shame at what you did. Or didn't do.

But I have no shame.

Some people, if they drink enough, can completely black out. They don't know how they made it to bed, what they said or texted. Unfortunately, I remember every thing about last night. I can still feel the weight of Jackson and Mom's heavy gazes and how, out of everything, their silence was the most terrifying to me.

I take a deep shuddering breath and close my eyes.

I may feel like shit right now, but in twenty-four hours' time I'll be feeling as good as new. And you know what? I'm going to do this again. I found a form of medicine that makes me feel absolutely nothing. And I'll keep doing it for as long as I can.

I smile at the very thought.

33

YOU KNOW WHAT I am not?

A liar.

No, I stay true to my word. When I say I'm going to do something, I do it.

I sleep the day away. I occasionally wake up to run to the bathroom and vomit or chug some water, only to collapse back into bed. By five in the afternoon I'm up, smelling like sweat and vomit. Strands of hair are sticking to my temples so I take a shower.

As the water pour downs around me I try to shake the images of last night. As much as I want to have Mom and Jackson back in my life, last night was all wrong. They weren't there for good. They were there to torture me.

I tilt my head back and let the water wash away the shampoo.

You can Google why good things happen to bad people, think about the concept until you're blue in the face, but the truth of the matter is that you'll never understand why things turn out the way they do. I know I won't give up on looking for Mom but a very small part of me thinks that it might be healthier if I accept the things I cannot change.

I finish showering and change into clean clothes and feel refreshed. When I sit down on my bed, I grab my laptop and re-read the message I sent to Jackson.

> ***Jackson,***
>
> ***Haven't heard from you in a while and I'm getting really worried. I've tried calling your phone but it's shut off. Is everything okay?***
>
> ***-Selah***

To me that sounds like someone who's calm, cool and collected, not someone who's on the brink of insanity. Yet there's no reply from him. And maybe that's all the answer I need, but it doesn't sit well with me. Like Mom, I know something has happened to Jackson. The not knowing is killing me.

I jump up from my bed. If I remain idle, dark thoughts will creep back into my head, showing me all the bad things that could be happening to them at this very second. I need to keep myself occupied.

I grab my laptop and go downstairs. I turn on the Christmas soundtrack again that Mom has always loved. Apparently, I made it back downstairs last night and turned it off. Already I feel a bit better when I hear the music.

A new bottle of Svedka is just where I left it in the cupboard. I clean the shot glass from last night, though I don't know why since I'm using it again. Before I start another rousing night, I open up my laptop again on the off chance there's an e-mail reply from Jackson.

Pathetic? Absolutely. But I lost my pride around the same time I lost my sanity. I pour a drink and stare down at the clear liquid before I take a deep breath. "Bottoms up," I mutter before I take the shot.

THERE'S A BANGING on the door that rouses me from my computer. About an hour ago Svedka and I made our way to the living room. "Go away!" I shout, thinking it's Mom and Jackson back again to torture me.

"No!" someone replies.

"I said, go away!"

"I said no."

"Fucking ridiculous," I mutter to myself as I push aside my laptop and stand up. It's a long walk to the front door, filled with a lot of stumbling and righting myself. When I finally get there, it takes me a few minutes to work the bolt lock. The pounding continues.

"You banging on the door isn't going to make me open up any faster, asshole," I say loudly.

The pounding stops around the same time I unlock the door. I make a small opening and peer out, only to see Noah standing on my front porch. My shoulders slump.

"What are you doing here?"

He looks haggard. He's dressed in gray sweat pants and a Northwestern sweatshirt that looks like it's seen better days. "I'm here because your music is too loud. That's why I'm here."

"So?"

"So?" He arches a brow. "That's all you have to say?"

"Well, I don't know what to tell you." I turn away from the door, knowing that he's going to walk in behind me. He does. And I'm okay with that. Because somehow I know that if he's here, the chances of Mom and Jackson torturing me are slim.

Noah quietly shuts the door behind him, which I find ironic considering I have the music blasting. I walk into the living room and pick up the Svedka where I left it. I take a drink directly out of the bottle before I hand it to him. "Want some?"

"No, thanks. I already drank half a bottle of Jack Daniels at home," he says sarcastically.

"Really? You handle your whiskey well," I say with a smile.

He doesn't smile back. Instead he makes a B-line toward the sound system and turns off the Christmas music. The silence that follows is almost louder than the music. It hurts my eardrums. Makes me want to hold my hands against my ears to make the aching stop.

"What is going on with you, Selah?"

I slowly circle the room, vodka in hand. "Do you know that you're the umpteenth person to ask me that?"

"A lot of people are concerned about you."

"Okay. I lied. You're only the second person to ask me that. But the question has been asked multiple times," I concede.

Noah doesn't reply.

I stop my journey around the living room and look outside. I love this time of night. Well, technically morning. I love that everyone is asleep and everything is deathly still. The world aligns better for me at this hour. I can think clearer. Be myself and do the things that I always want to do in the daytime but don't. During the day the world is alive and bustling. I find that overwhelming. Everything feels on hold and all I can focus on is breathing in and out and making it through the day.

You'd think Noah would interrupt the peace, but it's oddly harmonious with him here. Who would've thought?

"How long have you been drinking?" Noah asks.

"You mean tonight or other days, because that might be difficult to answer."

Noah flexes his jaw. "I mean this drinking binge of yours. How long has it been going on?"

"Define drinking binge."

"*Selah.*"

To end the questioning, I give him an honest answer. "A few days."

"So that's why you've been locked away in your house."

"Ding, ding, ding, ding, ding. We have a winner."

"You can't drink away your pain, Selah."

"Thank you for the PSA, Dr. Phil. I'll keep that in mind."

"Can you just listen to me for one fucking second?" Suddenly he's in my way, ripping the vodka bottle out of my grasp.

"Give me that!" I shout.

He holds it up in the air, out of reach, before he goes to the kitchen. I know he's going to wash it down the drain. "Don't waste good vodka," I say as I trail behind him.

My words fall on deaf ears and I watch in abject horror as he pours the vodka down the drain. Noah slams the bottle onto the counter. His hands grip the lip of the counter. His shoulders are slumped. He takes one deep cleansing breath before he pushes away from the counter and stands up straight.

"I'm not leaving until I see with my own eyes that you're sober and okay to be by yourself."

I cross my arms. "Well, get a pair of glasses so you can see better because I'm sober and okay to be by myself."

"Selah, I mean it."

I throw my hands in the air. "What's it to you?"

"Oh, I don't know… just a few days ago you came to my house in the middle of the night on the brink of having a meltdown. And now I see you're self-medicating by drinking yourself to death."

"I can assure that I'm not drinking myself to death."

"Then what are you doing?" he asks.

At that I hesitate; this conversation is becoming way too serious for my liking. "I don't want to talk about this."

Noah's lips form a thin line. "I'm just worried about you. That's all."

I stare down at the floor. "I know that."

We stand like that for a long moment, before Noah says, "Let's go to the living room."

I don't budge from my spot. "Only if we turn the Christmas music back on."

Noah sighs. "Fine. Christmas music it is."

Shoulder to shoulder we walk back to the living room. I can feel my beautiful buzz wearing off and I know that I'm going to have a massive hangover tomorrow. Noah gestures to the couch but I shake my head because all I can see is Jackson sitting there, staring at me with unblinking eyes.

Instead I sit with my back against the wall, facing the couch. I pat the spot next to me.

"What's wrong with the couch?"

"I just want to sit here," I say; it'd take too long to explain.

Noah shrugs and slides down the wall. He rests his elbows on his knees as he looks around the room. Neither one of us says anything for a few minutes. Surprisingly, it's not stiff and uncomfortable, although every few seconds I can feel his eyes on me.

"Am I making you uncomfortable?" he asks.

"Honestly?" I say, my gaze facing forward. "You staring at me is."

I turn my head to face him just in time to see his smile. It's warm and genuine. Of that I'm certain. And I smile back.

"You want me to leave?"

"No," I reply honestly.

Now that he's here I realize how I've been the past few days. It might not be a bad idea for someone to keep me company.

"Good." He nudges me with his shoulder. "Because I'm not leaving."

"Fine. But you're going to miss out on your beauty sleep."

"I can sleep sitting up."

At that, I snort.

There's more silence and soon it starts to get to me.

"I wrote to Jackson like you suggested. Still no word," I blurt in one big rush.

Noah averts his gaze. "Maybe he lost his phone or is traveling."

I sniff at his words. "No, I think something has happened to him. Just like Mom." I glance over at Noah. "Don't give me that look."

"What look?"

"The one that says I've been catfished but you don't want to come out and say it." He doesn't say anything and that furthers incites my anger. "We were together," I insist.

"If you were together then show me a photo."

Most couples take photos together. Not Jackson and me. Right now, I don't know why we never did.

"Okay. So I have no photos of him. But he's real!"

Noah looks at me from the corner of his eye. "When you told me he was missing, I looked him up, Selah. There's no Jackson Cooper."

I push away from him. "You're lying."

"I'm not lying," he says gently. Which just pisses me off because he's talking to me like I'm a crazy person and I'm not.

"I can't show you proof, but he exists and he's real."

I'm not a wuss but tears start to well up in my eyes. I'm so sick of having to defend myself to everyone. My tears soon turn into sobs. Noah's arms go around me. He guides me toward his chest. I don't fight him. Even though I want to punch him for what he said just minutes earlier, his touch is soothing in the strangest of ways because I feel something where I shouldn't: my heart.

His hand curls around my head, holding me tightly to him. "I want to help you," he says into my hair. "You just need to let your guard down because your mind is powerful and brilliant and all-consuming and I think you are wonderful." Gently he pulls me back so we're face to face. "Please. Let me help you."

"If you want to help me then you can start by believing in me."

"I want to believe in you, but I also think that it's important that I don't lie to you."

"You think Jackson doesn't exist. I guess that also means you think I made up my mom disappearing too, huh?"

He hesitates and that's the last straw. I extract myself from his hold and quickly jump up.

"You're wrong, you know." Before he can say anything I quickly speak up. "My mom had a home security system put in. I found it upstairs in her closest."

That instantly grabs his attention. He sits up straighter. "What did you see?"

"A man breaking and entering."

"You saw that?"

"Well, not exactly, but he was trying to get in. He was in the backyard moving toward the back door when the tape cut out."

Noah's face falls a bit and somehow I feel like I've disappointed him. "So there's no definitive proof that someone broke in."

"No. But I know something bad happened."

"Did you tell the police?"

"Yes. I gave them the video."

"What did they do?"

"Nothing." I drop my hands helplessly into my lap. "They were absolutely useless. When Detective Fatass saw it he said he couldn't do anything because the video cuts out before he's actually caught trying to break in. I tried to argue the fact that he was trespassing but he wasn't having it."

Very slowly, Noah stands up and approaches me carefully, like I'm a wild animal that's getting ready to pounce. I drag my hands through my hair and start to pace back and forth.

"No one believes me. No one understands. Of course they don't because it's not happening to them. If it were happening to them then it would be a completely different story. Everyone just wants to look down on me and judge me, instead of trying to help."

"I'm not judging you."

I stop pacing and whirl around. "Oh, but you are. You don't think you are. You just don't realize it."

"Selah, if you'd just let me explain—"

"No!" I shout. "Don't explain. Just help me and if you can't help me then just leave."

Any other time, I would stay and fight but everything he's saying is unsettling and I just can't handle it. Stubbornly he stays put. I grab my keys and hurry out of the house, not caring if Noah stays behind or not.

"Selah, where are you going?"

"Out," I toss out over my shoulder.

The headlights flash as I unlock the car with my key fob. I hurry toward the driver's side. Noah grabs my arm in a painfully tight grip and turns me around. There's a wild look in his eyes that causes the hairs on my arm to stand up.

"I'm not trying to upset you," he says way too calmly.

"Let go of me. I need to get out of here."

He doesn't let go. "Selah, just talk to me."

"I said. Let. Go."

His eyes remain locked on mine for a second longer and finally he lets go, slightly shoving me away.

Fine by me. I slam my car door and put the car into reverse. I peel out of the cul de sac with Noah watching me the entire time.

34

YOU DIDN'T HAVE to tell me about the video.

I saw you uncover the surveillance in your mom's closet. And I saw you go to the police station and walk back out thirty minutes later. You were so angry. Your hands were curled into fists so tight that your fingernails dug into your skin, creating little crescent moon indentations.

To be honest, it was nice to see you angry for once. Your eyes were blazing, making them brighter than they've been in months. And your cheeks were bright red, which is a step up from the deathly pale look you've been sporting.

I can't tell you what to do next—as much as I want to. And I can't give you another gift; I'm fresh out. You have to figure this out on your own. I have to let you go; I'm tired. So fucking tired. Can't you tell?

Of course not. Because you're too busy wallowing in your pain to notice that I need just a moment to breathe. When I think about how narrow-minded you can be sometimes I get angry, and when I get angry I have these dark urges to hurt you. To let the depression and anxiety and all of it crush you to a pulp.

You're starting to remind me of a fragile baby bird who refuses to leave the nest. You've watched everyone else fly away and a part of you wants to join them on their journey, but you're too scared of what's on the other side so you sit there and slowly starve. All because of your fear.

"Do something!" I want to scream. "Do anything! Just don't waste away!"

Then it hits me. This is my fault. I've always protected you. Always helped you. You've never had to think about leaving the nest. The option was never there. Well, your nest is getting ready to fall. So it's either fall or fly.

Little bird that I love the most, what are you going to do?

35

THERE ARE CERTAIN streets in Decatur that you steer clear of during the night.

Eldorado is one of them. Sure, in the daylight when everyone is busy working and running errands, it's fine. But at night it's a different thing.

"Just be careful," Mom once pleaded.

I told her I would and then dashed out the front door where Sam was waiting in the car. I laughed off her words; I was sixteen and I knew everything. Sam and I drove around, stopping at a Mexican restaurant not far from Millikin University. We sat there, giggling, pretending what it'd be like when we were eighteen and in college. *Grown up* is all we could think of when the word 'eighteen' rolled off our tongues.

Afterwards, we drove around some more until it was close to my curfew. We drove back down Eldo toward South Shores. It was at a stoplight that I glanced at the bus stop and saw a woman sitting there. She had a stack of Wal-Mart bags between her feet and a ratty hoodie on. Her brown frizzy hair was greasy at the roots, her jeans streaked with mud. She looked filthy.

I took one look at her and she stood up slowly, her chest slightly jutting out like she was getting ready for a fight.

"What?" she shouted at me.

I sat there, motionless, riveted by the wild look in her eyes. She was crazed. She was erratic. She looked scary. But she also looked lost. It was only when she started walking toward me that I scrambled to lock the door. She stopped walking once she saw me lock the door and roll up the window. My heart was racing. As we waited for the light to turn green she just stood there and continued to stare pointedly at me.

That was over ten years ago yet it still stands out in my memory. I find myself constantly thinking about that woman. Especially lately. Maybe she wasn't as dangerous as I thought her to be. Maybe I jumped to conclusions. Maybe she was just scared. Maybe she just wanted someone to listen to her.

In a way we were a lot alike.

For the past few hours I've driven around with no destination in mind. I just go with the flow of traffic, taking random turns here and there. Soon the sun starts to rise. People wake up and begin their day, but I'm still not tired.

I stop and get some gas and continue to drive around, surprised when I finally look at the clock and see it's 10 a.m. I find myself on Water Street driving past businesses and restaurants. It's at the stoplight on Pershing road that I notice Jackson's car.

My heart starts to pound at an erratic tempo. The car is ahead of me in the lane to my right. I try to see who's driving but I can't tell. The light turns green. In order to get into the right lane, I press the gas pedal to the floor and narrowly avoid getting hit. Someone presses down on their horn but I ignore it.

The car's right blinker flashes, then the brakes light up. The car turns into Brentwood Village, a small shopping complex. I brazenly follow and when it turns toward the Kroger I turn right and find a parking spot a healthy distance away so I won't be obvious.

I turn off the car and watch as a pretty brunette gets out. I grip the steering wheel and lean forward. She flings her hair over her shoulder and grabs her purse before she opens the back door. She smiles. Lips move, but I can't make out what she's saying. She's wearing a navy blue trench with the belt tied around her non-existent waist. She has on black tights, black turtleneck and black ankle boots to match; so put-together and chic. She leans into the car and seconds later, she stands to her full height, a little girl in her arms.

The little girl is stunning; her mop of curly dark hair is pulled into pigtails. She couldn't be more than three years old. My heart thuds wildly in my chest as I watch the beautiful woman place the little girl on her feet.

I feel like I've been duped. Or that I'm on of those prank shows. Any moment some host is going to jump out from behind my car, laughing and telling me this is all a joke.

Yet the longer the seconds tick by, the more I realize this isn't a joke. This isn't in my mind. This isn't a dream.

This is real.

It's a general rule of thumb that everyone in this world has secrets. Everyone. They just come in different sizes and shapes. So it shouldn't be shocking to discover that Jackson has another life that I didn't know about. People have affairs all the time. I just never pegged Jackson to be that someone.

He's quiet and somber. That's something that we had in common. At least I thought it was. But maybe that's how I chose to see things. Maybe I created this picture perfect relationship just so I could ignore the negative side of Jackson.

The brunette sets the little girl on the ground, making sure to hold her hand. I see a ring on her left finger. My heart cracks in two. They walk across the parking lot, the little girl hopping around, barely able to contain herself. The brunette smiling down at her as they hurry toward the grocery store.

I watch her pick the little girl up and put her in a cart. The doors slide open and they step forward. She stops and grabs the weekly ad with all the savings on groceries and home goods. She flips through the ad and I imagine that she is trying to figure out what to make her family for dinner.

She's probably a great cook. Slaves in the kitchen making delicious meals that she, of course, never eats. (Has to watch her figure.) Every morning she religiously goes to her spin classes. She takes her daughter to play dates. Has coffee with her friends. And she does all of this with a smile on her face. Why? Well, it's simple: she has the perfect life. She has the man and the beautiful daughter.

They are her world.

Everything she could ever ask for.

She will never love anyone the way she loves them.

My head falls back against the seat. I close my eyes and try to take deep calming breaths. My heart won't stop pounding.

Why did I never see this coming?

All this time I'd been under the impression that something bad had happened to him. That he would never be so cruel as to just stop talking to me out of then air; it just didn't seem in his nature to do that.

I want to get back at him. Find him and hurt him. But he doesn't want to be found. Especially not by me. And why would he? I just put a spotlight on a part of his life that he never wanted me to see.

A sane person would leave but I stay there and wait.

Thirty minutes later the woman and the little girl emerge with a cart half full of groceries. The woman brushes her hand across one of the little girl's cheek before she hurries to Jackson's car.

I'm riveted at the sight of them together. What is the little girl's name? Are there any other kids?

I have questions that demand answers and I'm going to get them.

36

IT'S BEEN SAID that the definition of insanity is repeating the same thing over and over and expecting different results.

So why do I keep coming back to you in hopes that you will remember me? Why do I keep spoiling you with gift after gift?

Am I obsessed with you? No. I prefer the word involved. I'm involved in your happiness. Your well-being. Your sadness. All of it. Every single bit, I want to be involved.

Yet you ignore me.

You're really starting to make me mad, Selah.

I know I can be fickle. Up and down. Hot and cold. Sometimes, I love you. And sometimes, like now, I hate you.

Hate is a strong word but I love it. Let the word roll off your tongue, slowly and deliberately, and it becomes powerful. A sharp object that can cut a person to shreds.

Hate, hate, hate.

I hate you.

I think you hate yourself, too.

We both know that you're letting go. Everything is piling up. One on top of the other and you're not lifting a finger. You need to put up a fight. Rage. Refuse to give up.

Everything you want to know is in plain sight. I left clues for you. Open your damn eyes and you'll see them. Put one foot in front of the other and you'll reach them.

Just do something.

Or do nothing.

I hate you.

The noise in your head? You can silence it all. You can take the easy way out. There's a knife in the kitchen. You hid it from your mom because you were afraid she was going to hurt herself. One good cut to the wrists, or if you really want to get the job done, the throat. Slice. You're done.

Or perhaps you want a much cleaner death? There is always the option of sleeping pills. I think I saw them in the bathroom cabinet. I've watched you glance at the bottle longingly. A few times you've taken some.

You know the option is there: suicide. But you just don't have the guts to do it and that, out of all your thoughts, makes it even worse.

Last night, as you got out of the shower you walked over to the mirror. You wiped away the fog with your left palm. You tried your hardest to focus on your reflection but your eyes couldn't focus.

Slowly, ever so slowly, you're slipping down the rabbit hole of insanity.

You're so conflicted and confused you don't know what to do.

I'll give you four options: Grab the knife. Open the bottle. Jump off your roof. Or fight. Hold onto everything that you love and if you let go make sure you leave marks. A sign of your struggle. Make sure everyone knows that you tried.

Do whatever you want, but do it yourself.

Consider yourself a bird that's been pushed out of the nest.

Good luck.

I hate you.

PART III

37

I'M A STALKER in every sense of the word.

Yet there's not a single bone in my body that gives a shit. The only thing coursing through me now is adrenaline. My heart's pounding so hard I'm convinced that it's going to burst out of my chest.

With both hands gripping the steering wheel, I make sure to keep two cars behind his black BMW. Not going to lie, I feel slightly elated at the prospect of seeing him. Which goes beyond the realm of pathetic. I have no words for myself. But… answers. I need them like my next fucking breath. God, I need them so bad.

Luckily, traffic is on my side and I easily remain behind. I try my hardest to peer past the two cars between us and into the back windshield but it's impossible. That'd require binoculars and super-stealth stalking skills. Even I have my limits.

Sleet readily falls from the sky, making it momentarily hard to see. I turn on my windshield wipers and keep my gaze straight ahead. A snowstorm could be coming our way for all I know, but that doesn't stop me.

I wonder for a second what Sam would say if she could see me right this minute. I can just picture her: lips pursed, shaking her head in disapproval before she says, "Really, Selah? Since when did you start stalking?"

Since everything in my life became fucked up, would be my reply.

We drive through Decatur, and soon we're in Forsyth. Her blinker flashes. She moves to the left lane to turn onto Barnett Ave. There's now one car between us but she hasn't looked in her rearview mirror once.

The light turns green and we turn with the flow of traffic. Her turn signal comes on yet again. Another right. This time into the Texas Roadhouse parking lot. It's packed to the hilt, which is good. I don't want to park too close. She gets a parking spot way in the back. I find a spot two rows back and immediately turn off my car.

She gets out, this time with an umbrella. Of course she has an umbrella. She's one of those ready and prepared women, whereas I can't tell you the last time I had an umbrella on me when I actually needed it.

I watch as the two of them run toward the building. The beautiful woman manages to shield the little the girl's face *and* keep herself dry all at the same time.

So perfect.

They disappear into the building. Maybe they're here to have dinner with Jackson. The very thought makes me sick to my stomach.

This is my opening to put my car in reverse and go home, but I can't. I've come this far. To give up now would be a huge waste. So I adjust my seat and make myself comfortable, turn the radio down to a soft murmur and wait.

ONE HOUR LATER I'm done waiting in my car. I get out, slamming the car door. Ignoring the sleet that's pelting the side of my face, I stand outside of the entrance of Texas Roadhouse, watching people coming and going through the front doors. Unbearably loud country music blares through the speakers whenever the doors open and becomes a soft murmur when they close.

Get out of here, my mind whispers. *You look crazy. Deranged.*

I think there's a good chance that I started going crazy the minute Jackson and Mom disappeared on me, leaving me with thousands of unanswered questions.

"Ma'am?" I see a man holding the door open. "Are you coming in?"

I've been outside for only a few minutes and already I'm drenched. My hair is plastered to the sides of my face. My clothes feel heavy and itchy against my skin. My toes are so cold I'm convinced that I'm getting hypothermia.

"No." I pause. "I'm waiting for someone."

It's obvious that he's wondering why I'm not waiting inside, but he doesn't say it. He just nods and lets the door shut behind him.

With my arms tightly folded across my chest and my chin tucked down, I try to imagine what I will say when I encounter the beautiful woman. I had an hour in the car to figure it out, but I kept drawing a blank. The only thing I can think of is to be honest and up front. 'Hey! How do you know Jackson?' seems to be the best approach.

Although, I could accidentally bump into her, say sorry. Ask if the girl next to her is her daughter. And if she says yes, I'll say she's so beautiful. And she'll say thank you. And there's my perfect intro. Perfect, but long and probably time consuming. Plus, that would take finesse. And that's definitely something that I'm lacking right now.

No, the best course of action is to be blunt and up front.

The double doors open. Laughter filters out and suddenly there she is, directly in front of me. I stand there, soaking wet, looking fucking ridiculous. She has the little girl in her arms. An older couple that wasn't with her when she walked in now flanks her on either side. Her head is turned toward the woman, in deep conversation. The woman says something that makes her kick back her head and laugh. She has a pretty laugh.

I bet that's what made Jackson fall in love with her.

A guttural noise tears from my throat, surprising her and me. She stops short. The woman next to her veers back. She has the same look I had when that homeless woman screamed at me. The beautiful brunette's face becomes pale, like she's looking at a ghost.

She knows me.

I don't know her, but she knows me and that makes this all the more gut-wrenching. Swallowing loudly, I take a step forward, which makes the woman take another step back, like I'm a monster.

"Do you know Jackson?" I whisper, ignoring their stares.

The older woman's mouth is agape and the man looks distinctly uncomfortable. As for the beautiful one, she looks ready to rip my head off.

"What are you doing here?" she demands.

"I…"

Holy shit. What can I actually say to her that doesn't make me sound like a nutcase? Nothing. I'd followed her to a grocery store and now to a restaurant. She could call the cops on me. File a restraining order. She could do just about anything and get away with it because I am the other woman.

I just never realized it.

"He's. *Not.* Here," she enunciates slowly. I can tell she wants to say more but she does a double take at the little girl in her arms. She looks out of the corner of her eye toward the older woman and gestures for her to hold the little girl and move out of hearing distance. Immediately the woman takes her, cradling the little girl like a precious treasure. She kisses the girl's head and walks away with the older man, who shoots a worried look in my direction.

When they're a few steps away, the beautiful woman takes a step closer. She says in a firm and level voice, "You need to leave us alone, all right?"

"You don't understand. I didn't know—"

"I don't care," she cuts in, enunciating her words slowly, as if I'm deaf. "I don't care what you have to say. Just leave us alone. Can you give us that, Selah?"

She knows my name. She knows my name. Out of everything she just said that's all my mind can fully grasp. She knows my name and yet I know nothing about her.

Jackson obviously told her about me. But what did he say? Was I painted out to be the villain? A woman that fell for a married man, almost destroyed a family and now wouldn't take no for an answer? If he gave his wife any image of me, it had to be negative. No positives.

"Are you ready, Claribelle?" the lady behind her asks.

Claribelle.

What a beautiful name.

She gives me scathing look. "Yes. I'm ready."

She turns on her heels and hurries back to the people she'd dined with. The woman holding the beautiful little girl keeps turning around to stare at me. She doesn't look at me with hate like Claribelle does, but with interest and pity.

It eats at me to think that his wife is going to walk away thinking I'm this huge whore that's stalking her family. I'm not the villain. And I'm sure as hell not a vixen. I'm not any of those things.

"I'm sorry!" I shout.

She doesn't acknowledge me.

38

COME BACK, MY sweet Selah.

I'm almost done being mad and you're almost done with life. Together we create balance. Not harmony. Hell no. But the discord that's happening right now? It's not there when we connect.

I didn't mean for it to go this far. I hate to see you this unhappy. But can you understand why I was so upset with you? You weren't trying. Here I am, working right alongside you when no one else is and I still don't get any acknowledgment. I'm not looking for a trophy or something.

Just a thank you.

Just two words.

What is it going to take to capture your attention? I've had it a few times over the course of these past few months and it was delicious. Like tasting freshly-baked cookies.

I saw you outside of Texas Roadhouse with the rain pelting down around you. I saw you talk to that woman and the devastating look in your eyes. You walked away, slightly hunched over as if she'd delivered a swift punch to your gut. You didn't want to believe what she was telling you—what was standing directly in front of you—but you had no choice.

So you numbly walked back to your car. You don't remember much of the car ride home; you were on autopilot. Just going through the motions.

When you pulled up into your driveway you softly shut the car door and walked inside. You locked the door behind you and flipped on the lights. And you took your drenched clothes off right there in the foyer. You walked upstairs, naked and went directly to the bathroom where you grabbed the sleeping pills. You took a few and went to your bedroom where you turned the light on.

39

TWO DAYS LATER I force myself to go out.

I'm so afraid that if I stay at home, locked up with my memories of Mom and Jackson, I'll never emerge. It's too easy to fall down the rabbit hole of insanity and I know that I'm so close to the edge. My feet keep slipping, but I refuse to fall because there's no one to catch me.

Well, there's always Sam and Noah. But I can't rely on them forever. At some point I need to fix myself. Something tells me that'll never happen until I find Mom and Jackson.

Both of my hands clutch the steering wheel as I drive down North Street. Winter still fiercely hangs on, refusing to let spring peek its head out. Snowflakes dance in the air as I drive toward downtown Decatur. The thermostat in the car says it's 40 degrees but it feels like 20.

There are so many choices when it comes to restaurants in Decatur, yet I choose Donna's Diner. Small and quaint with no memories of Jackson. Or Mom.

It's your typical nondescript diner with a black and white

checkered floor, long counter with barstools and booths lining the windows, letting you glimpse outside. The seats have small tears with cushioning spilling out in some places. The place smells of greasy fries and it makes my stomach growl.

There's a waitress behind the counter. She nods her head in my direction. I nod back and take a seat in the booth near the very back of the counter. I grab a menu, idly scanning the items. I'm hungry yet I can't seem to find anything good.

"What can I get for you, Sweetie?"

I lift my head to see the same woman who was behind the counter earlier. Her nametag says Ang and has a few star stickers on it. She looks as excited about being here as I do. It makes me wonder what's going on in her life that has her stressed. Certainly this job doesn't help. But is she married? Have kids? Or is she alone, like me?

Part of me wants to ask those very questions but I push them down, down, down so they have no chance of slipping out of my mouth.

"A coffee and some toast would be good."

She arches one brow. "That's it?"

"That's it," I confirm. I drop the menu and slide it across the table toward her.

Ang shrugs as she grabs the menu before walking back to the front register.

The diner is quiet. My left leg nervously bounces up and down. Why? I don't know. Maybe it's because I wanted to escape the silence. I didn't expect it to follow me. I cough loudly, causing the few customers that are here to lift their heads.

I fiddle with the salt and peppershakers, putting them on their sides and spinning them around and around until I'm practically in a trance.

"Thought I'd never find you alone."

I lift my head and see Jackson sliding into the seat across from me.

I swear my heart stops for a millisecond before it resumes beating. Furtively, I look around to make sure that everyone else is seeing the same thing. No one takes any notice. I close my eyes, thinking it's all in my head. But when I open them back up he's still there. I gasp loudly. It's like some part of me has been dead and has suddenly woken up, greedily gasping for air.

I lean forward and fight the urge to reach out and touch him.

"Jackson?" I whisper.

He tilts his head to the side and smirks. "Who else do you think it'd be?"

This can't be happening right now. It can't. "You left." I lean in toward him. "I haven't heard from you in so long."

He leans in and tries to grab my hands. At the last second I snatch them away. "I know. But it's for the best."

"How? How is it for the best?" I can't help the anger that seeps into my words because all I can picture are the lies and deceit that started the second I met this man.

Confront him, my mind hisses. *He can't do this to you. He can't make promises that he can't follow through on.*

As if he can read my thoughts, his eyes lock with mine. He doesn't look shocked. No, he looks sad for me. And that one single look fills me with an unexpected rage.

Sorry? For me? Impossible.

Yet I realize that I'm pathetic. And yes, sad. Because here he is, right in front of my very eyes. Nothing bad happened to him. Nothing bad happened to me. The only thing that happened is he lost interest in me.

I can theorize that maybe he became bored and moved onto some other woman. Perhaps he realized that he truly loved that woman and child and wanted to give it a second chance. From the way she looked at me with hatred it was obvious that he told her all about me.

"Jackson, I followed you yesterday."

He doesn't look surprised.

I continue. "I followed your car and I met a woman. She told me that I've already caused enough damage." I put air quotes around the last word.

Still no response, which by now should be no surprise. But it still pisses me the hell off.

Jackson remains rigid in his seat, unmoved by my words and the pleading look in my eyes. He looks down at the table at the salt and peppershakers on their sides before he lifts his gaze back to mine.

"I'm sorry, Selah. You have no idea how sorry I am. For everything."

"Go into greater detail. I'm not okay with you using the word everything. Tell me exactly what you're sorry for."

He swallows. "I can't."

"You can't," I repeat dully. "The whole time you've been talking to me you've had a completely separate life. Do you know how badly I want to reach across this table and choke the shit out of you? I don't think I've ever been so angry in my life."

"I know you're upset. But there's no time to explain it all."

"You're sitting across from me at a diner in the middle of the day. How much fucking time do you need?" I ask, my voice rising with each word. "Tell me the truth!" I slam my palms on the table. "All of it. Please!"

"Is everything okay here?"

I lift my head and see Ang staring down at me with a strange expression.

I give her a false smile. "Yes."

She points to my half-empty cup. "Would you like a refill on your coffee?"

"Ahh… no. I'm good."

"All right." She walks toward other customers but looks over her shoulder at me, like I'm nuts.

I ignore her, intent on continuing my conversation with Jackson. I turn back to him but his seat is empty. He's gone.

Poof.

Like a magician he just disappeared on me.

Again.

Twisting around in my seat, I frantically look at each person in the diner.

No, no, no. I'm not done talking to him. I want him to explain why he led me on for so long. Was he even sorry? Who was the little girl? Better yet, who was Claribelle? He can't be gone!

I drag all ten fingers through my hair and squeeze my eyes shut. My palms settle against my temples. I want to squeeze as hard as I can so that my skull breaks open. I picture all the black pieces of me spilling out like ink. Maybe the madness can escape and maybe I can rifle through the remnants and piece my life back together. And maybe everything can be okay because I know I can't keep fucking doing this to myself.

I'm not a person right now. I exist solely on memories of Jackson. Conversations with Noah. And in between those fragmented thoughts and feelings I should find portions of my life, but they're nowhere to be seen.

Think! Keep thinking; you're so close to the truth, my mind frantically screams at me.

My hands are shaking as I pull out a ten and place it on the sticky surface of the table. "Keep the change," I say to Ang and flee the diner.

My breaths come in short gasps as I make my way to my car. I refuse to look around at my scenery, afraid of what I might see. Will I see Jackson standing across the street? Or perhaps this time it will be Mom? What an idea. I can picture it my head, telling Sam and anyone who asks that I found Mom on the corner of North Street. How simple.

It's only when I'm in my car that I cry. It's so cold in the car that I'm certain my tears will freeze in place. Still, I don't turn on the heat. I curl my fingers around my steering wheel. Everything feels so convoluted and twisted that even if I attempt to disentangle one thought from the other, it'd never be enough.

40

THIS NEXT INTERVIEW is going to have to be handled with kid gloves.

There was an agreement made beforehand that we would treat these two people with the utmost respect, all the while trying to get answers to hard-hitting questions. That was the difficult part: straddling the line between caring and callous. I had all the faith in the world that we could pull the truth and emotion from the both of them.

To keep most of the interviews cohesive, we're still at the Homewood Suites. I'm getting fucking sick of this place. Sick of looking out of my window every morning and seeing a mile of space defined by an empty parking lot for an ever-dying mall.

In fact, the only thing keeping my spirits up is this very interview. Everyone on set is working quietly and in unison. I think we all feel the same: this is going to be an interview to remember. Last year, when everything happened, Jonathan and Catherine practically went into seclusion. Anything said to the press was through a close family member or their lawyer. They clung to their privacy like some crave their next breath. And who could blame them?

Catherine's a woman in her mid-fifties. Her light brown hair is cut in the typical mom haircut. Crows feet curve around the outer edges of her eyes. What were once laugh lines around her lips are now downturned, making her look like a mild version of the joker. A full year may have passed but Catherine is clearly still not okay with what happened. She's quiet. Lets her husband do all the talking.

Claribelle is also unfortunately on set today, but she brought her little girl. It's only when that girl is around that Catherine's face lights up.

It isn't that I dislike Catherine. She just makes me uncomfortable. There's something about how freely she embraces her sorrow. Not only that, but how it spreads around to everyone else. She stares at you with these imploringly eyes that say, *Do you understand my pain now?*

For me it's just easier to speak with Jonathan. He's a rugged man with a head full of snow-white hair. He has slightly droopy eyes that make him look perpetually sad but it's his thin lips that are always set in a straight line that show he puts up with zero bullshit. He calls it like it is.

Weeks ago, we asked Jonathan to bring in some photos of Jackson throughout his life. I could've asked Catherine but I know what the answer would've been. A big fucking no. She probably has a shrine of every single thing he's ever touched.

But Jonathan? He has a haggard, life has tried to beat me but I've won, look about him. I think that's partially from being in the military for his whole career, but mostly from the cards life has dealt him. Either way, he was the person to ask. At first he was reluctant, until I told him how important it was for the viewers to see the other, softer side of his son.

He told me he'd think about it.

This morning when he came into the conference room he handed me a manila folder filled with photos of Jackson. Catherine had shot me a scathing look, like she couldn't believe I'd go behind her back and ask such a question.

At the coffee station, I flipped through the photos. They were perfect. Pictures of Jackson's first birthday. Jackson's kindergarten photo. The awkward photos from middle school. Some prom photos. A handful of photos of him with Claribelle.

I close the folder and pat Jonathan on the back. "Thank you so much for these. We'll take good care of them. In fact, during your interview we'll go through these photos."

He nods briefly. "How long will this interview take?"

"Not long. I will go through a string of questions, centered mostly around Jackson and—"

"And what happened," he supplies.

"That'll only be at the end," I quickly explain so as to not to push him away.

Before he can reply, a makeup artist taps him on his shoulder and says, "Sir, we need to see you over there." She points to behind the opened black curtains where Catherine is looking at her finished makeup. Jonathan looks at me with concern.

"Everyone wears makeup on camera. It'll be just a bit of powder. That's all," I supply.

Jonathan relents, muttering things under his breath as he follows the makeup artist.

Catherine approaches me. "I picked out those photos you asked of Jackson."

For a second, I'm stunned by her words. "Thank you for that," I finally say.

"You didn't have to go behind my back and ask my husband. This has been a brutal year but I can handle more than you know."

That stops me in my tracks.

"I have to live with the tragedy that happened just like everyone else. I deal with both anger and sadness every day. And it's agony," she says, her voice wavering. But there's strength in her eyes that I never quite expected.

"When we talk to you and your husband, show them you're both a mom and a human being with feelings. It's imperative the world sees that, Catherine."

Thirty minutes later Catherine and Jonathan sit across from me. Everyone is perfectly still. The boom operator is standing close to the cameraman, ready to catch every word.

"How would you describe your son?" I ask.

Catherine sighs and her eyes take on a faraway look. "Jackson," she says and then a burst of laughter spills from her mouth. "Jackson was Jackson. From the day he was born that kid was giving me a run for my money. Growing up he was so mischievous. He loved playing sports: soccer, basketball, and football. You name it."

"Was he good?"

"He was amazing. But he was mostly interested in soccer. He could've gotten a scholarship to Millikin if he'd applied himself more."

"So he didn't do well in school?"

"If it didn't interest him, he wanted nothing to do with it. And going to class was not interesting. He barely graduated high school and the minute he did, he got a job at Caterpillar."

"Did that bother you?"

"Not really. It was a steady job and he seemed relatively happy."

"Did he date a lot?"

"Of course. Jackson was quiet the catch. Growing up he brought home many girls for us to meet."

"Did any relationship ever stick?"

Catherine smiles thinly. "Just one or two."

I glance down at my notes. "When did he start writing?"

This time, Jonathan answers. "He's been writing for as long as we can remember." He looks to his wife. "When did he present us with his first novel?"

Suddenly, a bright smile graces Catherine's face. She looks at the ground, deep in thought. "Seven or eight. He was so proud because he got to type it on the computer. It was only twelve pages long but he printed it out and made Jon and I copies."

Jonathan and Catherine look at each other. Their smiles fade right along with the sweet memory of their son. Quickly, I glance at the questions in front of me.

"So you read his stories?"

"Only when he was a kid. As he got older he became protective over his work."

"Did he ever mention the website JustWrite?"

"Just in passing," Catherine replies. "He seemed excited to have a place to talk to other people that shared the same passion for writing."

"And Selah Kerrington was one of those people."

Catherine hesitates briefly. "Not at first. For a while I think they were just two people who read each other's stories. It was later on that he started to become secretive."

"Secretive how?"

"I'd ask more about this Selah but he'd be evasive. Tell me that they were only talking. He'd offer up no other details."

"Did that bother you?"

Catherine thinks over her words carefully. "A mother is only as happy as her unhappiest child. He really struggled in his twenties but lately he seemed really happy. It was so refreshing to see. To me, that's all that mattered."

"Struggled how?"

"Unfortunately he started taking drugs. It really had a hold on him and put him in a dark place. For a long time I questioned if he'd ever be clean. It took him a while to finally pull away from that lifestyle."

"How did you find out about Selah?"

"In early February. I remember he came home to visit and sat down at the kitchen table and said 'I think I've met my match.' I was so happy for him."

"Did you ever get to meet her?"

"No." Catherine adverts her eyes. "Everything happened so swiftly after that. We never got the chance…"

41

I KNOW I saw him.

I know it. Some people might say that it was a figment of my imagination, but he was a full-bodied, living, breathing male. And he was only just steps away from me.

And I swear when our eyes met a jolt slashed through me, from my fingertips to my toes. Right when I was getting answers to my most burning questions, I turned my gaze elsewhere and he was gone.

I realize that I should be furious at him. And I am. But more than anything, I just want an explanation as to why he left. Like anyone, I just want closure—a reason for his actions. At the diner he said there wasn't enough time, which is ironic because that's all I have. The clock keeps ticking away, threatening that I just might never find out the truth.

I start to pace my bedroom, fighting the urge to call Noah. He would know what to do. He always does. But even the kindest people have their limits and right now my thoughts are a fucking mess. Everything about me screams mess. I need to get my shit together before I call him.

Over and over I pace the room until I'm convinced I've worn a trail onto the carpet. We'll call it 'the trail to insanity' because that's where I feel I'm heading.

"You didn't make it up," I say into the quiet room. "You saw him with your own two eyes."

And that's when I hear the automated voice.

"You've got mail."

I pause and turn around slowly and look at my laptop sitting open on my bed.

"You've got mail."

Pause.

"You've got mail."

Pause.

"You've got mail."

The phrase repeats itself until it's all I can hear. I run over to the laptop and see all of Jackson's e-mails being resent to me.

All the blood drains from my face; what the hell is happening?

Outside the wind picks up, sending hundreds of white flecks of snow against the windowpane. It's freezing out but inside my blood is boiling. Nothing is making sense.

"No!" I shake my laptop in frustration. "What is happening?"

There's no reason for this. I've heard of this sometimes occurring, but only with an an e-mail or two. Even then, it's typically a glitch. Nothing to this extreme. No, this feels on purpose. It feels like someone, possibly Jackson himself, is resending every single e-mail just to get a rise out of me.

"You've got mail."

This is all too much.

I cover my ears. "Stop it!" I scream. "Stop it! Stop it!"

And all of a sudden, it does. My ears are slightly ringing as I slowly lower my hands. They drop heavily to my sides. Except for the wind, it's deathly quiet in the room. I take a deep breath. I approach the computer. My palms rest on the flat surface of the desk as I lean in and see that each e-mail is marked unread, as though this is the first time I'm seeing them.

It's a ridiculous thing to do but I click on the first e-mail and read it.

To: Selahk85@aol.com

From: Jackvan.dosis9@gmail.com

February 2nd

2:27pm

Hello.

So innocuous. So simple.

But I remember impatiently looking for a job when that e-mail first showed up. And I remember deleting that e-mail.

"What the hell is going on?" I groan.

I slam my hand on the keyboard. I'm half tempted to rip the laptop off my bed and throw it against the wall.

Suddenly, out of nowhere, the printer kicks into action. When I hit the keyboard I must have hit the print button. Completely stunned, I listen to the steady thrum of the printer and see a page fall out of the dispenser, float to the ground, and softly land upside down. I bend down to pick it up and it's then that I notice it. Something I've never seen before. It's fleeting, like catching something out of the corner of your eye. But slowly the letters start to move around before they settle in their correct place: Jackvan.dois is Jackson Davis.

Of course. It makes sense now. If he had a double life, why wouldn't he change his name? He wouldn't want the two intermixing.

Ignoring the e-mail, I pull up a new window and Google his name

Seconds.

That's all it takes for information to come up. There are multiple links, but all I see is the one from the Yellow Pages. The address is across the street, one that I know so well: Noah's.

PART IV

42

DON'T STOP NOW, little bird.

You are so, so close to the truth. You hold the key in your hands. The lock is only steps away.

I suppose I should be scared because everything is so close to becoming exposed. I don't know how you'll handle it. There's a very good chance that you'll crumble and never get back up.

But this is meant to happen.

All good things must come to an end.

Are you ready for the truth?

I know for damn sure that I am.

I've been waiting a long, long time fore this.

43

WHO KNEW THAT with all the secrets and confusion around me, he had the answers the whole time?

Slowly, I raise my head and look out into the hall. Before I leave the room, I grab the printed-out e-mail. My steps are slow and steady as I walk down the stairs. I skip putting on a coat and grab the first pair of shoes I can find. My heart is pounding, begging and pleading for me to hurry up. But something inside of me is growing numb. Something inside of me knows that what I uncover over there will destroy my whole world.

I walk outside, not even bothering to shut the door behind me. All around me the snow falls, making the street into a winter wonderland. Ice-cold wind bites into my skin, pushing my hair up and away from my face.

At this time of day, I'm sure he's at work. Yet I still walk up the steps to Noah's front door. I try the door and just as I expected it's locked. But sweet, trusting Noah is probably like ninety nine percent of the people out there who keep a spare key somewhere near their front door. Since he doesn't have any flower pots, I look under the doormat.

Bingo.

I hold up the silver key and shake my head as I break into Noah's home.

There should be some part of me that feels a small amount of remorse for what I'm doing. But I'm so determined to find answers there's no room for remorse. Somehow Noah's intertwined in this, and I need to know why.

All the lights are off except for a lamp in the dining room. I creep forward, but pause when I hear footsteps. I sigh with relief when I see Duke standing in the doorway. He cocks his head to the side. His tail starts to wag slowly. I approach him with a small smile.

"Hi, Duke," I whisper, which is ridiculous. No one is here.

He sits and cocks his head to the side, like he knows something is wrong with me being here and can't figure out why. Seconds later he stands up, brushes past me and then walks to his pillow in the corner. So much for being a good watchdog.

Noah's house is a bi-level. Almost an exact replica of ours, but completely different in one way: it's virtually empty. Where Mom's home is packed to the hilt with belongings, Noah's house looks like no one is living in it. There's a pop-up table in the dining room. The living room has a simple black leather couch and a flat-screen TV mounted to the wall. It looks like a man cave, only halfway decorated.

I move into the dining room. Besides the lone pop-up table, there are stacks of boxes lined up against the wall. His laptop is open on the table. A half-drunk cup of coffee sits next to it. I can picture him abruptly getting up from his seat and leaving the house to run a quick errand. Which allows me a small window of time to search through his things.

On the opposite wall from the stacked boxes is a massive dry erase board that you'd typically see in schools or conference rooms. On it was my family tree.

My name is written at the top in bold, block letters.

Beneath me is my family.

Dad, David Kerrington is to the left. To the right is Susan Kerrington. Birth: September 10th, 1963. And her death: March 6th, 2016.

Impossible.

Just seeing the words makes me almost collapse in the nearest seat.

I was right. This man is crazy. A stalker. He's been watching me this entire time. How could I have let him dupe me like this? Anger makes a red haze appear in front of my eyes. If I had a gun and Noah walked in, I'd probably shoot his balls off.

"Calm down," I say out loud. "You need answers."

I need a lot of them. Starting with, how are Noah and Jackson connected? Why does he have a date of death listed for my mom?

My heartbeat echoes in my ears; it can't be. She's not dead.

Missing? Yes. But dead? No fucking way.

Sitting back in the seat I take a deep breath and press my palms against my eyes until white spots appear. When I open them back up, I look down at the table at a CD. On the plastic wrapping is a post-it note:

Noah,

Thought you might like to see how the taping has gone so far. It airs in March.

Keep in touch.

-David.

My hands are shaking as I remove the CD and slide it into the CD port. It takes a few seconds for the laptop to download it. The screen turns black for a second and then a woman's face appears. I move in closer and see that it's the same woman who I saw driving Jackson's car. She's looking away from the camera but it's obvious from her body language that she knows the spotlight is on her. I want to say she likes that, but there's a slight tremor to her hands.

Someone snaps together a clapperboard and a man's voice says, "Claribelle, how well did you know Selah Kerrington?"

My eyes are riveted to the screen. "I hardly knew Selah. I'd met her only twice."

She looks away and you can tell that she can barely get my name out without feeling disgust. She tucks a strand of hair behind her right ear.

"And what are your thoughts about her?" the man continues.

Claribelle leans in and I find myself doing the same. "She's an evil, manipulative bitch who can't be trusted."

I press pause.

This woman clearly knows me. But how? Other than the one time at Texas Roadhouse I've never spoken to her.

All the unanswered questions rushing through my brain are driving me crazy. I drag my hands through my hair and groan before I press play again.

Claribelle's face cuts out, only to be replaced by Sam's. Her face staring back at me gives me a jolt. How is she involved?

44

THERE ARE PEOPLE you interview that you enjoy, and then there are others who hold the missing puzzle piece.

They are the key that you desperately need to unlock the truth. Samantha Gulick is that key.

It took me five tries to get her to finally call me back. There was a brief second where I was convinced she'd reject my offer to be interviewed, because she wasn't flattered like some. She saw this as a chore.

But finally, after much coaxing and promising that it would only take up one weekend (traveling included), and that we wouldn't hound her again, she'd agreed.

The makeup artist is trying to apply more blush on Sam's cheeks but she shoots the poor woman a look that makes her slowly step away, brush in hand.

"At this point I'm going to need a chisel to get all this makeup off," she remarks dryly.

"I know it's a lot but it's needed for all the lights that will be shining on you."

Her only reply is a cursory nod as she picks up her Blackberry.

Who the fuck still uses a Blackberry? Sam, apparently.

I gesture to it. "You still have one of those?"

"Of course." Her fingers fly across the keyboard with a finesse that can only be learned through practice. "It's the only way I can get work done."

"It's ancient."

Finally, she lifts her head with an impatient expression, as though I'm a child who won't stop with the 'but why' questions. "Time is money. And I don't have time to learn a new fucking gadget. There's an iPhone every other year. Something newer and greater. I'll stick to what I know."

This woman is so matter-of-fact that it's hard to argue with her.

It's hard to get a good read on Samantha Gulick in general. One minute she's polite and kind, and the next she's all business, making you feel like you're slacking off on the job.

"Can we hurry this up?" she asks as she slowly lowers her phone onto her lap. "I have a conference call in forty-five minutes."

"Yes, yes. We can get started right now."

As we get ready to film, Sam puts away her phone and sits up straight in her seat and very deliberately puts up a wall. We may ask questions and get answers but the chances of us pulling out her emotions, gathering tears for the viewers, is incredibly low. If this woman is going to cry, it's going to be in the privacy of her own home.

I immediately jump in. "What type of friendship do you and Selah have?"

"We're incredibly close. We are a year and five days apart."

"Are you the oldest?"

At that, Sam smiles. "No, I'm not. It was always funny growing up. Selah may have been the older one but I always felt like I had to be the one to protect her. She loved too hard, which made her vulnerable."

"And when she started to date Jackson. What were your thoughts?"

Samantha shrugs. "Not much, to be honest with you. I live up in Chicago. I hadn't met him in person yet. First impressions mean a lot to me and it bothered me that the two of them met online. I warned her that it could be dangerous, but she's too stubborn and shrugged off my words. After awhile I came to the conclusion that if Selah was happy then I was happy."

"You wanted that for Selah… didn't you?"

"Of course. My sister deserved it."

In the video editing process, we'll have pictures flashing across the screen—the ones that Aunt Ruby gave me of Selah and Sam growing up with their mom.

I pull back from questions about Selah and direct them toward Susie. "How hard is it for you to fathom that your mom was found dead?"

Samantha takes a deep breath. Her fingers are still linked together. "Not as hard as you may imagine."

"What does that mean?"

She looks me straight in the eye. "What I mean is that my mom may have had some traits that were difficult to deal with, but overall she was a kind and caring person. She saw the absolute best in everyone. Like Selah, she was very vulnerable."

"A lot of people have accused your sister of bringing this addict into your mother's life. They say she'd still be alive if it weren't for Selah. Do you believe that?"

If it were anyone else I think they'd take offense to this line of questioning, but Samantha Gulick has balls of steel. She's never going to show her pain. It's all mind over matter for her. Especially when it comes to her pain.

"Absolutely not," Samantha says with such conviction that even I believe her. "Ultimately, at the end of the day people are going to make their own decisions, and if it wasn't one person that preyed on my mother it would've been another."

"If you could go back and change one thing, what would it be?"

Sam goes quiet. She stares at the ground for a few second before she looks back up at me. "I would change how quickly I gave up. From the beginning I had a bad feeling about Jackson, but I chose to ignore it. Maybe if I hadn't, none of this would've happened. That's what I would go back and change."

45

KEYS JANGLE AND I gasp as the doorknob slowly turns and the door opens.

Duke barks once and rushes to Noah's side. His head is down as he's rummaging through the mail, completely unaware that I'm standing in his dining room.

"Hey, how was your day?" he says absently to Duke.

"Not good, since I've discovered that you're a fucking liar," I say out loud.

Noah's head snaps up. The mail drops from his hands and scatters all around him. He takes in the scene. The laptop in front of me. The newspaper and the dry erase board.

"How did you get in here?"

"You have a spare key underneath your doormat. You have to find a better hiding spot than that."

Noah doesn't reply.

He knows that I know him. The real him. I can tell by the look in his eyes. Very slowly, he approaches. He raises his hands to show he means no harm.

A few days ago, hell, even an hour ago, I would've believed he wouldn't. But now I don't. I jump up and move across the room, until we are facing each other, and the table is between us.

"Selah, let me explain."

"Tell me what's going on," I say calmly even though my heart is pounding.

"Selah—"

I feel like I've been left in the dark, pulled this way and that. I've obviously been made to appear crazy and I can't take it anymore. "Tell me!" I scream because it's that or break down and sob. "Tell me why your address is Jackson's."

"He didn't live here," he says. "His parents were the last people to live here." He selects his words carefully. Delicately. It's driving me crazy.

"Do you know him?" I demand.

Noah shakes his head. "I didn't."

My mouth opens, but no words come out. "So where is he?"

Now it's Noah's turn to look speechless. He looks away, his jaw clinched before he moves toward me. Hesitantly, I glance at him, unsure of what he's about to do. But instead of coming closer he rummages through one of the many boxes against the wall. He flips through a stack of newspapers before he pulls one out. He looks me in the eye when he holds it out. I snatch it from him and scan the front page. It's dated from last year. The headline reads:
Decatur Man's Body Pulled From Lake Decatur

Beneath the headline is a colored photo of cops lingering along the waterline. Some are speaking to each other. Others look out into the water. There's yellow caution tape behind them. Cop cars and ambulances are all around with flashing lights. There's no sign of Jackson's body but there might as well be.

It feels like someone is punching me in the gut over and over.

Laying both palms flat on the table, I hunch over the

newspaper and continue to read the article: *Authorities confirmed that a male body was pulled from Lake Decatur on March 22nd at 8:30 p.m. The man was identified as Jackson Davis, according to Macon County Examiner's office.*

I try to read the rest of the article but my vision goes blurry from tears. I take a deep breath.

"There's this, too," Noah says quietly. He slides over a small newspaper clipping. I read the obituary even though I know I shouldn't.

Jonathan Jackson Davis, 31, tragically passed away on March 22nd, 2016.

He is survived by his parents, Jonathan and Catherine Cooper-Davis of Forsyth; sister, Claribelle (husband, Roman) Sandoval of Forsyth. Services will be held at First Baptist Church, Mt. Zion, Saturday at 1p.m. Officiating is Pastor George Riney. Burial: Greenwood Cemetery. Moran and Goebel Funeral Home is in charge of arrangements.

Out of everything I've just read what sticks out to me is the year—2016—that I can't comprehend. How is that possible? A man has been dead for over a year yet I saw him less than two weeks ago?

With my hands curled into fists I press them against my temples. I can feel my entire body shake. "No…" I breathe.

When I pull my gaze away from the obituary I see Noah staring at me with sadness. I brush past him and move toward the door.

He is wrong. And that newspaper? Also wrong. I'm being set up. Maybe Jackson wants me to believe he's dead. It's some kind of sick joke on his part.

"Selah! Just listen to me!" Noah calls out behind me. "You need to read this."

I stop dead in my tracks and turn around and stare at him. What more can he possibly have to show me?

He holds out another newspaper clipping. This time the headline reads: **Police Discover Body at Twin Oak Apartments**

On Tuesday, March 22nd 2016, police were called to apartment 2B at the Twin Oak Apartments after a landlord reported complaints of an overwhelming smell coming from the location. When the police arrived they discovered the body of Susie Kerrington, who has been missing for over two weeks. She was found in one of the bedrooms, her body dismembered and shoved into black garbage bags. Police confirmed that the apartment belonged to Jackson Davis.

Chief of Police, Anthony Cooke, said, 'It's always a crushing blow to be called to a scene like this one. We can confirm that the body found is Susie Kerrington, who was reported missing by her daughter. Our thoughts go out Mrs. Kerrington's family at this time.'

In a strange twist of fate, Davis's car was reported abandoned on East Lake Shore Drive at around four-thirty p.m. the same day the body of Susie Kerrington was found. His keys and wallet were found inside the car. Search and rescue teams were called out to the scene. Four hours later, divers found his body. His death has been determined as a suicide.

I think I'm going to be sick. Jackson didn't kill my mom. He wouldn't harm a fly.

And Mom isn't dead. Can't be.

I have to get home. I have to wait for Mom. Maybe she'll come back. I open the door and step out onto the porch right as Noah grabs my arm. I whirl around.

"Let go!" I shout, before I violently try to extract myself. I need to go home. I need to be in my own home; it's safe there. He puts up a small struggle before he finally lets go. I take a step back and point a finger at him. "You're wrong," I hiss.

Noah approaches slowly, like he's coming close to a wild animal.

"That newspaper was wrong," I say, my voice slightly breaking. "It's not true."

"Yes it is!" he says more forcefully. "Jackson killed your mother and hid the body at his apartment. He killed himself the day your mom's body was discovered!"

"Stop it! You're wrong!"

"No I'm not. I wish I was wrong but I'm not."

"Jackson wouldn't do that. He wouldn't."

"He was a drug addict, Selah! He needed money. He would've killed anyone for his next high!"

"But not my mom," I say, breathing heavily. "He knew she was mentally ill."

"Your mom was fine. Everything you thought was happening to her was happening to *you*."

I shake my head in denial but that just makes him grip my arms tighter.

"Dammit, listen to me!" he says sharply. "You need to listen to this! After your mom died last year, *you* were the one who was crying and laughing on the sidewalk. *You* were the one who was put on seventy-two hour hold.

"I didn't have ulterior motives when I first moved in but then I started to watch you. You were talking to yourself and I had to find out why. So I started to digging through old newspapers and that's when I discovered what happened. A college friend of mine, David, is an executive producer for *Dateline*. I knew they were taping an episode about your life and I asked to see the interviews they've taped so far." Noah swallows. "Selah, I'm sorry. I didn't want you to find out like this."

"No." My lips quiver. "You're wrong."

"I'm not."

When I try to pull away this time, he lets go. I turn back around, intent on going home but stop short when I see the neighbors outside. Some are standing on their lawns. Others on their porches. Parents are standing next to their kids, a firm hand planted on their bony shoulders. They're all staring directly at me.

A feeling of deja vu hits me. I'd seen that look so many times. But it was always directed at Mom. My breath comes out in shallow gasps as I close my eyes. When I do, a curtain slowly pulls up. I see memories in a different light. I am now acting out the role my mom played, the crazy person of Wildwood. Walking down the street in a ratty robe and house slippers, laughing and crying at the same time. A cop slowly asking me if there was anyone that I needed to call. "I'm fine," I told him, but the words came out in Mom's voice.

Very slowly, the fog is beginning to lift. The images are becoming clearer. I don't want to watch this play out in my head but it's like someone has their hands on my head, forcing me to look forward.

I can see myself sitting across from the doctor as he told me that he was worried about me. That if I was brought in one more time, he'd be forced to find a 'suitable place' for me. I can distinctly see my sister, Sam, signing me out, assuring the doctor that she'd make sure I was okay.

I see myself sitting at my mom's kitchen table, staring into depths of the murky brown coffee, wanting to drink it, but not having the stomach for it. I see myself blindly watching the TV.

I see myself going to interviews and sitting in the waiting rooms. My head bent to the left, talking in hurried whispers to the empty seat. The people around me giving me strange looks, leaving a wide berth around me.

My knees start to buckle.

I can hear Noah say my name behind me.

A small, keening noise escapes my mouth. It's a sound I didn't know I was even capable of making. Pain rocks through my body. Everything Noah's told me tries to squeeze its way into my brain. It's all a jumbled mess.

I lift my hands to my face. Feel my fingernails dig into my skin as I drag them through my hair. All outside noise has been put on pause, leaving me to face the truth. I can't accept this. It isn't the truth. I press my fingers deeper into the skin around the base of my skull. Harder, harder, harder until I'm certain I've drawn blood. I lower my head until my forehead rests on the ground.

Then I release a blood-curdling scream.

The truth is a powerful thing. When it's suppressed for such a long time and then suddenly set free, it doesn't come quietly; it attacks you from the inside out, forcing you to feel every last lie and deception you were holding onto.

No matter how painful it is.

46

One month later...

"HOW ARE YOU doing, Selah?" Dr. Clowds asks.

He sits behind his desk, not bothering to look up from his paperwork. He has a yellow binder (my binder) open in front of him. To his left sits a cart with about nineteen binders. The names of each patient are written on the spines.

I've been here at Sacred Heart Behavioral Health Facility for thirty days, and for a place where people normally stay for five to seven days, that's a long time. My file is so large that I have two binders. The other one sits on the cart. A couple of times I've tried to see what's written in them, but the doctor's writing is so sloppy I can't read a damn thing.

"Selah?" the doctor prods.

Rapidly, I blink and turn my gaze away from the file back to the doctor. I try to think of the last thing he said to me. "Uh… I've been great."

One thing I quickly learned here is that everything you do and say is closely monitored. A male patient muttered underneath his breath that a female patient was a bitch and he was removed to Ward 1 where the more severe patients are sent. Three days later he came back, looking stable but definitely subdued.

I couldn't help but wonder what would happen if I had a complete breakdown. Would they put me in Ward 1, too?

"That's good to hear," the doctor comments. "How has your anxiety been? Is the Effexor helping?"

"I think it is," I answer truthfully. "I can concentrate better lately and I'm not as nervous going to the cafeteria."

He nods his head thoughtfully, his pen flying across the page.

When I arrived I was instantly put back on Seroquel to treat my depression and Remeron to help me sleep during the night. I still had horrible anxiety when it came to interacting with other people or overly-large crowds. It was almost like my brain became over stimulated by it all. So they put me on the Effexor.

My mood may be stable but that doesn't mean I'm one hundred percent well. In fact, I'm far from it. But Sacred Heart helps to treat the mentally unstable, not the broken hearted. I know my time here is running out.

"When do you think I can go home?" I ask.

The doctor hesitates for a second. "Within the next few days."

It's hard to tell if he's saying that to placate me or if he's telling me the truth. Either way, I'll take it. The thought of leaving this place fills me with happiness and fear. Fear because I don't know how I'm going to survive in the outside world. Sure, I may have tricks up my sleeve for handling my anxiety and depression, but using them is a whole other thing.

"You can send in Michael now," he says.

I nod and stand up.

When I walk out of his office I scan the rec room. One patient is doing a jigsaw puzzle. Another is leaning against the nurse's station, trying to coax one of them into letting him have another smoke break before lunch. A few are sitting in the uncomfortable chairs, quietly watching TV.

"Michael?" I say. He pulls his gaze away from the TV and looks at me. "It's your turn," I say and make my way to my room.

Since I hardly remember my brief time spent at DMH, I was terrified when Sam took me here days after my breakdown at Noah's house. My only knowledge of psych wards came from movies like *Girl, Interrupted.* I'd walked into the main recreation room and stared at the people, wondering who would be the Lisa of the ward. Who would be the Janet? Or the Georgina?

Yet it was relatively quiet. There were two wards: one for the more severe patients and others that ranged from just needing medication adjustments to people wanting to commit suicide.

I see my psychotherapist, Kim, twice a week. Some days there is nothing that I have to say and I'm in and out of her office in just a few minutes. And then there are other days when I talk for a good hour. We talk about my anxiety and how I'll thrive in the outside world.

There's an order here that I find oddly comforting. People who would normally never speak to each other in the real world become your closest confidants. You'll take their confessions and darkness to your grave and you know they'll do the same for you.

I walk into my room and see my roommate sitting on her bed. Colored pencils are spread out in front of her as she dutifully colors.

Her name is Michelle and she's been here for three days. I've had three roommates since I've been at Sacred Heart. One constantly wore long-sleeved shirts to cover up the cuts on her wrists. Another was a girl with PTSD who regularly screamed out at night. And the other was a pissed off woman in her thirties who was only at Sacred Heart because she had told her doctor that she was suicidal.

I'm not sure what Michelle is here for; she's kind but very quiet. Keeps to herself during group therapy and only talks to me while we're getting ready for bed. For all intents and purposes, she looks normal. But that's the thing. We automatically assume that the strangers we see walking down the street have it all together when in reality they're fighting a battle of their own.

She looks up from her page. "How was your visit with Dr. Clowds?" she asks.

"Good." I flop down onto my bed. "He said that I might be able to leave in a few days."

She nods and doesn't say anything for a few minutes. I close my eyes and take a few deep breaths.

"Are you excited to get out of here?" she asks so quietly that at first I don't hear her.

"I don't know yet," I confess. My eyes open, I stare at the ceiling. I still think about my mom constantly. So many times I've wanted to Google her name and see how many articles pop up about her death and Jackson's involvement.

The knowledge that her death could've been prevented if I never brought Jackson into our lives eats at me constantly. Kim tells me that I can't think that way. That I had no way of knowing what the future would hold. She tells me that I have to work through my guilt or I'll never be able to move on with me life.

Have I come to terms with her death? Yes. But sometimes I think I'm still in shock. My grief is like a blindfold. Every day I take steps forward. Some days I walk without falling. Other times I trip and fall and the pain is so raw it feels like I'm finding out the news all over again.

Then there are moments when I feel a strange sort of empathy toward Jackson. I've only confessed this morbid feeling to Kim because saying the words aloud just feels fucked up. She'd asked me to explain. I was silent a few moments and then I said, "Because I think he was so blinded by his addiction and depression that all he wanted was a way to feel nothing. I think if he didn't kill my mom it would've been someone else."

"Can you relate to the pain he was going through?"

My reply was yes.

I was diagnosed with Bipolar One in my mid-twenties. For so long I thought I was simply struggling with depression and that it was normal to have incredible highs and alarming lows. I thought it was common to experience grandiose thoughts and reckless behavior. The turning point for me was when I'd been struggling through depression for close to a year before I realized something was wrong.

There's a negative connotation attached to Bipolar. People instantly picture the two white masks: one smiling and the other sad. But it's so much more complex than that. Some think you're a loose cannon and you can't be trusted. But mental illness is not a collective sum of bad days and moments. It's a chemical imbalance that no one would choose to suffer with, any more than someone would choose diabetes.

You have to learn to live with it. And a lot of times that is a daunting, terrifying task.

"IT'S VISITING HOURS," Cynthia says, turning off the TV in the recreation room. Some people holler at her because she's standing directly in front of the TV.

"If you want to keep watching the game, go to the therapy room."

The therapy room is where we have group therapy twice a day. Everyone on the ward comes together and we do activities that center around dealing with PTSD, anxiety, and addiction. You name it. Most times I'm a cynic when it comes to the therapy bullshit, but there have been a few times when I've applied the techniques or tools in dealing with my anxiety and found them incredibly useful.

I close my book and head to the nurse's station. I lean against the wall and wait patiently for one of the nurses to bring out the bath cart. Each patient here has a toiletry box. It's placed on a cart that's brought out in the mornings and at night. This is my favorite time of the day. Sometimes I'll spend up to forty-five minutes in the shower. I'll let the scalding hot water beat against my skin until my it's red. Until it feels like every emotion that the day's therapy has drudged up is washed off of me.

A red-headed nurse named Carla pushes out the cart and stops it in the middle of the hall. I grab two towels on the first shelf and bend down to grab my toiletry box.

"Selah. You have a visitor."

I frown because today isn't Friday. That's when Sam comes to visit me. She hasn't missed a single Friday. She always comes with a gift. Typically books, or a toiletry item or a new shirt. While we're talking she'll hand over the gifts to the nurses; they make sure she hasn't snuck in any contraband and when she leaves they hand it back over to me.

But today is Tuesday.

I drop the towels and walk back to the nurse's station and see Noah there. This is the first time I've seen him since I've come here.

I think about him almost daily. About my last moments spent with him before I came here. Sometimes I feel anger toward him that he didn't tell me sooner. During one of my sessions, Kim once suggested that I was placing most of my anger on Noah because I had no one else to direct it toward.

She had a valid point.

Other times I feel grateful that someone out there cared enough to try and untangle my story when I couldn't.

Slowly, I walk over to where he's waiting, using the time to figure out what I'm going to say to him. But I can't think of anything that would lead to a light-hearted conversation.

There's a nervous energy bouncing between us that has my heart racing. It doesn't help that he came today without any warning. But it's not like I can turn my back and walk back to my room, like this never happened.

"Let's sit here," I tell him, pointing to the table closest to the kitchenette. When I sit here, I have a perfectly angled view of the room, putting me at ease. I pull out the chair across from his and sit down. I lace my fingers together and place them on my lap to hide how much they're shaking.

He sits down and rests his elbows on the table before he gives me a small smile that doesn't quite reach his eyes.

"Wow… this is a surprise," I say.

"A bad or good surprise?"

"I'm not sure yet. Ask me after our visit."

"Will do."

There's a small silence between the two of us. Honestly, I have no idea what to say. It's not like this is a coffee date between two friends catching up. It's two people who were brought together by tragic circumstances, and no matter how much time goes by that will never change. I'll always think about my mom when I see Noah.

"How have you been?" he asks.

I shrug and look down at my laced fingers. "I have good and bad days, but that's to be expected with everything that's happened." I lift my gaze. "How are you?"

"I'm all right."

"And Duke?" I ask with a hint of a smile.

"Still the worst guard dog in the history of dogs."

"Well, it's good to know that at least something has remained the same."

Noah smiles broadly before his gaze wanders around the rec room. He takes in everything from the small kitchenette in the corner to the table against the wall with art projects drying on it. There's a piano in the corner and one available computer. All social media is blocked, so we can only check our e-mail. Some patients are constantly on there, furiously clicking the refresher button as they wait for loved ones to write them back. I occasionally log on, but all I get is junk mail.

"So what do you do around here?" Noah asks.

"We keep busy: there's art class, group therapy, and free time."

"What do you do during free time?"

"Typically read."

Noah smirks. "Why am I not surprised?"

I smile back, but it quickly fades because there's no use in pretending things are normal between us. "Noah, why are you really here?"

His mouth opens and closes before he leans closer. He looks left and right before he speaks. "I just had to see for myself if you were okay. I've talked a few times to your sister."

"So she's the one who told you I was here?"

"She was," he confirms.

"Why does that not shock me?" I mutter to myself.

"Don't be mad at her. I saw her at the house and asked about you. I hadn't heard anything and I was getting worried."

My skin starts to tingle underneath Noah's scrutiny. I take a shaking hand and tuck a lock of hair behind my ear.

"You know that if things were different. If—" he starts to say.

"Don't," I whisper. Noah has a pained expression on his face. "Please."

I already know what he's going say. In a perfect world, maybe we could be together. But I don't ever see it happening.

"I don't want to entertain the idea; that will just lead to disappointment," I confess. "Right now, I take everything day by day. Moment by moment. Second by second. I go to bed thinking that it's another day and I've made it."

Noah doesn't say a word.

We stare at each other while other patients and their visitors talk around us. I swallow, trying to ignore the pain in my chest. It feels like my heart is being smashed into thousands of pieces.

I watch Noah very carefully, taking in his appearance: his hair's grown out a since I last saw him, he has thick stubble on his cheeks, peppered with silver. I fight the urge to place my hand against his cheek.

One of the biggest misconceptions about psych wards is that they're lonely places. But we don't want for company here. There are nurses and doctors constantly walking through the doors. In the four weeks that I've been here, I've seen patients form tight friendships with other patients.

But there's a silence that settles deep into your bones. You become swept up in the monotony of each day and getting better, and when you look out the window you can feel the outside world just vibrating with life.

I feel that energy coming off of Noah right now. I want to smell his skin. See if the magic of life clings to him like I imagine.

"Visiting hours are over," the night nurse calls out from the front of the room.

I can hear the commotion of patients peeking their heads out of the room, like people hiding in storm shelters, waiting for the severe weather to leave them in peace.

Slowly I stand from the chair, ignoring the way it squeaks against the floor. Noah stands up, his hands digging into his pockets. He grabs his car keys and stares at me for a moment before he moves in and wraps an arm around my shoulders, guiding me closer to him. My head rests perfectly against his chest and for a second my eyes close. My arms go around him. My fingers have a mind of their own and tightly curl around the back of his shirt.

Because he's good.

Because he's stable.

Because I know that we will never be.

Noah is the first to pull away.

"Thank you for coming," I say.

He nods somberly. "I'm really glad I came."

We stand there, both of us refusing to be the first one to leave.

He reaches his hand out and curls it around the back of my head, then leans in, pressing his forehead against mine.

One, two, three, four, five…

I count the seconds with a feeling of dread. With all of my strength I ignore the urge to beg Noah to take me with him. The words are on my tongue; I can feel them. I can hear them like they're being whispered in my ear. Finally, I push back.

Noah's eyes sweep over my face. He gives me a sad smile. "Take care of yourself."

I nod. "You too."

Then he walks away, leaving me with my misery.

"Med time!" David hollers behind the nurse's station. Everyone lines up, single file. Some keep to themselves, others talk to the people in front or behind them. Typically I'm one of the last people to take my nighttime meds. Tonight I'm the second person in line.

When I step up to the counter, David hands me a cup with my name written on the side. I take all my pills at once and swallow them down with some water. I stick out my tongue for David to examine before I turn around and make my way to my room, hoping that I will immediately fall into a dreamless sleep.

EPILOGUE

HELLO.

You've heard me speak a few times over the course of the last few months but I don't believe we've been formally introduced.

Throughout time people have described me in numerous ways:

A prison.

A tool.

A blank slate.

Fickle.

Powerful.

Dangerous.

But I'm not any one of those words; I'm all of them.

Sometimes we can't live together but we certainly can't live apart.

I'm your mind, Selah, and I remember what you refuse to.

Think of me as one big house. There's the main room, or command central, where I reside and many small ones that split off from where I live. I keep everything in working order.

There are days when things become… overwhelming. For the most part, though, I've done a damn good job at keeping everything together. On good days, I can easily find my way through the whole house. I slip through the halls, open up doors one by one, enter every room. And on bad days, the doors lock. Whatever room I'm in, I know I'm going to be there for a while.

But even then, the door eventually opens.

When tragedy struck your life, your grief became so powerful and overwhelming that the whole house shut down. The doors locked. Lights turned off and it was deathly quiet. I was the only one alive. You went on autopilot, thanks to me. Yet it was terrifying because I couldn't hear you. Couldn't find you.

In all our years together that has never happened.

Of course, I still had the keys to each room. When I finally found you, you were stuck in what I like to call the grey room. It's the room between sadness and complete madness. It isn't necessarily dangerous there, but it warrants concern.

Oh, I wanted to join you. And some days I easily did. But I have one job to do. And that's to keep you going.

I tried many keys to get you out. I tried the Sam key, thinking that if you talked to your sister, the one solid link to your mother, you might perk up. And you did, for only a brief moment. I wiggled the key in the lock, intent on getting you out. But the door would become jammed and I was back at square one.

I suggested that you write. Yes, writing! You've always loved to escape into the busy, endless world of your imagination. Yet when you opened your laptop and pulled up one of your many unfinished manuscripts you would stare at the screen. You couldn't string together a sentence if someone paid you to. Another dead end.

I recommended running. That didn't pan out.

Then reading. But you could never focus on the story long enough.

Options were running out. I had to do something to mitigate your pain. Because if I didn't do something, I was scared it would be impossible to pull you out. Somehow misery found its way into the room like a squatter, plopping its useless self on the floor and refusing to budge. It became your companion and best friend. No one was better than your misery.

And then I thought of it: the one key I hadn't used. The key to where all your memories were stored. But when I opened this door it was like Pandora's box. All of them hit me at once. For months I rifled through memory after memory. And not just any kind—the good ones. It seemed so foolproof. Why did I not think of it sooner?

Yet how was I supposed to know that every time you access a memory it's constructed differently? Time becomes irrelevant. Minor details shift, such as the weather, day of the week, or what you were wearing. How was I supposed to know that you'd latch onto each memory so readily? That you'd sink into them so deeply that they became your reality?

Almost instantly I saw the error in my ways, yet I continued to hand you gift after gift after gift. I became so obsessed with you that I lost keys to doors that should always remain closed and forgot to open the doors to your happiness. It all became a fucking mess and for that I'm sorry.

But look at you. You came out on the other side alive. You're better than before. At least I think you are. Though it's hard to tell if that's your own doing or the medication.

Either way, I've taken a small step back. Control of your life is now yours unless you ask for my help.

You grip the chair in front of you and watch as the last page flutters onto the tray. You grab it, enjoying the feel of fresh ink before you place it upside down on the stack in front of you. If it weren't weird, you'd put the pages close to your nose and smell them. Instead, you flip over the manuscript and stare down at the title.

Pride and accomplishment rushes through you, causing the smallest of smiles to appear. When you came home from Sacred Heart you immediately delved back into writing. The words became filled with the darkness of your heart and the blood running through your veins. If you're ever going to have a magnum opus, this book is the one.

Why? Because this is more than just a story.

You wrote this book because the truth gets lost inside of rumors. Trapped inside of souls. You didn't want that to be a possibility for you.

You have no kids but you imagine that this is just a small portion of what a parent feels toward their child. You put the heavy stack of pages in your messenger bag and leave the library. Before you go, you give the librarian a small smile. Like everyone else she only knows your story through the media's eyes, but she's always been so nice to you so you're nice to her.

When the *Dateline* episode aired in late March you were still at Sacred Heart. The episode brought a whole new round of magazines covering the story and journalists wanting to talk to you. It's now July and the media is still knocking on your door for a chance to get an exclusive interview with you.

Through Sam, you declined each and every interview. She stepped up and became a watchdog for you. She told the journalists you had no comment. Once you were discharged from Sacred Heart she pleaded with you to find an apartment and to continue therapy sessions with a psychotherapist.

You agreed to everything.

Sam found you a small, one bedroom apartment in Mt. Zion.

It was in a fairly quiet area, where no one would hound you or stare at you with fascination. Sam found furniture for you. It was minimal. (Personally, I think she was afraid that more items and furniture would lead to you hoarding like your mom.) Overall, she created a cozy place for you.

Of course, people still recognized you. Some of them were bold enough to talk to you. 'I'm sorry,' they'd say quietly, but you don't know if they meant it. The words were instinctual, like saying 'bless you' after someone sneezes. You always said 'thank you' and hurried away.

Some days were good for you. On those days you talked your psychotherapist's ear off or happily answered the psychiatrist's questions about the medication she prescribed for you. She recommended consistent treatments.

But on those bad days? Oh, your thoughts were dangerous. You felt uncontrollable and downright dangerous to yourself and others. It scared me. Hell, it scared you, too, because if you hadn't sought treatment and just lived in your own world, there wasn't much chance that you'd make it out alive.

It's been a while now. Long enough for the drugs to kick in. You're taking upwards of 1000 mg of Seroquel a day. And let's not forget Remeron. At night, the sleeping pills make you drowsy before they knock you out, but you always wake up thinking of your mom, convinced it was a bad dream before reality sinks in again.

Something has to give.

I know the danger of giving you too many gifts now. So I bestowed my last gift as an idea: move out of your apartment. Move out of Decatur altogether. You love that idea and spend days on the Internet searching for places you can settle in. Wherever it is, you know it isn't going to be in Illinois.

Ultimately, you settle on Kokomo, Indiana. It's small enough not to be considered a big city and big enough to be considered a town.

I tell you to stop taking your medication. Because what people don't understand is that drugs are just a band-aid placed over agony. They may hide it and a lot of times, numb it. But at the end of the day the agony's still there. Still waiting for you.

You don't tell Sam any of this.

You throw your medicine in the trash.

You pay next month's rent. You place it in an envelope along with your apartment keys before licking it shut. You drop it off at the community center.

According to your navigation system, the drive to your mother's house takes approximately fifteen minutes. Twelve, if traffic is good. You make it in nine. (You told yourself not to speed but you couldn't help it). It has been months since you've seen the house.

We miss it so much. I swear we sigh in unison when you pull onto the street; it doesn't matter what heinous moments happened here. There is something indescribable that keeps us tethered here. You park near the sidewalk instead of in the driveway.

There's a Brinkoetter Real Estate sign planted in the front yard. The grass is a healthy green thanks to a good amount of rain. The oak trees are once again covered with leaves that gently sway in the direction of the house, almost as though they're pointing you toward the door. When you step out of the car you hear the birds chirping. The wind carries the sound of kids' laughter and lawnmowers.

When Sam decided to put the house on the market the real estate agent gave her a key to the lock box. She also, albeit reluctantly, gave you a key. I think she thought you were going to become a squatter and refuse to leave, but you're proud of yourself that this is the first time you've used this key.

The door easily opens and when you step inside you're momentarily frozen in confusion; this isn't the house you grew up in. It's a cleaner, sleeker version. It looks like it belongs on one of those before and after shows on HGTV.

It has Sam written all over it.

It's been staged to the nines to attract more buyers but you're skeptical. You imagine that once people discover what happened behind closed doors they'll become too nervous to buy it.

The floors are real hardwood and the walls have a fresh coat of off- white paint. Windows have been replaced. So have the holes in the walls. The putrid smell is gone. The old bannister that was on its last leg has been replaced. Your hand curls around it as you slowly walk up the stairs.

The walls start to speak.

You hear the laughter and giggles of you and Sam as you both raced up the stairs. You can smell your mom's famous meatloaf and it's so real that your stomach rumbles. The flash of a camera goes off behind you. You turn around and see your sixteen-year-old self standing on the stairway with your date. Your mom takes pictures as he puts the corsage on your left wrist.

The memories make you smile faintly. You continue up the stairs and go directly to the your old room. The team Sam hired to stage the house put a simple twin bed up against the window and dresser on the opposite side of the room. Even though there's fresh carpet a rug has been placed in the middle of the floor. You wonder if Sam had anything to do with that.

When you go back into the hall, you look to your right. The master bedroom door is open but you can't walk down there. The emotions swirling through you are ones that I deal with every damn day. Surprise. Nostalgia. Sadness. Fear. Some of them I'm closer to, like sadness. The bond we've created can't be helped. When a person experiences trauma like you have, it's impossible for the human psyche to go back to normal.

You slowly make your way down the stairs and realize that even the front door has been replaced. How did you miss that? You must have been too busy trying to get inside. The door is one of those 'fancy ones' as your mom would've called it. It's a stained mahogany, four-panel print with sidelites.

The dinning room table is staged, making it look like some fancy dinner is minutes away from starting. You marvel at how clean the table is. You sit in one of the chairs. It's stiff, from lack of use. You stare at the grainy wood of the table surface. When it was just you the dinning room table was so packed with junk you could barely put your plate down.

You get up and tour the kitchen. Sam had someone do a full gut because it doesn't even look the same. There's new flooring, new cabinets and appliances. New countertops, too. But the biggest difference is the wall that's been removed, replaced now by a kitchen island.

You have to tip your hat in Sam's direction; she did an amazing job.

You close the front door and make sure to lock it behind you. Your head is held high as you walk down the sidewalk, past the FOR SALE sign in front of the yard. You cross the road toward Noah's house. You know he's at work so your steps are sure, confident even.

Instead of moving toward the door, you stop in front of the mailbox. You take one of the heavy manila packages and put it inside. You don't worry about how long your manuscript will stay out here, neglected. Noah's responsible and he'll have the pages in his hands within a few hours.

For a brief second you shudder with relief and fear because everything you could never say aloud—all the pain and dark thoughts—is written in black ink and enclosed in this package. You give the weather-beaten mailbox a small tap before you hurry back to your childhood home and put the house keys where they've remained hidden for years: beneath the door mat. You don't need them anymore.

You move toward your car. The second folder is in your arms. As you back out of the driveway you keep the folder in your lap. Once you're on the outskirts of Wildwood you pull over to the side of the road, in front of the blue collection mailbox. The package is addressed to Sam Gulick.

Just like the first package, you hesitate for a second. You're so nervous to send out your manuscripts you think you might vomit. It's one thing to write your feelings down but a whole other matter to send them out into the world where anyone can see them. Feel them.

You're so nervous because you know you're strange, not altogether whole. Your brain is constantly on the go. You can't help but wonder what it would be like if I could step outside your body and show you everything you're doing wrong. It's in interesting idea, but who's to say that I'd want to step back in?

Dark things live inside of you, Selah. But I'm part of that darkness.

"Fuck it. Just do it," I urge you.

"Fuck it," you mutter to yourself as you drop the package off. You take a deep breath because you can't take it back. It's officially out of your hands.

Your hands curl tightly around the steering wheel as you drive out of Wildwood. You go ten over the speed limit. You're driving like someone on a mission. A person who's late to something important.

You drive into South Shores when the light goes red.

You turn your head to the left and see a woman behind the wheel of a silver mini van. One hand is curled tightly around the steering wheel and the other is wildly waving around. Her eyes are glued to the rear view mirror. She's probably yelling at her kids. Maybe she has one. Or maybe four.

Either way, she looks close to tearing her hair out.

Seconds later she looks forward and closes her eyes. Then she turns and her eyes connect with yours. She looks at you with envy because you're alone in your car and she'd do anything to get a break from the kids screaming in the back of her car. And you'd do anything to have a solid family. Maybe a kid or two, but you don't think those cards are in your future; you're not stable enough for a man, let alone kids.

You want to tell her to hold on a bit longer. You want to tell her that she's lucky because much worse things are happening in the world to people. Yet that's the thing about pain; it's equal opportunity and yet never strikes every person the same.

I whisper into your ear that what needs to change is everyone. Everyone needs to acknowledge that everyone is fucked up. Everyone is broken. Everyone is going through their own shit. And that's okay.

So you give her the faintest of smiles, to let her know that it's all right. For a brief second her face slightly relaxes and she smiles back. I feel momentarily proud. Two strangers connecting.

The light turns green.

Purposely, you keep your foot on the brake and wait for her to pass. People behind you start to honk their horns. You put the turn signal on and merge in behind the van. You don't focus on her van, though. In fact, you barely notice it. You have tunnel vision, convinced that what's been done is done. And what will be will be.

You near the next intersection. The light is red but then suddenly turns green. Your heart speeds up because you think it's a sign.

Go, go, go as fast as you can.

You press down on the gas, inching closer and closer to the South Shores Bridge. Seconds before you rear end the Sienna you make a sharp left. Your body moves left and right and if it weren't for your seatbelt you would pitch forward. The front bumper makes a hideous screeching sound as it hits the sidewalk.

Your foot never leaves the gas pedal. It's pressed all the way down. You have no intention of letting up.

You keep the steering wheel turned right and burst through the guardrail. Your car flies into the air. It feels like minutes but it's only seconds that your car hovers in the air.

Before you crash into the water, you close your eyes. There's a moment of fear. A moment where you want to back out. Maybe life will be easier. You can turn it all around!

But then I ask you the most important question that you'll ever be asked: do we really want to go through this darkness and pain for the rest of our lives?

And for one second we think in unison.

"No," you whisper.

"No," I whisper back.

Some people are just not meant for this world.

ACKNOWLEDGEMENTS

A HUGE thank you goes out to my beta readers: Darla Williams, Tosha Khoury, Vanessa Proehl, Holli Buck, and Alyssa Cole. Thank you so much for reading through the rough draft of Selah's story, giving me your honest feedback and being so supportive. It means the world to me.

Thank you to Anna from Cover Couture for creating an AMAZING cover for *Figure Eight.* I absolutely love it. You did an amazing job!

Thank you to Mare Piquette Editing for doing such a fantastic job!

Thank you to Angela from Fictional Formats for making *Figure Eight* so pretty.

A big thank you to Autumn H. from Wordsmith Publicity for all her hard work. I appreciate it SO much!

Last, but not least: thank you to my husband, Joshua for watching the kids and playing both Dad and Mom while I was in my own world. Most of all, thank you for believing in this book.

ABOUT THE AUTHOR

College seemed like too much stress for me. Traveling across the world, getting married, and having four kids seemed much more relaxing.

Yeah, I'm still waiting for the relaxing part to kick in…

I change addresses every other year. It's not by choice but it is my reality.

While the crazies of life kept me busy, the stories in my head decided to bubble to the surface. They were dying to be told and I was dying to tell them.

I hope you'll enjoy escaping to the crazy world of these characters with me!

For more information on Calia Read visit her blog:
caliareadsandwrites.blogspot.de/

Or visit her Author Page on Facebook
https://www.facebook.com/CaliaRead

Follow Calia on Twitter
@ailacread

ALSO BY CALIA READ

Sloan Brothers

Every Which Way

Breaking the Wrong

Ruin You Completely

Fairfax Series

Unravel

Unhinge

Made in the USA
Middletown, DE
03 June 2018